THE LAST NEANDERTHAL

THE
LAST
NEANDERTHAL

A Novel

CLAIRE CAMERON

Little, Brown and Company
New York Boston London

Copyright © 2017 by Line Painter Productions, Inc.

Little, Brown and Company
Hachette Book Group
1290 Avenue of the Americas, New York, NY 10104
littlebrown.com

First Edition: April 2017

Little, Brown and Company is a division of Hachette Book Group, Inc. The Little, Brown name and logo are trademarks of Hachette Book Group, Inc.

The publisher is not responsible for websites (or their content) that are not owned by the publisher.

The Hachette Speakers Bureau provides a wide range of authors for speaking events. To find out more, go to hachettespeakersbureau.com or call (866) 376-6591.

The image on page 273 is adapted from a photograph by Dagmar Hollmann / Wikimedia Commons, License: CC BY-SA 4.0.

ISBN 978-0-316-31448-0
LCCN 2016955674

10 9 8 7 6 5 4 3 2 1

LSC-C

Printed in the United States of America

Our deeds still travel with us from afar,
and what we have been makes us what we are.

—George Eliot, *Middlemarch*

The Family[1]

Big Mother[2]

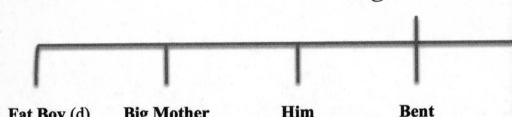

Fat Boy (d)
Killed by bison horn

Big Mother
(born Big Girl)
Moved to new
family won at the
fish run

Him
Now first male of
family

Bent
Born with crooked
forearm

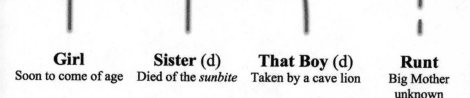

Girl
Soon to come of age

Sister (d)
Died of the *sunbite*

That Boy (d)
Taken by a cave lion

Runt
Big Mother
unknown

1. At its peak, the Neanderthal population numbered only in the hundreds of thousands. They were dispersed across a vast area of modern Europe and Asia. However, when this family lived, the sum total of members of their species could be counted on a pair of human hands.

2. Neanderthals didn't track paternity. Monogamy wasn't held up as a virtue, as it could hinder reproductive success in a small population.

Glossary

Aroo: A tonal word; the precise meaning changed with pitch and context. Most often used as a sharp warning but could also be a call for help or a term of endearment.

Bearden: An expression of fear, as in the quiver you feel when you suddenly find yourself too close to where a bear sleeps.

Boh: The blowing sound made by a bison. They were the staple food of this particular family and therefore at the front of their minds much of the time.

Chewfat: Most often used in reference to a strong body. One interpretation might be "I would like to sink my teeth into that meat." It was a phrase of active encouragement, not a direct compliment.

Crowthroat: Someone who talks too much. Derived from the despised crow, the worst offender when it came to mindless chatter and making a racket.

Cu-cu-cling: A phrase meaning "My head is a bison" that was often chanted in singsong. It expressed the feeling of a deep hunger that occupied the mind and body.

Deadwood: A body on the other side of the dirt; used as an equivalent to our idea of death, though it expressed a change of state rather than a permanent end.

Pitch: A tarlike substance distilled from a pine or birch tree. When directed at a person, the word could be roughly interpreted as "Keep your head attached to your meat," as in "stay alive." It had a double meaning, as it also conveyed the importance of, and the skill involved in, keeping one thing attached to another.

Stone tooth: A handmade stone tool.

Sunbite: A disease with a high mortality rate that started with flu-like symptoms, followed by red spots all over the body that turned to blisters; believed to come from the sun burning the body from the inside out.

Warm: It meant "family," but the word had a connotation of physical warmth and safety of the kind that brought peace of mind.

Wintersleep: Literally translated as the sleep that occurred during the height of the winter storm season. While not technically hibernation, it was the process of becoming languid, slow, and inactive during winter to keep the energy needs of the body low.

THE LAST NEANDERTHAL

Prologue

They didn't think as much about what was different.

There was good reason for this, as they lived in small family groups. Every day was spent among people who were similar to them. The bodies that sat around the fire shared the same kind of cowlick at the backs of their heads, or the same laugh, or teeth that were equally crooked. Every time a head turned to look, a body could find one part of itself in another.

It's because of their similarities to us that I can speak for them when I say that much of what you've heard isn't true.

They were kind and clever. They had hands with opposable thumbs and a light dusting of hair on the backs. They had hearts that throbbed in their chests when they saw certain people, and this happened more than you might expect. Their brains were larger than ours by about 10 percent. Many of us have inherited up to 4 percent of their DNA, and now that both genomes have been sequenced, we know that theirs differed from ours by only about 0.12 percent. To be fair, these slight variations are significant. They had a sensitive patch of skin on the gums above the front teeth; by curling up the top lip, they could feel the heat of a body from a mile away. Their ears could pinpoint where a drop of water had fallen in a pond long after the

3

ripples were gone. Their eyes could see the unique pattern of bark on each tree and this allowed them to tell one from the next, just as we can with human faces.

If they knew I was telling you this, though, it would embarrass them. They did not like to focus on inward thoughts, as this lay the body open to outward dangers. They would hold up a hand, lower their eyes, a slight pink to the cheek. If they were still alive today, they would want to make clear one pressing point: They were much like you.

But they aren't alive. They are extinct. The knowledge that something is extinct often leads to worry. You are probably already feeling guilty because you assume that I'm about to place the responsibility for their end on modern humans. We compare ourselves to them through one stark reality: We survived and they did not. The space between those two things, life and death, is where our trouble starts. We focus on that one difference and it dominates our thoughts. Blame comes next.

But the last thing they would want you to worry about is their passing. They didn't dwell much on difference, and it was the resemblances between seasons, bodies, and species that stood out to their eyes. They were so few in number. The world in which they lived was vast and empty. As a matter of survival, they tried to focus on what was the same.

If you happened on one in the woods—say, a female named Girl with a shock of red hair—it would not be by accident. She would have sensed you coming long before, felt curious about another upright primate, and allowed you to approach. She would make a noise in the brush to let you know she was there. Maybe she would drop her spear to show that she didn't mean you harm. She would spread the fingers of her left hand and raise that palm to greet you.

The polite thing to do would be to raise your right hand the same way. Walk slowly toward her.

Her body is streaked with dirt and only partially covered with a loose cloak of bison fur. She is often too hot and doesn't like the feel of tight animal hides on her skin. Her breath comes in plumes from her nose, expelling heat from her broad body into the cold air. Look at her densely packed muscles. They hold a kind of strength more on par with a bear's. As you get closer, notice the earthy smell of bison meat and sour stomach. There is nothing wrong with her; that's just from how she lives.

Take a deep breath because you will feel intimidated. And you should. This is your instinct taking hold. You've never seen such a magnificent creature before, but your ancestors did. They knew from experience that she could close up your throat with one squeeze. They passed this sensible fear on to you.

Don't run, though. You feel scared because on an instinctual level you acknowledge that you are weaker. Remember that she isn't worried about you. She knows she is stronger and she can afford to stare. The thing to focus on is that you are the most spectacular thing she has ever seen. Because the Neanderthal population was always small, she has seen only a handful of other upright bodies in her lifetime, and never anyone like you. What she feels is a sense of wonder.

Hold up your palm. Spread your fingers out like hers in a greeting. Walk up to her, slowly.

When you are close enough, press the skin of your palm against hers. Feel her heat. The same blood runs under the surface of your skin. Take a breath for courage, raise your chin, and look into her eyes. Be careful, because your knees will weaken. Tears will come to your eyes and you will be filled with an overwhelming urge to sob. This is because you are human.

When you look into her eyes, you will feel an immediate connection. All the difference drops away. You each know with certainty that you can feel the mind of the other. You share a single thought: *I am not alone.*

PART I

1.

It was the warmth that Girl would remember. The night, the specific one she often thought about later, the one that turned out to be among the last they had together, had been filled with warmth. Spring was in the night air, though the ground was still hard with frost. Cold nipped at exposed skin.

When they slept, they were the body of the family. That is how they thought of themselves together, as one body that lived and breathed. The forms curled into one another in a tangle; the curve of a belly rested up against the small of a back, a leg draped over a hip, and a cold set of toes found heat in the crook of an arm.

As the sun had turned its face away, they were all exhausted from the work that came with spring. For once, there had been no nighttime shadow stories, talk, or laughs—though when they had all settled, Him, the oldest brother, issued a tremendous fart. He could have split a log with the force. Runt replied with a messy blow of his lips to the back of his hand. Bent laughed, just once, and Girl let a smile curl her lips but was too tired for more. Big Mother said, "Hum."

And then it was quiet in the hut; heavy breathing, slow.

Deep in the middle of the pile of bodies lay Girl and Wildcat. Girl usually slept soundly, but that night she woke too early and pulled her cramped arm out from under the large cat. Earlier Big Mother had shooed him away to the edge of the nest. The sneaky cat had waited and, once he heard a whistle of air running evenly through Big Mother's large nose, crawled back in. Wildcat was gray with pointed black tips on his ears. He was thick-boned and robust and had a dense mat of fur. A set of black rings ran the length of his tail. He had made a single chirp, a sound he had trained Girl to know, and moved in to cuddle up to her. He rubbed his head and ears against hers. She made a faint chirp in reply. They were good friends and Wildcat was the softest thing she knew.

Girl scratched at a flea that was attempting an escape from her armpit. She ran her sleepy fingers across the skin to try to flick it off. A shift and a slight grunt and she couldn't reach. A moment later a thick finger pressed on her back. It skimmed across the shoulder blade and pushed. It was her brother Him, she knew from the feel of the rough skin on the tip of his finger. A pinch and a pop and the bug body crushed between his teeth. Girl didn't say thank you. There was no need. It was built into all the times that she would pick a flea or louse for Him. Words could be empty. It was the return of a gesture that held meaning.

And then it was quiet. Girl sighed and fell back and became part of the tangle of bodies again. The protective layer of bone and muscle blurred. The edges of their shapes melted into the warmth. Thick lashes hit cheeks, breaths came slower, and the weight of long limbs fell away. When one had a dream, the others saw the same pictures in their heads, whether they were remembered in the morning or not. It wasn't just their bodies that connected in sleep; it was also their minds.

The family lay in a pile on top of two thick, stretched bison hides. Under those hides was a bed of fresh pine boughs, crisscrossed to lift the nest away from the cold dirt floor. Girl and Runt had just changed the boughs that day, so the air was heavy with the scent of pine. Over the bodies were hides that had been cured and chewed until they felt soft against the skin. A layer of furs was spread on top to keep the family cozy. This nest lay inside a hut that was tucked into the side of a granite cliff, a carefully chosen position, as it was perched on a ledge with steep rock above and a sharp slope below. They had to slink along a narrow trail to get to the hut. While not convenient, it limited the routes that a predator could use to approach.

When going to sleep, the family imagined that they were crawling into the belly of a bison. The hut was roughly the same shape as the bison they ate. It had a low, tight back end to hold the heat in close. The front was stronger and made with more support, horned and watching. A long tree limb formed the spine of the structure. It was propped up at one end with a forked branch and wrapped in place with twine made from strips of the inner bark of a cedar tree. Once these main supports were up, long sticks were laid across the center pole, like ribs. Thicker branches were secured with stones at the front and back to form legs for stability. A first skin, cured with brain oil, was pulled tight enough over the frame to quiver. Dead pine boughs were then placed on the skeleton, like a thick slab of fat. The outermost layer was rough hides made of the densest fur from the backs of two old male bison, thrown over and tied on with cured tendons.

With body heat, it was snug inside the hut. The strength of the animals remained in their parts and gave the family a special kind of protection. In a land full of peril, protection of any kind was precious. What comforted the body was also solace for the mind.

When Girl was inside the hut, she had a habit of murmuring a word: "Warm." She craved the feeling of being connected to so many beating hearts, to ears that listened, and to all those pairs of eyes that would watch to ensure that something wasn't sneaking up behind another body. It was how her blood spread heat to the bodies she loved. It was how she stayed alive.

And much later, when the family was all gone and Girl was alone, the warmth was what she would remember about that night. She would let her longing out in a lonely moan: "Warm."

2.

When Girl peeked her head out of the hut that morning, she could smell the struggle of spring. It was the first day of the hunt and the land had come alive. The sun worked hard to peel the winter ice away from the earth. As it did, it uncovered a deep hunger in the land. The same kind of craving lived in the bellies of all the beasts who roamed the valley of the mountain. Girl watched as the trees below swayed with worry. They could feel the vibrations from the growling bellies through the soil around their roots. Cold air clung to the pine needles and each sprouting cone at the end of each branch quivered in anticipation. The ground shifted in discomfort as the ice let it go. Spring brought life for some, but it brought death for others.

Down the slope at the hearth, Big Mother stirred the coals to rouse the morning fire. The old woman wore her bison horns, which were secured in a soft hide and tied onto her head. The two horns protruded straight out at the spot where her short forehead met a thick hairline. With only a glance, any beast could tell that Big Mother was in charge. She was old by then, which meant that there were more than thirty springs she could remember. She had lost count of them all, but her milky eyes could still pick out shape, light, and movement. Her nose could still catch the scent of a fresh green shoot from a hundred strides away.

As the head of the family, Big Mother would decide on the particular beast they would try to kill that day. Though her hunting days were over, she would still make the trip to the bison crossing with the rest of the family. Girl wouldn't risk leaving Big Mother, or any of the other weaker-bodied ones, alone at that time in the spring. A young leopard had recently come slinking around near their hearth. He was new to their land and unsettled. In earlier times the family could have driven him away easily, but that spring their numbers were especially low. They didn't dare allow the leopard a chance. Only some meat got to eat.

As Him, Girl's brother, walked over to the fire, Big Mother started to laugh. It took Girl a moment to see why. Him often had an erection and, given the loose arrangement of his cloak, she could see that this morning was no different. Big Mother laughed with joy, as an erect penis signaled good health. It was happiness.

Many things had dropped away from Big Mother's body by then, but not her smile. Her laugh came out as a sharp cackle and showed her missing teeth, all gone except for a few mid-teeth in her upper left jaw and two molars on the right. When she laughed, she put a hand to her cheek, and Girl knew the old woman wished those teeth would also fall to the dirt. The pain made her body feel like dry meat. A clutch of wiry gray hairs lifted from her chin, and large breasts lay proud and flat over her belly. The thick skin on her face showed the trail of a tear. Big Mother believed that the measure of a life could be reduced to such small things, a count of the wrinkles to see how many laughs versus how many frowns a body had produced. Because of this, Girl knew that the old woman made sure to laugh often.

The smells of spring and her aging mother mixed together in a way that caused Girl some unease. Realistically, she knew that Big Mother could drop dead at any moment. She often said her breath smelled like the hindquarters of a bison after so many years of eating just that.

While the back end of a bison had a distinct smell, it wasn't necessarily bad. Shit came out of it and stank of life in a sweet way. If mixed with sand, bison shit could be stuck around the pine poles of a hut to fill up the cracks and keep out the wind. There was nothing bad about stopping a damp wind from blowing down your neck, just as there was nothing bad about aging. If Girl was wise enough to live so long, she would also earn that breath.

Big Mother's wisdom was needed. Only the best instincts could get a body to reach old age and she had taught Girl that living a life, riding the back of the churning seasons, meant that change was constant. Everything around them sprouted, grew, and, at some point, reached its peak. Its strength would start to recede when the thing was no longer able to renew itself. It would then die—be deadwood. A leaf that falls starts to decompose. It soon becomes nutrients for the soil. The rich soil will take in rain and become food for the tree. And in that way, in time, things didn't really die. They only changed. But all changes came with discomfort and unease. And Big Mother did her best to give comfort to the family by keeping what she could the same. Over all her years, she made her tools with the same source of rock, ate the same kind of foods at close to the same time of year, and built huts in the same way again and again.

Girl looked at Him and admired the shiny brown hair on his head. Its glossiness was a sign of health. Raked back above his ears, the hair was pulled away from his sloped brow and tied with a lash. His back was broad and flared out wide from his waist. He had gone through a change of his own. It came later than it had for some, as the years before had been lean and his fat stores were low. The change included moods that alerted Girl to what might be happening. Given the close quarters, moods were endured in a fairly stoic way. Though she pretended not to notice, she knew he might catch the eye of a woman at the fish run that summer.

Just thinking of the bright colors of the fish run was enough to make Girl's heart quicken. Saliva flooded her mouth. Her hunger deepened. She thought of the soft fish eggs in her fingers. The year before she had held one up close to her eye and it looked like the river was trapped inside. That small river held the next generation of fish and so she wanted their strength inside her body. She had put the eggs between her back teeth, crunched down, and listened to them pop. She imagined the slippery skin of the fish in her hands and eating the soft, orange flesh underneath, and her blood felt as though it boiled under her skin.

When the spring sun climbed high enough to kiss the cliff that stood behind their hut, the family would start moving toward the meeting place. Other families who lived on separate forks of the river would also make the journey. It was by a broad stretch of the water that flattened into a series of shallow rapids where the river's branches came together.

At that time of year, it was also the meeting place for the fish. As they flung their bodies up rocky steps, some were smashed on the rocks, some found themselves in the waiting reed nets of the family, and some fell into the jaws of bears. And a few of the fish made it through. Each was as long as an arm and as thick and muscled as a thigh, with two fangs that protruded up from the lower jaw. They were as smart as crows and as quick as snakes. Their scales were speckled gray, but the tastiest ones wore a blaze of orange across their backs to show they were ripe. The family believed that those were the best fish. They were not necessarily the strongest, but their traits—cunning, strength, size, or eyesight—were best matched to the conditions of that particular year. They were the ones who continued on to lay their orange eggs in the shallows higher upriver. The new generation of fish would come from them.

Girl's mind was full of inward thoughts of the meeting place, but she knew she shouldn't be distracted. She quickly snapped back to the present as she looked at her family by the hearth—Big Mother, Him, Bent, and Runt. They were a small group and some of them looked weaker than other beasts. She knew from their previous visits to the meeting place that they might not be the most attractive of the bunch. But she didn't let worry about their chances flood her then. Like the skills of hunting, repairing, and building, learning to hold some of her worries back was part of growing up. She had to focus on the hunt. She shouldn't divert the attention of her body from the present moment; it could put them all at risk. The world was so easily lost.

Him had been the first to climb down the steep slope from the hut to their hearth that morning. The land of the family was still in the grip of the ice, but he didn't mind the cold. He was driven by his urge to mate. He knew that he would mate only if he looked in good health at the meeting place, and health lay in the food he ate. In the spring, it was only bison meat that could fill the needs of his dense muscles and large frame.

Him didn't stop working when Big Mother laughed. His erection stood for the desire to eat and mate and it only drove him harder. He smiled, kicked the embers of the fire to extinguish the flame, and scraped the ashes to the side with a stick. Using a hide to protect his hands from the heat, he lifted a slab of stone with a concave surface that was used for making sticky pitch from birch bark. Someone in the family long before had found the slab and it had since been passed down from one body to another. As they moved frequently to find or follow food, it wasn't a practical thing to carry. They cached the slab each year near where the spring hut was likely to be. Him handled it like a treasure. It was one of the few objects that many generations of the family had used. That was how a thing was made precious, by how many hands of the family had touched it before. The work he did linked him to the family through time.

The day before, Him had put layers of bark from a birch tree into the concave slab of stone and let the heat of the fire coax black ooze from the bark. Once hot embers were added, he used this sticky pitch to seal a triangular flake of stone onto the end of a wooden thrusting spear. Him quickly worked the pitch before it set. He licked his fingers often. He pressed and molded the pitch to get it just right. Once happy with the shape, he dipped the new tip in cool water.

As Him waited for the tip to set, he watched his younger brother Bent, who had a forearm that was curved like the horn of a bison. The thumb pointed away from Bent's body, and his wrist was fixed. He was attempting to tie a hardened hide onto his shin for protection in the hunt, and the guard was difficult to get in place with his crooked arm. He could turn his hand only by twisting his elbow. It looked like Bent's arm was aching too, as it often did when the weather changed. Bent spat in frustration.

"Runt." Him let out the word in a loud, piercing bark. His larynx was short, which gave his voice a high pitch. This shrill sound shot through his broad nose cavity with a nasal quality. At the same time, it resonated through his deep, muscled rib cage. When he spoke, his voice came out loud and it tired his throat.

But Him didn't need to stress his throat with words very often. Big Mother had set the quiet tone of their social customs, and living in such a small group meant that many things didn't need to be said. Big Mother's throat was even more prone to strain and she discouraged too much chatter, though those who witnessed her occasional flashes of rage might question her commitment to quiet. She called a body that talked too much a crowthroat; with a hand out, she would flap her fingers against her thumb, a gesture that stood for the beak of the bird she despised the most. The crows squawked and shit with no regard for what lay around them.

Runt heard his name and followed Him's eyes to see Bent's struggle. Runt had lived through six or seven winters by then, though no one knew his true age. It was difficult to tell, given his frail appearance. Him was glad to see that the boy had started to look for ways to be useful. Runt scampered over and put a skinny finger on the middle of Bent's knot and used the other hand to pull one strand through. Together they tied the hardened hide to Bent's shin.

Him thought that Runt's position in the family was still uncertain. The boy had been found along the river before the fish run began. Another family had brought him to the meeting place, but they had not treated him well and barely fed him. Soon they had kicked him out of their hut and he had been left to wander around like a stray wildcat begging for scraps. Big Mother had finally taken pity on Runt and given him a nice piece of fish. The boy had attached himself to her side and had managed to hold his position ever since.

But Runt wasn't growing up and out like he should. Him often suspected that the boy was sick. The morning before, Him had made the boy stand in front of Big Mother so that she could sniff his breath. He was worried about sunbite. The family knew it started with a particular kind of stench on the breath. Soon after came a deep fatigue, pain in the joints and back, and vomiting. The next and often fatal signs were flat red spots that appeared on the face, hands, and forearms and filled with pus, then turned to blisters. The sunbite burned the body and consumed it—the body had got too close to the sun. But Big Mother didn't think Runt showed any signs. There was nothing obviously wrong with him.

Still, Him wondered. Even this spring, the boy wasn't taking on muscle. Bulbs of knees and elbows stuck out from thin limbs, his eyes bulged, and his skin was darker than it should be. Him did not know why Runt was so small or if more meat would help him grow. He knew that the boy was a risk to feed. Each piece of food they tossed his way might compound the loss. Life was a moving set of decisions. Even reaching to pinch a flea had to be worth the saved blood.

Him sensed that the balance of the family was off. Perhaps it was his strong urge to mate that made him feel it more acutely than the others, a constant pressure on his skin.

3.

When Girl was ready, she made her way down the narrow path toward the hearth. She walked up just as Him was admiring their new spear. They all had a role in most of the things they made, and constructing this spear was no different. Bent had collected and shaped the shaft, Runt had prepared the tendon that was used to wrap around the spearhead before the pitch seal, Girl had made the pointed stone flake, and Him had assembled the parts into a tool. None of them could conceive of themselves as separate from the others.

Girl reached out her hand to touch Him's shoulder. Him didn't look back and didn't need to, as Girl's scent was so familiar. She felt his heart throb. All of them could feel the physical reaction of another body on the soft parts of their skin, the inside of the wrist, a cheek, the base of the neck. Girl noticed that Him's penis stood up again. One whiff of her was all it took. She knew how she looked, dressed for the hunt with hardened hides strapped tight to her shins and forearms. The black ocher paint on her face showed the two streaks of the family on each cheek. A shock of red hair stood up from her head. She wore a single shell on a thin lash around her neck. Her skin smoothed over muscles and gleamed with hazel oil. She could feel the effect of her strength on him. He made her teeth want to sink in. But she kept her eyes down and pointing away. If Big Mother caught her looking, there would be trouble.

In the years before, after a hunt, they would spend time eating and digesting in the protection of the cave that was tucked into the side of the cliff near their spring hut. They would build up the fire so that the flames licked up into the dark. Big Mother would stand in front of it so that her shadow cast shapes on the stone wall and, with shadows and singsong yowls, she would tell them stories. She felt it was worth straining her voice.

The story she told most, the one they loved to see, was one that Big Mother meant as a warning. It was about a brother and sister who had developed a taste for each other. It was a time when there were many families at the meeting place. When the brother and sister wouldn't leave each other alone and one man in the family was chosen to kill them. They managed to escape, but the only way they could get away was to follow the fish.

The brother and sister traveled out toward the sea, to a part of the land where the families did not go. There were no bison, and the water was not fresh. They drank only salted water and ate only creatures with pinching claws. All the salt poisoned their minds and they went crazy. They had babies that became the sum of their experience. The children grew with eyes that stayed open in their heads like the fish in the sea. Their lips became crusted with the salt water that they drank. They grew claws for their hands and started to look like the creatures they ate. Big Mother would crouch over and pinch her fingers to show their ghastly shapes in the shadow. It was a story they all loved, the horror and the delight twisted together tightly.

To reinforce the message, Big Mother had given Girl a shell from the sea the size of a walnut. Girl strung it on a lash and wore it around her neck. But passed down for generations, the story changed in texture through time. The telling of a story using shadows was not as precise as Big Mother might have wished.

Girl understood the tale in the context of when it was told. It had been after a hunt, when she had a full belly. And Girl also saw the story against the backdrop of the change that was happening to her body at that time. Big Mother's narrative became a new thing in Girl's mind. To her, it was a tale that reinforced their way of life. It reminded her of why they preferred to live the same pattern every year and why their ability to hunt bison made them the strongest beasts on the land. Staying close to her brother could get them through the hardest times. That was why she always wore the shell, which she called the Sea, around her neck.

"Girl," Big Mother shrieked now when she turned to see that Girl had emerged from the hut. Big Mother had given each of them a name that was relative to her. It was a way of distinguishing one body from another but without separating them too much. She believed that anything elaborate in the way of naming put unnecessary strain on the throat. Rather than words, rituals formed the pattern that guided their lives, and it was time for the morning meal before the hunt. The shriek meant Big Mother wanted Girl to feed her. No more words were needed.

Calling Girl was also Big Mother's way of showing preference. It was rare and special to have two generations alive at one time. Most of them knew they would probably not live to see three for long. In Girl's time, she had rarely lived with more than eight bodies at once. And to Big Mother, she was the last girl. It was a position so precious that she felt especially protective of Girl. No more breeding females would come from Big Mother's old womb. Her body had become like a smooth pan of sand. Nothing could grow there, but something could take root in Girl.

The time for a succession was coming. Ensuring the family would live was Big Mother's most basic concern, and their survival strategy hinged on the fish run at the meeting place: The oldest male, Him, would try to entice a new woman into the family to become a new Big Mother for their group. The female, Girl, would try to win a place as Big Mother of a new family. If both these things happened, the family was strong, like the fish in a good year. Their kind would return to run with the river again.

Girl took a piece of dried meat into her own mouth and started to chew. The meat had to be worked just right to get it ready for the near-toothless woman to consume. Too much chewing would drain all the juice; it had to be just enough so that the meat could slip through gums and down a throat. Girl chewed until it felt soft and took out the pulpy mouthful. She knelt beside her mother and dangled the piece of meat, holding it up for inspection.

Big Mother glanced at the chewed strip, taking heavy breaths through her nose. The wiry hairs on her chin caught the sun. She nodded okay and opened her lips. The smell of her breath came out in plumes. Her lips pulled back, and she snatched the meat with her gums.

"Hum," she said.

She sucked at it until she swallowed.

After the old woman had eaten, Bent gave each of the other family members a handful of roasted hazelnuts and a slab of dried meat from the cache. Girl hungrily gnawed her piece of meat. It was slightly bigger than usual, as she was important to the hunt, but to her eye, it was not big enough. No portion ever was. She was always hungry.

Girl had noticed a feeling under her skin too, like a chewing sensation. She tried to soothe her mind by picturing herself after the hunt, a warm hunk of meat in hand, sucking at it for juice, surrounded by the smell of a fresh kill; her feet with their light brush of hair on top would twitch with happiness as she licked and chewed, the blood dribbling down her chin. The memory of meat filled her with hope. Her memories weren't necessarily of things that had happened to her; they might be the experiences of someone else in the family. They could be transferred through dreams or through a body she ate. They were for keeping the body safe in its present state, finding food, or making sense of something unfamiliar. So Girl closed her eyes and let the good feelings from the fresh meat flood into her body. She thought of all the times the hunt had been successful for both her and the members of her family who came before. This hunt might stop her hunger.

Behind her she could hear Big Mother sniffing. The woman's old hand, strong like a claw, wrapped around Girl's shoulder and held on. The sniffing was closer and the old woman scented something on her. "Hum."

Girl quivered like a leaf too heavy for its branch. Big Mother was sniffing her like she was checking for the sunbite. Girl pressed her own hand to her forehead. She seemed slightly hotter than usual, but none of the other symptoms were present. She didn't feel sick; quite the opposite. Her muscles were twitching with want. Maybe more hunger than usual, if that was possible. She didn't yet sense what Big Mother had already discovered with a sniff.

Girl found out when she went to squat behind a bush, the final step in getting ready to go. She saw a line of mucus on her thigh. It made her giggle, as it looked more like egg white than something that came from her. She wiped at it with a leaf and found it surprisingly slippery. It wasn't like the blood that had come in the year before. She didn't feel pain, only a slight cramp inside her hip. A cold trickle crept down her spine as she realized that this was the heat. It was the first time she had got it. The heat gave out the scent that told others she wanted to mate.

Girl knew she had to wait until they were at the meeting place for that. Big Mother had given her extra meat over the winter and signaled that this year Girl might be fat enough for the heat to come in time for the fish run. With it, she would be old enough to win a family of her own. Big Mother wanted her daughter to make her proud. Just as Girl's sister, Big Girl, had done before.

But even as Girl had eaten the extra meat that winter, she worried. She didn't want to leave this family as her sister had. Big Girl was quick to laugh. They had played and whispered and picked bugs off each other's backs. Many had thought the two were the same body, with their broad noses that flared and their shocks of red hair. There was one difference that distinguished them, though. When Big Mother was confused about who was who, she would tell them to smile. Big Girl had had a particularly hard collision with a rock, and she had not managed to keep her front teeth attached to her head. The gap made her smile all the brighter. When Big Girl wanted to make Girl laugh, she would stick her tongue through the gap and hiss like a snake. Girl was scared of snakes. They would duck and weave around the camp, shrieking and laughing until one of them fell. The body who was still standing would fall on the other and start tickling. Or sometimes it was Big Mother's large foot that would end the game. The gap in the front of Big Girl's mouth was a source of great fun.

From Girl's perspective, Big Girl was the strongest kind of woman because she had won a family at the fish run. But now she was gone. Maybe she lived well with ample meat, but Girl had no way of knowing. With the exception of going to the meeting place, she had never lived away from the family's land. She did not know what life elsewhere was like. When she tried to imagine Big Girl's life, all Girl felt was the bite of bugs with no sister to pick them off. That's also how the idea of leaving felt to Girl, like a flea that her fingers couldn't reach. And now the heat had come and Girl would change too. What lay ahead was dark and shadowy, like the back of a cave.

Girl knew this feeling wasn't useful to the family. Thinking forward was distracting. It left the body vulnerable in the present. All she wanted to do was push it away. But everyone in the family would know. With the heat, the eyes of beasts across the land would take in her snowy skin in a new way. If not immediately, then soon. The sheen of her hair would look deeper, to show the heat that came from between her legs.

Girl hoped to hide it for now. She quickly found moss to wipe with and lessen the smell. She kept her head low and flicked her eyes to the side, a new fear to stay alert for meat-eaters. She straightened and walked back out to join the others. She took her place at the front of the line, just like she always did. As many in the family had before, she tried to pretend that nothing had changed. She focused on what was the same.

Dr Pepper

Why does life exist? I'd been plagued by doubt about my purpose for much of my life. The day I found her, a Neanderthal long buried in the dirt, I was relieved of it. As an archaeologist, I knew that the essential difference between something living and something dead is heat. Only living things are able to capture energy from the land and use it, but somehow, more than forty thousand years after her death, that Neanderthal was able to capture me. I felt as though her big hand reached through time to grab me by my grubby T-shirt and pull my nose to the spot where she lay. When I found her, I finally knew why I was alive. I wanted to learn her secrets.

By that time, I had already discovered one male skeleton in the cave. The remains belonged to a modern human, one of the *Homo sapiens* (meaning "wise man" in Latin), who are the only surviving species of the genus *Homo*. One of us. Some kind of geological activity had resulted in his bones fossilizing. Based on his pristine condition, I felt it was worth draining my savings to extend my teaching leave and assess the potential of the site. Andy, my assistant, and I camped at the cave, carefully staked the area inside, and started the slow process of excavating one thin layer at time. Soon after we began, I brushed aside a coat of sediment and uncovered a rounded fragment of skull.

"Andy?"

He pushed through the thick plastic that we had hung to protect the entrance from outside contaminants. "Rose?"

"I found her," I said, my voice shaking.

"Who?"

The soft hiss of carbonation came from behind me. Andy carried a can of Dr Pepper most places he went. I had forbidden him to bring it into the cave, assuming that one splash had sufficient corrosive power to instantly dissolve the artifacts that had survived all other threats. But Andy had developed a survival strategy of his own over forty-odd years of marriage to his wife, recently deceased: his hearing was highly selective.

"It's a second set of remains," I said.

"Really?" Andy sighed and took a big slug. "I see a tiny piece of bone."

We were in a small cavern that was attached to a cave network not far from the Gorges de l'Ardèche near Vallon-Pont-d'Arc in France. It was part of a larger system that had become well known thanks to the Chauvet caves, where spectacular paintings made by modern humans had been discovered in 1994.

"We don't want to get ahead of ourselves," Andy said as he tapped his watch. "I'll get your notebook, but remember, it's quitting time. We'll come back to work on it tomorrow."

"Her," I said instinctively.

"We'll come back to *her* first thing in the morning," he teased. "Does she have a name yet?"

"I need to keep working, Andy."

"My vote is Patricia, but we'll have to firm up the christening details tomorrow. You made me promise that I'd force you to stop working at five. Remember?"

"Andy?"

"Rose?"

"There is no way in hell I'm leaving the site right now."

Andy let out a longer sigh. "Is Jane too plain?" He took another big swig from his can.

I leaned back to look at Andy and noticed that weariness had settled about his kind face. Perhaps I was driving him to his carbonated addiction? But he smiled his big, wide Oregonian smile to let me know he was fine. I did the same by giving the slight round of my belly a pat.

"Get yourself a fresh can," I said. "And my notebook and the camera."

"Does this mean we aren't stopping?"

"I'm pregnant, not deranged."

"Hum." Andy shrugged and pushed back through the plastic.

"Andy?" I called after him.

"Yeah?"

"Jane is far too plain."

I waited until Andy was gone to rub the sore spot in my lower back. I was well into the third month of my pregnancy. I wasn't showing, but I hadn't needed a test to know my condition. I'd had to tell Andy. You can't hide the fact that you're experiencing morning sickness when you're sharing a tent with someone. My plan was to visit my doctor when I got back to London in two weeks. Then, after I had confirmation, I would break the news to Simon, my partner. He was holding down our fort in London, since the courses he was teaching went through the spring. Part of me wanted to grab the phone and shout the news to him, but another part of me felt it was premature. Simon had wanted a baby for a long time. I was thirty-nine and I knew that on some level, he had given up hope. Quietly, I'd watched him resign himself to a different kind of life than the one he'd imagined. If I was going to shift his life view again, I wanted to be completely sure.

At sixty-two, Andy had decided that life was short and had taken early retirement from a financial firm in order to pursue a PhD in archaeology—a late bloomer, he'd called himself. When I e-mailed around for help on a scouting expedition, he was the first to respond. He had been studying at Stony Brook University with a good friend of mine, Dr. Conn Bray, who specialized in Paleolithic technologies. I had been reluctant to take Andy on, as I'd assumed he was the sort of student who'd anticipate Indiana Jones–type adventures in snake pits and wouldn't be happy with the usual slow-moving nonaction of archaeological dirt pits. Conn tended to make paleoarchaeology look like a great adventure and was prone to carving up goats with stone tools in class. But the more Andy and I had worked together, the more I realized that he was the best kind of student—one who listened and learned but had much to add. He quickly became my willing coconspirator in all things archaeology as well as a good friend. I didn't know what I would do without him.

Andy pushed back in through the plastic. Holding my notebook, my camera, and a fresh can of soda, he twisted a wrist in an attempt to glance at his watch. "And Simon wants you to call when you're back in camp. Your mother called too."

I was listening, but not really. Andy knew. He tried again. "I'll take a photo, plot it, do a sketch, and we'll call it a wrap?"

"Who's the boss of this site?" I lifted my chin teasingly.

"That's a touchy subject."

"I beg your pardon?"

"Dr. Rosamund Gale, sir!" He tipped his Dr Pepper in a salute.

"And what time is it, Andrew?"

"Five thirteen p.m."

"Take photos. Mark this find."

"My boss will have me axed!"

"Andy?"

"Rose?"

"As your boss, I say put that damn Dr Pepper outside." I burst out laughing.

I'd taken a leave of absence from teaching to follow up on a few interesting features I'd noticed while caving in this area with a surveying team in previous years. With Andy working as support and paid with the last of the money from my savings, I retraced the route that I'd taken. But this time, in the silence, with no pressure from the group, I found a vent. A cave vents air like a body. When the pressure changes, the less dense, cooler night air is drawn in, like an inhale. When the sun heats the air, the cave seeks equilibrium and exhales. I'd found the vent when I stopped to take a water break. I felt it first, like someone blowing gently on my cheek. It took two days to find a channel that led to this previously unmapped cavern.

Maybe I'd suspected then that I was pregnant, but I had managed to delay my internal discovery of it for a few weeks—a time-tested way of ensuring that plans are easier to hatch.

When I first accessed the cavern, it was through a narrow channel of rock. I had to wriggle like a snake to make it through. The cavern on the other end had remained undetected for years, possibly because the narrow channel prevented men of even average girth from entering.

After I'd wriggled through and dropped down, it was only an hour or two before I uncovered the edge of a stone hand ax. I later identified it as an example of the Châtelperronian industry, part of a toolmaking culture that I believed was shared by modern humans and Neanderthals. Andy and I were able to punch through a wall of the cavern to expose the outside wall and make the site more accessible. The cave soon became more like a proper dig site, though the money and glamour of Indiana Jones was missing. Andy said he provided the good looks.

Within a month, Andy and I had found the first set of bones; they belonged to an ancient male who was a modern human.

The moment I'd uncovered the fragment of a second skull, I had a hunch we had found something big. I couldn't just put down tools because it was precisely five o'clock. We kept working, quietly and carefully brushing and plotting.

"Okay?" Andy asked.

"Yes, thank you." I forced a smile to mask my exhaustion.

"Nice mustache." He chuckled. I had an unfortunate habit of running my dusty arm along my face to wipe at the sweat. The result was that each day, I collected a thick line of dirt on my top lip. At least it kept Andy entertained.

Late afternoon stretched to evening. Before I knew it, it was dark outside the cave. Andy measured and charted while I slowly brushed away more layers of dirt. We had some nuts and granola bars on-site to keep us going. Somehow I found myself coaxed into taking a slug of Dr Pepper. I admit it gave me a little pep. As more of the skull appeared in the dirt, I saw that she seemed to be lying on her side with her head turned toward the modern human. They were clearly in the same stratum, or layer, of dirt.

I began to see that the skull was longer than expected. There was a distinct ridge of bone above the eye orbit. I looked up at Andy to see if he noticed too, but he continued to act like it was any other day.

"Should I switch?" he asked.

I realized that Andy had been talking while we worked, but about what? I was too absorbed by the visible bone to know. He easily decoded the confused look on my face.

"To diet," he said.

"Dieting doesn't work," I answered. "Our bodies evolve much more slowly than our eating habits."

"I mean to Diet Dr Pepper. I might switch to that."

"Diet cola is for fat people, Andy."

"I'm fat." He patted his gut.

"Be thankful it's not a baby," I muttered and turned back to my brushing.

"You ever wonder if we could excavate—"

"Have you ever tried cherry Dr Pepper? Isn't that a thing?"

"—your sense of humor."

"Or go crazy and switch to Fanta—do you like that? Maybe you just need a change."

"I was fishing, Rose."

"What, you want to take up fishing for exercise?"

"For compliments."

There was no need to bother trying to cover up my lack of attention since it was so readily apparent. I reached over and gave Andy's belly a nice pat, which pleased him immensely. I was his favorite person to tease and vice versa, but he was no longer looking at me. He was staring at my breasts.

"Really, Andy." I put a finger under his chin to lift it. "You are just like the rest of them."

"Did you spill water?"

Andy had a confident enthusiasm that usually rippled all around him. It was part of what made me agree to take him on. This might have been the first time I had ever heard him sound unsure. "Ah, you're leaking."

I looked down. He was right. I had a wet stain on my T-shirt over my left breast. "Shit," I muttered.

"Nope," Andy said, regaining his swagger. "I'm pretty sure it's milk."

"Colostrum." The word came out of my mouth as a wail. "It's too early, isn't it? How could I have already turned into a cow?"

"You'll make a good cow."

"I'm an angry cow."

"Did I mention that you told me to make sure you stopped working at five p.m.?"

"Oh, wait." I shone my headlamp on the spot on my shirt to take a closer look. "It's only a drop of Dr Pepper. Phew."

"Wow, you are jumpy, huh?"

"Perhaps."

"Well, quit spilling the good stuff or I'll start panicking too."

A few more sips of Dr Pepper kept me going. I would not have stopped for anything. This was the culmination of years and years of painstaking work; I'd sacrificed teaching money and time with Simon to explore this area. It was potentially the first big find that I could claim as my own. While I was considered old to be a first-time mother, I was too young to have made a significant mark on my field yet. Andy was right. I was jumpy.

As we worked, I let my mind run over the idea of having a baby. I had seen what happened to the women in my field who came before me. Most who had kids got sidelined, or sidelined themselves. Men who chose to be involved with their children tended to do the same. I had no reason to expect that my experience would be different. And if this was indeed an important find, timing was crucial. In archaeology, the discovery is important, but the person who interprets the find and publishes is the one who gets the credit. I knew that any absence from the dig could result in my name getting bumped to the end of the line of authors or, worse, dropped entirely. The list of female scientists whose contribution had been diminished or forgotten was depressingly long.

And then, with a few more strokes of my brush, in the dirt before my eyes, the story started to come together. It must have been about two in the morning when I uncovered enough of the skull to see the outline.

"Look." The word came out in a choke. I pointed to show Andy the profile of a prominent brow, a larger nasal cavity, and a receding forehead. "What do you see?"

"One ugly dude." He whistled.

"Andy?"

"Rose?"

"It's Neanderthal."

Andy let his breath out of his lungs then. The length of the exhale spoke of just how unsure he had felt about my theories of where and how we might find artifacts. There were no jokes or fresh cans cracked. We were both too stunned. Andy grabbed my arm, mouth agape. Neither of us could talk. We sat in silence and stared.

As we looked, the implications of this find slowly registered. Maybe on some level, I had begun to doubt myself too. We knew well from the recent advent of DNA testing that many modern humans had inherited genes from Neanderthals and vice versa, but beyond the obvious method of transfer, we knew little about the relations between them. In my quieter moments, I doubted we ever would.

But in the cave, the remains of a Neanderthal lay with those of a modern human. It looked like they had died together, maybe in a volcanic event, as there were records of those in the area. Perhaps they had been placed in this position by someone who thought they would want to face each other in death. They might well have lived together. Whatever the case, their position was evidence of more complex communication between the two, something that I had always assumed would be lost to time. Now it was found. A relationship, a feeling, or a glance—it's the things that don't fossilize that matter most.

4.

The family walked in a line to the bison crossing. Girl went first. She broke trail and snapped branches that had fallen across their path during the winter storms. In her mind were images of meat and memories of how the different parts tasted on her tongue. She would eat the first bite raw and later roast more on a stick. She would dry slabs from the round quarters. Though she ate greens on occasion when food was scarce, she didn't feel they were of much use to anyone. Her body preferred meat. She walked and let each step push out words in a forceful chant: *"Cu-cu-cling, cu-cu-cling, cu-cu-cling."* My head is a bison.

Girl's sidekicks, Wildcat and Runt, joined her. Wildcat stayed in the brush, but Runt scampered along directly behind her. The day before, she had taken a rare trek down to the thicker stands of trees where the small herd of bison grazed. The family couldn't hunt the bison in the forest, as the landscape didn't lend them any advantage. But Girl had wanted to know what they could expect of that particular herd when they hunted them at the crossing. She had taken Runt along because he needed to learn what to do when the melt came. If he were to survive, the boy had to build a clear picture of the land in his head. The context for every small judgment that would come after.

When they reached the trees, Girl's brow furrowed deeper than usual. The bison rooted through the melting snow for the first sprouts. They had long horse-like legs and shaggy beards under their chins and moved in the slow, measured way of beasts who don't expect a green shoot to sprout anytime soon. The more she looked, the more she felt the land had tilted over the winter. There were so few bison. Usually they lived in herds of ten to fifteen, maybe more, but this was just a small clutch of five beasts looking lost. It was too few to sustain the herd unless they joined with another. Two calves teetered on limbs that looked like long fingers instead of strong legs. They nosed through the dirty snow trying to find the stubs of grasses that had had little chance to grow the season before.

Girl had sniffed and pointed for Runt to look. The tremor in the bellies of the beasts sent a sour stench through the branches of the trees. It billowed in a cloud above their backs.

"*Ye?*" She'd touched his nose.

Runt twitched his round nostrils.

"Bearden." She nodded. *Fear.*

On the way back to the camp, Runt had dragged his feet. Girl sensed the boy's fatigue and assumed that even a walk of that distance was too much for him. As younger children in the family had made the walk many times before, her doubts about Runt increased. But Big Mother had decided the boy was one of them and Girl couldn't go against that. So Girl had lifted up his light body and put him on her shoulders to make better time. With her large hand on his leg, Runt seemed to feel more secure. The happiness rose up like a bubble in the boy's throat and burst. He had chattered. Rather than call the boy a crowthroat, she had tried to listen. She was amused by the sounds. Fast and scaly, the words slithered past her ears and into the wind. But she also worried. The points of Runt's small bottom had stuck into her shoulders and she knew it should be rounder and wider before the fish run. As she walked with the others now, she thought of the shrunken herd of bison and the mouths of the family. They badly needed strength.

Girl's other sidekick, Wildcat, also walked with them to the crossing, but under the cover of the brush and off to the side. He gave a chirp to let Girl know he was there. She turned and saw the tip of his tail disappear behind a tree. At the end of the line, Him heard the chirp too. Girl saw his nose wrinkle reflexively. He didn't like cats and there was no doubt that he would love to skin that particular one. From the brush, Wildcat returned Him's look with equally narrowed and wary eyes. Him kicked his foot out, but the cat darted away just in time. Girl held back a laugh, as she could imagine the cat's pride at having yet again successfully avoided Him's foot.

Big Mother came next in line after Runt; her swaying gait and rolling hips set the slow pace. Her horns jutted from side to side as she walked. Bent was close behind her and ready to help the old woman. Girl heard a crash and turned back to see Big Mother stumble and fall. But even as Girl stepped forward, Bent was already there with a hand out to pull the older woman up. Big Mother was too proud to give warning of a fall. When she did go down, getting her upright again was an increasingly difficult task.

From the ground, Big Mother glanced at them as if she wondered, *Did they wish her bones would stay deep in the dirt?* Bent tried to assure her with soft coos and pats. Of all of them, Girl knew, he was the most anxious about her weakening body. With Big Mother at the head of the family, his place as her son was anchored. Without her, his position would be weakened, and Girl knew he had trouble imagining what might come next. Bent helped the old woman up and looked at Girl. Their eyes met and Bent tentatively pulled his lips back to show his teeth—a gesture of affection.

"*Aroo?*" he said in a high, softer pitch.

Girl nodded and pulled her lips back too. Despite his physical shortcomings, or maybe because of them, he was the kindest of them all. She turned from her brother and continued walking at a Big Mother pace toward the crossing.

All the beasts who lived on the land let the family pass in peace, and for good reason: they knew what happened at this time of year. If the family made a kill, many of the animals would also get a good feeding. The family would leave part of the carcass for the cave bear, something they always did. It was clear from a large pile of shit that the bear was awake. She was probably making her way up to the river in the hope that the family would be successful. The large red doe and her young one had been through much earlier, probably to leave ample space between themselves and the bear. Their scent sat lightly on the melting snow and had a milky trace. The hyenas and badgers would come later, likely at dusk, to check for scraps. The birds would clean the carcass. The worms would wriggle through and churn blood into dirt. They would spread that dirt and the rains would come and wash the tiniest parts down to the river. The small silver river fish would gum on green algae that grew on the decomposing bones. The hunt connected them all.

There was no scent of the young leopard, which struck Girl as odd. When the leopard had arrived ahead of the winter storms, he had made himself known. He was looking for his own land. She was especially tuned in to signs of danger from him. She wondered where he was.

All beasts had their own characteristics and the family didn't see themselves as an exception. Like the bears, the family had the soft feet of predators that allowed them to sneak up on prey. Like the cave lions, they had eyes that faced front to judge the distance from a target. Like the birds, they could make sounds in their throats to call to one another and warn of danger. Like the foxes, they collected and stashed food for the winter.

The differences between their bodies and those of the beasts around them were not shortcomings but sources of inspiration. If a bear could rip skin with her claws, they would look for something to slash with. Long ago, one of the family had started to chip pieces of rock into talons. Over time, the techniques for shaping rock were refined. By rounding the back of a stone, the family made a hand ax comfortable enough to hold in their palms. With it, they too could claw into a hide. A wolf used a tooth to pierce a vein and drain its prey of blood; the family could attach a stone point in the shape of a fang to a sharpened stick. A bird could use his call to attract a mate; the family members could try to link gravelly sounds from their throats to turn them into something slightly sweeter.

All beasts were made of meat and blood. Their daily life often involved some kind of gore. When they sliced open any of the animals around them, the insides of the bodies looked much the same as their own. The blood of a red deer tasted surprisingly similar to one's own blood. A chip of the bone of a wolverine was hard to distinguish from a chip of a brother's bone. For all these similarities, there was a sharp divide that separated the beasts. There were only two kinds of meat: The meat that gets to eat. And the meat that gets eaten.

5.

The family hid and waited for the first bison in the small herd
to cross the river. This was at a wide part where the water pooled
before the river narrowed and the land steepened. Here the rocky
cliffs flattened out to make a way for all beasts to pass through. The
small bison herds often used this crossing to move from their winter
grounds in the trees to the open grazing meadows higher up. They
would enter the river on the far side of the bank, break through the
thinning ice, and swim across the cold waters as fast as they could,
trying not to get swept away. Once the bison gained the other side,
the only path funneled them into a narrow pinch. They had to pass
through this channel of rock single file to get up the bank.

Girl tucked her spear into the groove in her armpit. To hunt was to
wait. The family had worked the hunting grounds for as far as their
shadow stories went back, but the site wasn't theirs alone. All beasts
on the land either hunted here or crossed the river here. It was a good
place to drink and play, but it was also a dangerous place. Where
there was food and fresh water, there was danger.

Then: *Snap*. A sound. Where? Girl curled her top lip up to feel the
breeze on the sensitive patch on her gums. She felt a small ripple, a
heated current in the air. What? She twitched her head to the right to

listen. The tremor from the snap was like a sharp prick to the back of her neck.

This was the land where she was born and she knew it like she knew her own body. It was the only place she had lived. Because she came from Big Mother, her mind held the memories of all the hunts the old woman had been on too, and her mother before as well. And Girl also had the stories that came to her in dreams from the other members of the family. Every bump, dip, and curve of the land lay in the grooves of her mind, but they weren't only there. Her body held the memories too. There was a dent in her shin, like a dip in a path, from when she had fallen. There was the scar on her finger, a ridge that held the same curve as the cliff, from a sharp rock. When the hair on her arms stood up, it was like part of the grassy meadow where the bison grazed. Her body took shape from the land.

The small muzzle of a bison calf pushed out from the bare branches. The brush was still stunted and brown from the cold. Only a few small buds had managed to poke out. Girl saw a head, a small body, and gangly, weak legs. This would be an easy catch.

Girl heard the soft click of Big Mother's tongue. The old woman was off to the side for safety, but she paid close attention. She would never admit that she could no longer hunt. Instead, she had pointed to Runt and folded her hands over her eyes to say that someone had to watch him, then tucked herself into the roots of the tree. She watched closely and signaled with the tongue. Two clicks for the bigger cow and one for the smaller calf. There had been only one click, so Girl knew it was decided. Taking the calf meant that the young beast would not grow to breeding age and multiply. It was a short-term decision to gain meat, but it also meant that in the long term the herd would probably die out. The bodies of such a small bison herd could no longer replace themselves.

Girl took in a slow breath to fill her body. She looked to Him and lifted her top lip. She felt the surge of his pulse on her soft skin; this was the beat of his body anticipating the danger of a hunt. He sniffed and gave her a look. Did he know her secret? Could he smell her heat? She pulled her eyes away.

The mother bison came out from the brush. She picked her way carefully down the path toward the water. It was cold and the breath came from her muzzle in plumes. Ice clung to the edges of the mud. Few animals had crossed so far this year. The cow had to move out a little way to reach a place where the ice broke into the shallows under her hooves. The ice had held on later than it had in other years. Everything on the land had to shift around it.

The calf caught up to his mother, small hooves slipping. The cow took a good look around, slipped into the frigid waters, and looked back for the small one. The calf entered just upstream from his mother. He struggled to move forward in the current once his hooves left the muddy bottom of the river. The river was still strong enough to try to sweep his body down and swallow it up. A chunk of ice thumped against his hindquarters and threatened to push him under, but the mother's muzzle caught him. She guided him through the swiftest parts and they made it to the other side.

Now the calf's spindly legs struggled to gain the bank. The cow lumbered out and shook. The first flies swarmed in the warming sun and angled for a way into her matted fur. As she climbed up through the mud, it clung to her hocks. The bones of her ribs hung over a knobbed spine, the imprint of the hard winter clear on her body. The calf pushed into his place close behind his mother, a nose to her tail. From his skittish eyes, it was clear that he would have crawled back inside her belly if given the chance.

Ahead, the path up the bank pinched. It forced them to walk single file through the high-walled, rocky channel, a trap with only one way out: the other end. It was the shape of this land that fed the family. Some meat gets to eat.

Crouched on the high ledge, looking down, Girl held her breath and kept her body as still as the rock. She felt Him's pulse quicken, and her heartbeat kept pace as the mother led the way through the channel. Girl waited until the larger bison had passed by and took a deep lungful of air.

Girl leaped down into the narrow channel in front of the calf with a roar. The rock walls were head-high. The sound resonated in every direction and the calf must have felt as if he were already in Girl's throat. Her body burst with action. She waved her arms above her head, churning the air in a frantic flap, keeping her mouth open, teeth bared. She looked twice her size.

The calf's eyes widened; a bleat of terror ran along his quivering black tongue. The cow knew the grave danger but couldn't turn around in the narrows. She wouldn't be so foolish as to back into Girl, exposing her weak hind end to a spear. It was from that direction that both wolves and the family were able to attack. Instead, the mother lunged forward to run out of the channel. Once out, she could pivot and come charging back with her horns pointing at Girl. In the time between the mother's exit and her reentry lay Girl's chance. She had to drive the calf to where Him waited by the river before the cow made it back. Bent would do his best to distract the bison mother and slow her progress, but Girl knew that there was no room for error.

Once the calf was injured, they could all climb a looking tree and wait for the mother's rage to lessen and the calf to die. Or, if fury made the mother blind, maybe they could move in on her too. They tried to make the most of an opportunity while staying clear of the beast that could so easily kill them. In that way, their approach to hunting the bison was close to that of the wolves. The only difference lay in the choice of geography. The family couldn't run like the wolves. They needed the advantage of the narrow crossing.

The calf bleated twice and then reared. He started to back away from Girl, closer to the entry where Him sat in wait. Girl shrieked and spat, the amplified sound filling the land. The calf was small enough to turn in the narrows. If he did, she could spear him from behind. But instead of turning or continuing to back up, the calf froze on the spot. Girl shrieked again and the small thing huffed. His eyes rolled, his head lowered, and she caught the sour stench of an empty stomach. He was stupid with hunger. He charged at Girl.

Him saw what was happening and ran into the narrows toward the hind end of the calf. He was coming fast, but not fast enough. He wouldn't make it before the animal's head butted Girl. And that was clearly the calf's plan. His thin legs churned through the cold mud. His head was down. Even a calf had enough strength to break her ribs and legs.

Girl watched the calf come toward her. She knew the mother was turning and would soon be somewhere near her back. This smaller beast was still chest level, a mat of thick fur on a flat forelock and plumes of hot breath, only a stride or two away. The rock channel on either side was too high for her to jump out. At that moment, everything around Girl slowed down. It was as if the air turned into a thick sludge and made it difficult for things to move. She had time to be aware that her body felt as if it were divided in two. Half of her started to climb up the sheer wall to get out of the way. Maybe, if she were lucky enough to find handholds and if she moved quickly, she would live and hunt again. Her other half stayed in place to take a risk and spear the calf from the front, then scramble over it and gain the end of the channel and safety. Though aware of having only one body, she felt both things happen at once. She almost expected to see another version of herself run the other way.

"Aroo." A sound came to Girl's ears. Her two bodies snapped back together. It was a shout from Big Mother, a signal of danger. Girl turned her head to glance behind. That was when she saw the mother bison. The large beast was now charging back through the narrow rock channel toward her.

Girl could taste the desperate fury that came from both beasts. Their rage would feed their blood and give them more strength. One butt from front or back would easily crush her body. The gore of a horn in her chest would make her bleed out.

The large animal put more fear into her, but she remembered the winter ice had taken a bite out of the rock. Focusing on this difference sent her instincts astray. Girl started to run toward the mother. There was a slight slope that she hoped she could reach in time to climb. But the cow came too fast. The mother moved quickly to block Girl's path.

Girl's thoughts went faster than her feet. She knew the two halves of her mind had joined in a certain way. She should turn back in the direction of the calf. Killing him was no longer in her mind, but if her only choice was to run, she should head toward the point of greater weakness. Girl stopped. Cold, thick mud made it hard to find footing, but she dug in and turned.

"*Aroo.*" Girl let out her fear—deep, guttural, urgent. The cow would sense her fear. And she heard the large beast coming through the narrows like thunder. She didn't hear Bent or Him. Girl's ears had room only for the noise of her struggle. Her own gulping breath, the wet, furious heaves from the bison, the sound of sucking mud, all these were so loud that her eyes blurred. She smelled the acrid stink of her own fear. And then she felt the hot huff of bison come into the channel. The beast was so close.

Girl's hair stood up on her body all at once. The bison now had her head down and her horns ready to gore. With a muzzle of foam and a pointed horn on each side of her massive head, she brayed and huffed. There was nowhere for Girl to run. It was a moment they all faced, of life or death. There wasn't time for a conscious decision. She moved on instinct alone. The bison would be on her in three strides. The thick head would crush her chest. Hooves churned, mud flew, and hot, heavy rage thickened the air.

A long stretch of sky moved in front of Girl's eyes. Her arm was up and in front of her face. The bison's broad head tilted. Girl could clearly see her deep, dark eye. A long line of spit dripped from the bison's muzzle. The great hindquarters of the bison hunched up, bundling, curling. This was the last stride the bison would take before her head connected with Girl's chest.

The bison straightened her head to strike. That meant that Girl disappeared from her view. With her eyes on the sides, the bison was built to watch for meat-eaters coming at her from the rear. She could see a spot behind her own tail, but, like a horse, she could not see directly in front of her. Girl vanished in the spread between the cow's eyes. The enormous head was almost to her chest. Girl felt a last heavy breath on her cheek. With that, the bison hunched and lunged.

It wasn't until that moment that Girl saw Bent. He jumped into the channel and onto the cow's back. With a hand on one horn and the other horn in the crook of his elbow, he twisted her neck to the side. Both bodies fell roughly against the rock wall. Girl was knocked back. She saw hooves and horns and fur and spit and then everything went black.

Pink Lines

I'd spent hours on my cell phone assessing my prospects for funding a more substantial dig on the site. I was affiliated with a university, but its trustees were not sufficiently moved to cough up more than a paltry sum. It would cover my pay, Andy's, the help of one student on rotation, and the most basic tools. With those resources, and taking the weather and working conditions into account, the excavation would be finished in roughly three years. My internal clock was ticking at a far quicker pace.

Then I had a promising conversation with a trustee, Tim Spalding, at the Ancient History Museum in New York. I'd met him a few times, and he had been following my work for a while; he was interested and said he wanted to discuss the project with me in person. He seemed to share my need to proceed quickly. He talked of how the museum had fallen behind and was merely coasting on its past successes. The trustees needed to reinvigorate the institution by getting behind big discoveries. They had just hired a new director, and he had plans for innovation and ideas for collaboration with other countries. Tim asked me to fly out and meet him the next day. Excited, I agreed and paused to allow him to offer to pay my travel expenses, but all I got was silence. I took a deep breath and said I'd be there.

When I hung up, I realized the extent of the tricky timing. I'd meant to go home, visit the doctor, and, if it was confirmed, tell Simon about my pregnancy. Then there was the issue of money, or my lack of it. I hesitated for a moment and then decided that credit cards were invented for precisely this sort of circumstance. I called Simon, barely giving him the chance to get the phone to his ear before I said, "I've got to go to Manhattan."

"Go to Manhattan, or drink one?"

"Perhaps you can meet me there?"

"I have classes. My students would wonder where I'd gone."

"I'm meeting with people from the Ancient History Museum."

"What? It sounds like you and Andy got into the cocktails again."

"Ask someone to take over your courses for a few days?"

Simon paused to think. "There's been talk of consolidation in the department. Better not."

"The museum might fund my project."

"You'll need a few cocktails."

"I'd love to have you there," I said.

"I wish I could come."

"Me too."

Andy and I sat in our camping chairs and I told him about the upcoming meeting at the museum. "Can you guard the cave while I'm in New York? Will you be okay?" I worried about someone coming along and attempting to lay claim to the precious remains at the site. "Don't worry," Andy said, mistaking the reason for the concern in my voice. "I promise I won't get lonely."

His wife had died two years before and sometimes I was caught off guard by the extent of his grief. I felt terrible when he said this, realizing that I'd been placing the feelings of the ancient dead before those of the living. "Are you sure?" I asked.

"I'll be fine."

"You've been thinking of her?"

"I haven't had a spare moment, but I miss her. The warmth of another body at night, you know..." His voice trailed off.

"That's an awkward thing to say, given that we share a tent." I tried
to coax a smile out of him.

"I'd prefer someone who isn't nauseous each morning. Am I too
picky?"

I gave him a kiss on the cheek. "Don't let anyone near that cave." I
didn't want any other treasure hunters nosing around.

"I'll bare my teeth and snarl if anyone comes near."

I gave him a hug. "Thank you."

"You'll be great." He returned my squeeze, then made a show of
looking up to the sky. "Please, God, let Rose be successful so that I
can get my own tent."

My flight left from Avignon in the early hours. In the airport, I bought
a pregnancy test. I would have to fit the visit to the doctor into my
schedule later. When the plane was in the air, I shut myself into the
small bathroom, opened the package, and peed on the felt tip of the
stick, which looked oddly like a clear marker pen. I sat on the toilet,
shut my eyes, and slowly counted to sixty. Vapor from blue chemicals
in the toilet drifted up, the airplane engine vibrated, and the noise
of a sudden flush of the toilet next door made me wonder if I might
get flushed out myself. I imagined getting sucked down the drain
and dropped into the cold air outside the plane. Somewhere over the
steely waters of the Atlantic, I'd fly and soar above the clouds for a
few moments...until I fell.

My stomach lurched as I reached the count of sixty. I opened my
eyes and looked. The pregnancy stick had a small plastic window in
the middle with two sharp pink lines. Why pink? It was the most
patronizing of all the lady colors. And what did two lines mean? I
fumbled for the instructions in the box, only to realize that I'd thrown
them out. With a deep breath, I pushed my hand through the round
hole that held the garbage. Luckily, the piece of paper with the in-

structions was at the top of a garbage mountain inside. I scanned and saw that two lines meant a positive result. That stopped me for a moment—positive that I wasn't pregnant, or positive that I was?

Of course, in a way I already knew. Scientists work more within the realm of the hunch than we will ever admit, but it's the hard evidence that turns an idea into something concrete. That's when, as Andy might say, the shit gets real. My hands started to shake, but I couldn't afford to let my emotions take over. It wasn't like the baby was about to pop out at any moment. I could figure out what it all meant when I got in touch with Simon. For now, I wanted to focus on the meeting. I stood up, threw out the test, and smoothed my shirt. I pushed out of the stall, thought of ordering a shot of brandy, then caught myself with a laugh. I'd have to find new ways to be strong.

One last trip to the bathroom before we landed; I combed my hair and put on lipstick. Soon I found myself in the customs line, smiling sweetly. I swept past the luggage carousel. If I was adamant about anything in my life, it was that I didn't travel with more than I could carry. There was a driver with my name on a sign waiting to pick me up. I switched into low heels as we drove.

I felt satisfied with my choice of footwear as I followed an assistant, my heels clicking down the polished stone floor of the museum. He turned and showed me into a room, where I was surprised to find four people sitting at one side of a long table, a polished glass of water in front of each. One more spot, presumably for me, was set across from them; it looked like I would be facing a firing line. They were talking among themselves, and they stood when they saw me enter. The only person I recognized was Tim Spalding, the trustee I'd spoken with on the phone.

"Dr. Gale, wonderful to see you again. Thank you for coming."

"Nice to see you again, Mr. Spalding," I said.

"Tim, please."

His palm was dry and his grip firm. I pulled my hand back with a glance down. I still had dirt under the edges of my nails. I had given them a scrub earlier, but I hadn't worried about it too much. Every archaeologist in the field suffers the same. But then, under the grandly arched ceiling of the museum conference room, all that digging and dirt felt very far away.

Tim didn't seem to notice my hands. "You'll be sitting here," he said, motioning toward the chair that faced the other side of the long table. I put down my laptop bag. I had expected to sit in an office and talk. The last time I'd been in this intimidating configuration was when I'd defended my doctoral dissertation. The same kind of nerves crawled under my skin now.

"Dr. Gale, I took the liberty of assembling the committee. We all rearranged our schedules to come." Tim went on to introduce the others. There was a paleoarchaeologist named Maya Patel, whom I'd met when we were on a panel together a few years back. A woman named Caitlin Alfonso, whom I had heard of but never met, a fairly well-known primatologist. She looked the part, with her Jane Goodall hair—a gray ponytail held back in a loose band. The last person introduced had stood to the side as the formalities were under way. Now he took a crisp step forward as Tim said, "And this is Guy Henri."

The man held out his hand. I grasped it and felt the callus from my digging trowel bite into the edge of his palm. A slight flinch from him; I looked down. His thumb stretched across the top of mine. The skin was pink and fresh, and the thumbnail was a buffed and perfect oval. I caught a whiff of lemon with a hint of something spicy, a scent far too tasteful to be called cologne. He also glanced at our mismatched hands.

"Rosamund Gale." I pulled my hand back.

"Your reputation precedes you."

"You're French." I smiled, realizing that on the phone Tim had Anglicized his name so it sounded like it belonged to a part-time fitness instructor who insisted his beer gut was muscle. But this was Guy Henri, the well-known Parisian curator. I'd never paid much attention to museum politics, but even I had heard of Guy. He had built an extension on the museum in Arles, a shard of glass fixed onto the older, dour modernist concrete building there. It had put the museum on the map and it drew tourists in numbers that Arles had never seen, but the addition had come at a cost. With a conservative French government pulling back on the funding of regional arts programs, Guy had forged an unprecedented relationship to build the extension with an oil company as a sponsor. The perception in the archaeology community was that this was an American-style model of business, the first step in turning a public institution into a space for private gain. My French friends were of the firm opinion that Guy was the barbarian who had kicked open the gate.

"I didn't realize that you had been appointed to the Ancient History Museum," I said.

"You know my work in Arles?"

"Of course."

"My remit here is much the same."

"Invite a sponsor to chisel its name across the door?" I asked.

He let out an easy laugh, clearly unconcerned. "My dear, this is New York. The wealthy don't need to hide behind a company here. They etch their own names, in full. But the true problem is that this institution has become a dusty crypt for artifacts. I will make it into a center for didacticism and debate. The public will be engaged with a dynamic institution, as important as the public libraries of the nineteenth century."

"Carnegie funded the libraries," I said. "Private money."

"With a vision for public good. We can be the start of the next American revolution." The corners of Guy's mouth curled up in satisfaction. I could already see how he thought it would play out. My theories about Neanderthals were controversial enough to attract the kind of attention Guy needed. He had the connections to negotiate a working collaboration around artifacts found in French soil. He might have kicked open the gate, but now he invited me to step through.

Tim looked unsure about the tension between Guy and me. Was it a good sign or not? Aware he'd missed some of the subtext of the exchange, he waved a hand toward my chair. "We will let you get started, Rose."

I sat, swallowed hard, and made a show of taking a sip of water from the glass at my right. I plugged in my computer, using the quiet moment to think. Maya Patel, like Tim, would understand the significance of the find. Guy clearly knew that my theories were controversial, but what was the depth of his understanding? The primatologist would also need context. Eyes on the floor, I tried to summon whatever part of me had once been brave.

"Maybe start by telling us why you should get to spend our money?" Guy broke the silence and, in doing so, rearranged the room into his vision of its hierarchy.

"I've spent the past few years working on a detailed review of the archaeological evidence we have about Neanderthals," I said. "I compared it to similar evidence from modern humans who lived at the same time. We wanted to better understand the disappearance of the Neanderthals. As you know, their extinction is usually explained in terms of the so-called superiority of modern humans. It's commonly posited that *Homo sapiens* had the ability to innovate as well as a more evolved culture and a greater cognitive capacity, and that's why they survived when the Neanderthals didn't. Our review was an attempt to test this assumption."

Now that I was in my area of comfort, I started to warm up. Rather than being cool and imposing, the stone in the building strengthened me. All four people leaned forward, listening intently. "We reviewed most of the studies completed within the past ten years. In that time, there has been a huge shift in our conception of Neanderthals, especially given the new DNA evidence that has greatly deepened our understanding of their biology. We compared modern humans and the Neanderthals who lived at the same time, and we found that the archaeological record shows little difference between the technological or cognitive ability of the two groups. It is incorrect, in any of these areas, to call the Neanderthals inferior."

Maya Patel quickly raised a finger. "If I may, Dr. Gale?"

"Yes, go ahead."

"I read your paper and was intrigued. But—forgive me—if the Neanderthals were not technologically or cognitively disadvantaged, could you expand on your ideas about why they did not survive?"

"It's a good question," I said, knowing that it was also carefully phrased. Maya was probably on my side.

"It must be answered with perfect clarity." Guy pressed his forefinger and thumb together in the air; his polished cuff link caught the light.

"I won't claim to have a definitive answer for you," I said, addressing Guy directly. "If you are looking for public engagement, then I'd suggest the conversation about Neanderthals is what needs to evolve. It's unlikely that there was a single cause for their extinction. They had a stable culture that survived for more than two hundred thousand years, which is far longer than the modern human has endured or likely will. That said, living at low population density left Neanderthals vulnerable to disease, climate change, interbreeding, and, especially, violence and competition from modern humans. What they lacked was the safety net of a social network, but they were a magnificent people."

"So magnificent, they died off?" Guy asked skeptically. "That's the question we are up against."

"We've long assumed that it was our species' large brains that set modern humans apart. The studies show that Neanderthal brains were possibly larger than ours, though cognitive ability and brain size are not necessarily as linked as we once thought. In the physical evidence, we see a brain that might have worked similarly to ours, like in the way they made tools. What's more, the modern human brain hasn't evolved substantially in the past fifty thousand years."

"If a Neanderthal were sitting in my chair, would he give you funding?" Tim tried to lighten the tone.

"My point"—I tried to smile—"is that our brains haven't changed significantly since the time of the Neanderthals. We are running twenty-first-century software on hardware that was last upgraded fifty thousand years ago. If the modern human brain is largely unchanged and the Neanderthals lived in much the same way as humans did then, it is realistic to think that we might be able to communicate with one sitting in your chair. The question remains, though: Would his brow protrude as much as yours, Tim?"

Tim, bless his heart, laughed out loud.

"With apologies." I gave Tim a friendly nod. "I undermine my own position by making a joke. The point is that the archetype of the grunting, knuckle-dragging Neanderthal is not only outdated, it's wrong. That's what the conversation with the public should focus on."

"They were as intelligent as us?" Guy raised a groomed eyebrow.

"That's what I believe."

"And yet we were able to kill them all."

"Some died by human hands, I'm sure of that. But others must have been friendly with humans. We know, as one example, that the two groups interbred."

"Sex is interesting." Guy smirked. "Almost as interesting as war."

Caitlin, the primatologist, sat forward and addressed Guy in a crisp tone. "In my area, when we see a behavior once, we tend to ascribe it to the whole population. If one gibbon murders another, then the scientific community is likely to decide that all members of the species have murderous intent. But a careful study of individuals shows that the range of their behavior is as broad as it is in humans."

"I'm sure the same would be true of modern humans who met Neanderthals by chance," I added, nodding. "Some would be peaceful, others wouldn't. It would depend on the individuals and their circumstances."

"But this is all theory," said Guy. "Where is the evidence?"

"It has been well established that when modern humans move into an area, an extinction of the large animals in that area tends to follow. I have no doubt that there was conflict over territory and resources between modern humans and Neanderthals. Low population density meant the Neanderthals were vulnerable to violence, competition, diseases, and so on. As a result, they couldn't withstand the pressure from new neighbors. But I agree with the point that Caitlin made, that there was probably a range of reactions to contact, from violence to sex to friendship. But I'm sure, also, that modern humans back then developed a certain kind of story about the Neanderthals that played to their benefit. It's a story that we continue to tell. It's the story we should challenge."

I could see Guy's finely tuned gears turning. "Sex or violence— which is the more compelling story?"

"They are both rather fundamental," said Maya.

"But this is a museum." Guy shook his head. "We need to convey the ideas without a big long conversation. We need a message that the public can understand in a glance."

I knew what to do. I tapped my computer to life. On the screen: the photo Andy had taken of the two skeletons. The room immediately fell silent. At that point we had had their two skulls dug out only enough to show their profiles, but the outlines were clear in the photo. The two skulls lay together in the dirt. They faced each other, their eye sockets level, as though they had been looking at each other in their last moments of life. The Neanderthal was on the left, her brow protruding and her braincase sloping, with a prominent bump at the back. The modern human was on the right, his skull rounder and his knobby chin jutting out. Whatever their differences, they appeared to look straight through them. The connection between them felt fixed, like they had managed to keep their bond even in death.

Maya's hand went to her mouth. She let out a sob.

"Oh my God." It was Guy who first spoke, in a whisper. "They look like lovers."

The committee agreed to give me a large grant. Tim reiterated the rough timeline we had discussed on the phone. We were to complete the excavation by the end of August. Caitlin expressed concern about whether that was realistic, given that the artifacts were the property of the French. Guy waved this away, muttering about how much the French system needed an infusion of cash. He wanted to have his negotiations finished and a preliminary exhibition mounted as my results were published. We could make casts of the two figures in position and show photos of the site. Other details they discussed rushed over my head as I started to realize that I'd done it. I shook hands and didn't worry about my calluses. Maya gave me a hug, and Tim seemed thrilled to be working with me after so many years of conversation. Guy came over to shake my hand, but instead I leaned in and kissed him on each cheek. He looked at me. "This will be big, Rose." I knew enough about him to take this as both encouragement and threat.

As I was leaving, Caitlin came and put a brittle-looking hand on my arm. "Will that schedule work?" she asked, glancing at my waist.

"For what?" I asked, feeling equal parts shocked and violated.

"You'll be under a lot of pressure."

"Of course." I looked at her frown. "Why does that worry you?"

She didn't answer. She only gave me a hard stare and then nodded. "I'll support you." Then she left and I was confused. Did Caitlin have the power to see right through to my uterus? I didn't appreciate the implication that I needed help or that I looked weak. Just then, Tim clapped me on the back and showed me out, so I didn't have a minute more to think about it. Soon I was in a cab.

I got to the hotel room and flopped onto the bed. I've never seen the point of staying in a hotel if I'm not with someone I enjoy having sex with. I missed Simon. Time zones be damned, I had to call.

"Big news!" I said when he picked up.

"Hello?" Simon sounded baffled.

It was the middle of the night in London. "The project. The dig."

"Is this some sort of sex hotline?"

"I got the money."

"That's wonderful." He was probably rubbing his eyes. I pictured him in our bed, sheets hopelessly twisted. "Your meeting went well. I never doubted it. Do you have a glass of bubbly to celebrate?"

That gave me pause.

"Are you still there, Rose?"

"I shouldn't drink."

"Is there a cava shortage in Manhattan?"

"I'm pregnant."

"Oh." Now I thought I heard Simon sit bolt upright. I knew exactly what he'd look like. His eyebrows, often the most expressive part of his face, would have risen halfway up his forehead. I heard a lift in his voice, the sound of a spreading smile. "That's the best news."

There was silence as Simon collected himself and decided which question he wanted to ask first. He finally settled on "How far along?"

"Coming up on four months."

"So due in . . ."

"Sometime in the beginning of September."

He paused, maybe coming to terms with how much his life had just changed. "That's what you meant by news. To think I thought you were talking about your meeting."

"Your mind is always on my work."

"I admit I'm so happy, Rose. You know I've always wanted this. I thought we were too old."

"That *I* was too old," I corrected.

He asked if I'd noticed any changes. I told him the grisly story of almost throwing up on Andy one morning. My breasts were larger by a quarter of a handful, although my belly was still flat, and my nipples were maybe a touch darker in the most pleasing way. As I told him this, my mind went back to what Caitlin had said as I was leaving the museum. If I wasn't showing, what had she meant?

"You know what I'm most excited about?" Simon asked.

"Changing diapers?" I guessed.

"Of course. I can't wait."

"I prefer ancient, fossilized poop to the fresh kind."

"Guess again."

"Bedtime stories?"

"No," he said. "I'm most looking forward to what this means for us."

"What's that?"

"We will get to spend more time together."

"True."

"You'll stop hopping from cave to cave and country to country all the time."

"Where will I be?"

"Finally, you'll be at home."

PART II

6.

When Girl came to her senses, lying on her back in the narrow channel, it was quiet. All the beasts in the area surrounding the river seemed to stay still, but she knew their ears were pricked. What she did next could mean a chance to eat. It could even mean a change to the order of the land.

The tree branches swayed just slightly. The red squirrels stopped their chatter, only twitching their tails. The badger family, who kept hidden away during the day, had woken but stayed under cover with ears perked. The bear, however, didn't stir. Her interest in the action was vague, so she had dozed off. Her long-held truce with the family meant she could save energy now and, if they were successful, feel assured that she would eat later. The young leopard was careful to stay well downwind.

The only thing that continued unchanged was the river. It didn't care about such earthly matters as which meat got to eat. It concerned itself only with a search for the easiest way down the flank of the mountain. It ran. Nothing could stop it, and in that sense, it was the strongest force in the land.

In Girl's head, all thoughts went through her mind as pictures. The bison, Him and Bent, Big Mother and Runt—where were they all? She could feel the hard ground against the back of her head. The sun was trying its best to give her heat. She took a big breath in and was almost surprised not to get a mouthful of water. But the river was still partly frozen...was she on the ice? She lifted her head and looked down. Her feet were at the end of her legs. The toes wiggled to say hello. She was amazed to see that her head was still attached to the rest of her meat. "Pitch," she muttered. *Still attached.*

Girl felt for the shell that she wore on a lash around her neck. It was there. She pushed herself up quickly, spear tucked in. Her head wobbled and the land slanted. She stepped to the side, trying to stay upright. Where was Him? Bent? She felt her head—a big bump. It had hit the rock wall on her way down; her eyes had been filled with white fire. She rubbed her head and carefully walked along the channel to the relative safety of the rock ledge. Big Mother and Runt were tucked into the tree roots where she had left them. They didn't dare peek out until Girl called, *"Aroo?"*

It was Runt's small head that popped out from the roots. Big Mother had pulled the boy close to protect him. Worry caused his features to gather at the center of his narrow face. Hair like a patch of dark moss; the broad strip of skin on his forehead caught the sun. In that fleeting moment, Girl wondered how old he was. He was so small, it was hard to tell, but when she looked at Runt, she realized that he was okay.

Time moved within the cycle of the season, but the repetition was never precisely the same. When the land took a lot of rain, the timing for the harvest of hazelnuts would change. If the sun was strong, the harvest might shift again. When the ice broke, the fish started to run. Before then, the bison would cross.

But in that moment, she looked at Runt, and though the blow to her head had left her stunned, she felt how time might move ahead of her. The land would change and Runt would grow. The dirt would freeze as his soft feet turned shiny and hard. The river would swell with rain as his round belly flattened out like ice. The rocks would erode from the land as his flat brow hardened and protruded to protect his eyes. All at once, in Girl's mind, all those things happened. And none of them did. She shook her head to clear it. The distraction of her affection for Runt was dangerous in that moment. It took her senses away from the hunt. Was there danger?

The boy caught her eye and lifted his pinkie finger up to her. It was their signal. When Runt had first come to live in their hut at the meeting place, he had spent much of his time sitting quietly in a corner in the dark. Girl had pushed into the hut to recover from squashing her pinkie finger under a rock. She held it up in the air so as not to knock it. When her eyes adjusted to the dimness, she realized the boy was sitting there. He was holding up his pinkie in the same way. Since then, it had become their sign. It meant different things depending on their circumstances, but right then she knew he wanted to ask *Are you okay?*

She lifted her pinkie to signal *Okay*. Runt nodded and ducked his head back down. Big Mother's head popped up next. Her wrinkled mouth stretched to a smile when she saw Girl. Relief curled around them like a ray of sun. The warmth flooded in.

Girl looked down the path, and her eyes followed the tracks toward the river. She could see the mother bison had run over her body and out of the channel. How had she not been crushed? It could have been due to chance . . . or to Bent. Where was he? The ice hadn't completely let the river go. The hoofprints tracked in the mud and went out onto the ice where it was thick enough to hold the creature up. And there was the sprawled body of the mother bison. The beast still twitched, her side opened with a fierce wound. Girl judged that the bison wouldn't stand again. A broad smear of bison blood crept outward on the ice. Him stood guard by the bison, spear up and not too close but ready to thrust it as needed. He must have speared the mother bison from behind. It was dangerous to get near a dying beast. Like a wolf, Him would stand back until it died.

Girl scampered through the mud. Where was Bent? He had

jumped between her and the mother bison's fury. Girl looked back up the narrows and then along the side of the bank, but by then she already knew. Bent's body lay on the ground. He must have been dragged and gored in the chest by the cow's sharp horn and then trampled by her sharp hooves as Him attacked from behind. She checked for other beasts, but they had all been scared deep into the bush by the ruckus. She ran to Bent and knelt down.

Bent's pulse was faint. There was too much blood around. Bent was already changing. His skin looked like a hide that had been wrung out. A chip of bone was missing from his skull. The pulpy brain bulged out. His legs were sticking out at odd angles. The only thing that looked untouched was his bent arm. She felt a stab of pain at seeing this. It was the single part he would have wanted to be trampled. She picked up his body and cradled him in her arms. He already felt smaller and slighter, like his trip to the other side of the dirt had begun. She held his head against her chest and hummed so that he would feel her vibrations.

Carefully, she stood and carried Bent down the path and onto the thick ice. Big Mother must have already known. She was waiting in a sad silence, sitting on the ice, using a folded part of her cloak as padding for her broad bottom. Runt and Him made a circle and Girl lay Bent in the middle of it, his chipped, bleeding head on the old woman's lap. They hummed and swayed and tried to fill Bent with *warm* from the family. A body doesn't want to feel alone when making this last change. When a body died, it was often the last request, made with the gesture of hands to the heart: *Hold me close.* To be connected to the family was the most important thing. And so they took turns holding Bent. They all joined in the hum to let him know that he wasn't alone. As they did, the dying mother bison felt their vibrations too. Soon the hum soothed her. In that way, they all let the changes come.

Girl kept one ear turned out. She would rather have been swamped by her sense of sadness, but the time after a kill was dangerous. A newly dead animal held much more value for a carnivore than a living one. If another beast was going to risk challenging the family, it would be then. The commotion would have alerted all the creatures for miles around about what was going on in the valley.

Girl heard a sound from behind and turned quickly. What? A bleat. A light tremor of air hit her cheek. It did not feel like a strong enough current to mean danger, but she looked more closely.

The bison calf was huddled into the frozen mud of the bank. She could smell his young fear, an uncomfortable ripple across her lips. His small legs trembled. He kept his eyes low. He would not live. He couldn't make the journey to the summer grazing spot alone. The other animals, those from the herd that had turned back from the crossing after hearing all the noise, would probably not take him in. They would knock past him and leave him in the cold. Only in the best times, in the midst of a summer bloom, for example, was taking on a young calf worth the risk. And the ice of the moon or the wolves who lived that way would get him quickly after that. His last few hours would be full of agony and pain. To Girl, the calf looked more alone than a beast ever had. She couldn't imagine how that would feel, to be without the family. A lone body.

Girl walked on the ice to the calf. He didn't run and let her take a small horn in her hand. She braced his head against her thigh. She gave him a pat, a moment of warmth. She let out a breath to give him heat. She heard a step behind her and turned to see it was Him. She nodded and turned back to the calf. With a hand on each small horn, she held the calf in place. Him thrust his spear into the calf's flank, twisted it, and levered it forward to make sure it couldn't walk. Girl pulled back her spear and thrust it into the calf's neck. She twisted the stone tip to make the blood flow. The calf slumped down, his front legs bending so that his weight was on his knees. Another stab from Him and the calf was on his side. Blood spurted and throbbed out until he collapsed.

Him put a knee on the calf's neck, pressed down with his hands, and nodded for Girl to go first. She put her mouth to the vessel at his neck and drank. She felt the heat of his body directly. The calf's life would change. It would give the family strength before the fish run. Bent's life would go forward inside of her and the rest of the family. She drank back this promise. And Bent died soon after.

7.

Girl was bloodied to her shins, hands glistening red against the river ice. Even though grieving for Bent, she was hungry. Him held the mother bison's hoof in place for Girl to make the first cut. She placed her stone tooth, a hand ax made by Big Mother, at the base of the hoof, where it joined the bison's hide. She leaned in for leverage, then pressed the blade into the fur and sliced up. The tool was sharp and the cut clean. She pulled it up to the bison's knee, exposing red blood and the first of the mother's meat. She cut to the side of the tendon that ran along the back of the leg, careful to keep it in one piece, as it would be soaked and dried and braided to make the best lashing.

Next she worked the stone tooth the whole way up to the chest. The hide was thick around the core. Girl breathed hard, the air coming out of her lungs in huffs of effort. They cooked most of the meat they ate, but it was a custom to take the first bites from a fresh carcass raw. The warmth of the meat filled them with joy. Girl would cut them each a slab before they worked the meat.

Him pulled the hide tight on either side of her blade to help her make a smooth cut. He watched Girl's hands, strong and blood-soaked, as she worked and felt a stab in his chest. He sniffed and marveled at the way the muscles along her back rippled. She had peeled down her cloak, and the bare flesh was the smoothest hide he had ever seen.

When Girl was born, she had been a curled creature, tiny and pink. She'd smelled nothing like she did now and he'd had little interest, though he was able to steal her food on occasion. Once, when she was a few years old, she had held a piece of dried tree sap, a favorite treat, in her chubby fist. Him had pointed for her to look at the fire. When her head turned, he plucked the sap from her hand and laughed. He walked away assuming she could do nothing. He was licking the sap, gazing at the trees, when a small foot darted out of the brush and tripped him. The next thing he knew, he was facedown. He spat dirt from his mouth and looked at his hand. The sap was gone. Most children would have stayed to taunt, but Girl's mind must have been on securing the sap. He didn't even see her escape.

Girl had grown up big and strong. Her limbs were quick and her thoughts seemed to run ahead of her body. Those around her wanted to help protect her, the sign of a leader. With her instincts, Girl would clearly be one of the best hunters. The instinct of a hunter was like having red hair or a big nose—it was built into a body or it wasn't. It was also a skill that could be improved through careful watching, listening, and learning. Girl could combine the stories of Big Mother with what was observed. She was rare in that she could account for all the things that changed as well as those things that stayed the same.

Him's mouth was salivating in anticipation of the meat he was about to eat. And that feeling, the powerful craving of hunger and the drive to eat, mixed with the sight of Girl working. He sniffed and found his senses overwhelmed by the carcass and the sound of the river and the steam in the cold air that rose up from the beast. The meat. Soon he would eat. As he watched Girl's muscles ripple under her skin, her arms slicing and her legs bracing, all the reverence and respect for skill and strength mixed with the swill of his spit. His cravings and the powerful urge of a body to fill itself came together. She became all that he could see.

Him's eyes filled up with Girl, but then came a loud crack. A white light flashed in front of his eyes and his head snapped back. He lost his footing and fell on the ice. When he opened his eyes and pushed himself up to sit, he saw Girl watching him with concern, surprise on her face. She turned to look behind her.

Big Mother stood there on the ice. She had caught Him staring at Girl. Maybe she had felt his mind, because she had thrown the rock to warn him off. She had a second rock in her old hand, ready to go. Him lowered his eyes quickly. He rubbed the spot on his forehead to show it was sore and also to say that a second rock wasn't needed. Big Mother might be old, but she was still a great shot. Girl's job was to live outside their family by winning another place at the fish run. Him wasn't to touch her.

Another sound. This time it was Runt. The small boy shuffled up as close to the carcass as he dared. Eyes down, he stopped a body length from the hoof of the bison and looked at it intently, as if that hoof could give him permission to join in. Him turned his back to the boy.

Girl could see by the shake of his fingers that Runt still considered himself new. He hadn't been with them through a full cycle of the seasons yet and was unsure of his place. After a kill, he didn't know if or when he would be allowed to feed. His breath smelled sick with nerves. He kept the heat of his stare down on the ice. Girl clicked her tongue. She held the meat under his lowered eyes so that he would see it. At first he didn't respond. He seemed to stare in disbelief at her hand, as if the thick fingers with ridged nails dipped in bright blood were only in his imagination.

After a moment, Runt came to his senses. He clamped his hands around the meat and stuck his front teeth into it. He ripped and pulled with a snarl until a manageable bite came loose. Girl wasn't sure he even heard her delighted laugh, a ripple lost across the ice. His attention was completely consumed by the meat as it slipped in a slick into his mouth. His tongue found the juice. It was one of the best cuts, from near the fatty heart, and he had never been worthy of it before. He closed his eyes and chewed in the warmth.

And because Runt's eyes were closed and Girl got such pleasure from watching him eat, neither of them saw Him coming. One moment Runt was approaching ecstasy, sucking down the taste of blood, the next he had been knocked onto his bottom. Runt's eyes popped open in surprise. Girl shrank back. Him stood too close to the boy. His broad brow was lowered and he snatched the meat from Runt's hand. The boy cowered, hand over eyes, memories of his past mistreatment still fresh, head turned so he wouldn't see the next blow coming.

Him didn't hit the boy again. Runt wasn't worth more effort. As there was an abundance of meat, Him gave the boy part of a rib that he cracked off with his ax. It was still a good piece and Runt was careful to dip his head and give a grunt of gratitude. He scampered off to eat near the safety of a boulder.

Girl was about to scowl at Him but stopped short when she saw that Big Mother approached, slowly. They all stopped their petty squabbles and lowered their heads when she lumbered up.

"Hum," she said, sniffing.

Now it was Girl's turn to cower. She looked down quickly as the old woman came up to her. It was the custom that the older woman said how they would hunt and how the meat was shared. Before the winter storms, long and hard that year by any measure, it would have been that way. But by that spring, Big Mother had withered. It seemed as if Girl's body had burst with round muscles and breasts to fill the empty space. It was clear from how Big Mother was approaching that she had taken offense. Her eyes were narrowed and she peered down her broad nose at Girl.

Girl had to be careful to show that she still knew her place. If she challenged the authority of the older woman, it could mean a fight. This was the last thing Girl wanted, to fight the woman who loved her and had raised her. But though Big Mother was calm in her later years, her temper could still spark. There was a reason she had reigned over the family for so long. She was able to set sentiment aside to hold her position if need be. So Girl was very careful to make herself as small and unthreatening as possible. She put her arm across her chest to push her breasts down. But now that Girl had the heat, she knew that Big Mother's mistrust of her might worsen.

Perhaps in Big Mother's eyes, Girl had acted like the hunt was her own. From her vantage point in the tree roots, she might not have been able to see what happened in the narrows. Did she think Girl had instructed Bent to go after the mother bison?

"Ne, boh." Girl blew out of her nose like a bison and wagged her head from side to side to show a humble kind of sorrow. Killing the bison, drinking the calf's blood, and making the first cuts were honors of the one who was in charge of the hunt. Impulsively, she had leaped in and filled the void.

Big Mother came to stand near the hoof and glowered at Girl. Runt moved over to take Girl's hand, but she quickly waved him away. This was not the business of a boy. Girl took in the body of her mother and felt a tremble in her gut. She wondered if the mountain was shaking or the ice was breaking, but it was only the movement of her actions coming up on her. When the body first moved, it took some time for everything else to catch up. She felt her lip tremble and she knew what came next. She slowly walked to the old woman's feet and knelt down with her head lowered. Placing the head and neck right in striking distance of another body's hands meant *You can do anything to my body that you wish.*

Girl stared at the ice and at the feet of her mother. The old woman wore bison pads lashed to the bottom of her soles to protect them against the sharp ice. Her skin was so thin that it almost shone as it folded loosely around her foot bones. Her toenails were as thick as bark. Calluses on her toes and heels were closer to the texture of rock than skin. Girl had known the feet to be kind, but they had also delivered many kicks. She felt Big Mother's hand on top of her head. She flinched and held her breath. The hand pressed against her matted hair.

"Hum," said Big Mother as she took a sniff.

The hand pushed hard on Girl's head. It waited there, the pressure sending the message that a decision was in the balance. After a pause, the woman sat. She clicked her tongue once at Girl. She wanted to be fed.

Girl leaped into action. She took a slice of the fattiest part from near the heart. She put a piece of the softest white-marbled fat into the woman's mouth first. Next, Girl chewed a piece of meat, careful to preserve the juice. Then, kneeling beside the old woman, she helped Big Mother eat. Forgiveness was felt first in the stomach.

The balance in their family might have tilted, but Girl was young. She didn't quite know it, but she wanted something impossible. It was a new feeling, as fresh as the warm meat that they chewed. Despite Big Mother's obvious weakness, Girl, as many of her kind often did, wanted things to say the same. While she fed the old woman, she allowed a shard of hope to pierce her heart. She wanted to show the others that she was not yet in charge. She would stay young. That way, maybe—despite the coming of her heat—she would be allowed to stay in the family.

8.

They missed Bent all the more when they started on the long job of butchering the carcass and carrying the meat the short distance to the cave near their spring hut. Girl worried that they would be vulnerable to meat-eaters on the trips back and forth. Him wanted to build a shelter and camp near the carcass, but Big Mother said no, as the ice could melt under them at this time of year. She decided that they would move the meat to the cave and showed this by marching off toward it. Girl tried to hold back a loud moan, her grief and exhaustion mingled in a black ball in her chest. At least in the cave, she could rest. They could carve and consume the meat in a big feast within the safety of the rock walls.

At the camp, Girl put some of the meat they wouldn't eat immediately in short-term storage. They had dug pits down below the freezing line in the ground. Runt and Bent had lined them with rocks at the base. Girl now placed the extra meat inside the pits, then added more rocks on top and poured water from a leather sack over the meat. This would quickly freeze and hold the meat as long as the weather stayed cold. When they wanted to eat, they would pour hot water over it to thaw it. When they cached meat in a tree, Girl carefully wrapped large leaves around the trunk so that the red squirrels couldn't climb up, but the creatures would still spend their days trying. That was one reason for Big Mother's great aim. She could knock a squirrel on the head with a rock from ten bison strides away.

Bent would have been the one who watched over them, spear ready, lips poised to shout, while Him butchered and Girl carried the hunks to the cave. Bent would have walked with Big Mother and Runt back to the camp and checked the surroundings while they worked in the cave. As it was, they had to keep glancing up from their work of cutting thin strips of meat for the drying racks, boiling the brain to make fat, and stripping the tendons to soak for lashing. It slowed them down.

Later, they would eat and tell stories with their shadows by the fire. They didn't yet miss Bent because of what he had said or how he had acted, but they missed the jobs that he did to help keep them safe and fed. Grieving took on a practical place in their minds. A body amounted to the work it did over the course of its life. Getting over a death was a matter of figuring out how to do all the jobs without the one who died. And processing a large bison with so few people was difficult.

The weather was on their side. It was just above freezing at midday. Him cut up the carcass and submerged the cut pieces in an icy pool of water at the edge of the river so that roundworms and buzzing flies didn't move in. Him took the forelegs off first and then removed the back legs. He dunked these and passed them to Girl. She heaved them onto her shoulder and started the short trip to the cave. Next, Him severed the hip joints and worked on detaching the pelvis. As he did, he kept turning his head to scan the land.

Aside from the worms and the flies, the next biggest danger—the thing that would stop them from eating or harm them before they could—was the other meat-eaters. All through the valley, the beasts would know of their success. News traveled on the trees. Even the lightest breeze could carry the scents of a successful hunt for long distances.

Back when the family was larger, defending a kill wasn't such a problem. Even if all of them were tired or sore from the hunt, a few bodies with spears in hand were enough to deter possible attackers. Most of the carnivores were old and wise enough to know better than to disrupt a family. All the beasts who lived around the mountain were well versed in the complicated math of who got to eat. A meal had to yield more energy than it took to secure it. When the family had more bodies with spears, it was easy for all the beasts to make the calculation in a single glance.

But now the family's numbers were few. The loss of Bent tilted them into a precarious situation. Some of the family, like Runt and Big Mother, were weak, though they were loath to admit it. Girl had this in mind as she approached the cave carrying a large shoulder of the mother bison across her back. She could hear the crackle of the fire and see the smoke coming from the cave, but she let the meat thump down on the ground to take a rest. Better to do this before Big Mother and Runt could see her. She didn't want them to worry about how tired she felt.

Girl squatted on a boulder, letting the air huff out of her mouth. The heat of her body rose from her skin. Watching her heat release into the air, she imagined that she had a fire burning inside her chest. When it burned hot, the smoke would rise and her muscles would crackle with strength. Sometimes the fire burned low, and that's how she felt now. She didn't have more wood to toss on the flame.

A quiet crack of a snapped stick came from behind Girl's back. She tilted her head, suspicious and alert. The sound was made by the weight of a soft foot breaking a twig, the sign of a stalking predator. She felt it then; the pulse of a beast was near the tree, but Him was still down by the river. Who was it?

She lifted her nostrils up to the air. The breeze was blowing from the other way and it was hard to catch. She curled her lip to feel the heat. There was lightness to the body; not a bear, not a big cat. Where? Her large eyes caught the tip of a tail in the bush. There. It twitched. She snapped her head around. Rings curled around a tail. Ears with black tips. A laugh of relief bubbled up from her throat. It was Wildcat. She put her hand to her chest to steady her breathing.

Wildcat slunk out from behind the bush to make himself known. He gave her a look, a wrinkled nose, like she smelled of something bad. Maybe she did, but that wasn't what he was trying to say. It was the gesture he used when asking for meat. He had trained Girl to know this by wrinkling his nose and then showing affection when she did the right thing by feeding him. Most of Wildcat's days were spent tucked into shadows and brush. He didn't often show his body during the daytime, but he had an amazing knack for appearing at exactly the right moment when he did. That was no coincidence. He kept Girl's body under close surveillance. If she killed an animal or found a carcass or even some old nuts, he was there to ask for some.

The cat crept up close. His rough tongue licked her cheek and felt like tree bark. He rubbed his body along her lowered head. He looked at her with squinting, narrowed eyes and offered his nose to touch. She moved her nose gently in and felt the wet tip of his. He had taught her that, to kiss like a cat with a touch of the nose. She smiled.

She reached to the leg and ripped off a piece from the rough edge. The meat still had warmth from the life before. The cat snatched up the meat from the ground, gave her a rub on the leg, and quickly scooted under a bush to eat.

Watching him rip and chew for a moment, Girl caught a glimpse of his long canine teeth. They were sharp and strong and could easily pierce a vein, but he'd never turned them on her. She sometimes wondered if their friendship was a product of their sizes. He had assessed her and knew he couldn't win based on muscle strength. His jaw was not large enough to hinge around her neck. So, being a clever cat, he plucked food from her in different ways.

If something terrible happened and it was her leg lying on the path, would Wildcat eat it? If his jaws could manage to open wider and times were hard, would he take a bite if there was nothing to stop him, like Him's foot or a well-aimed rock from Big Mother's hand? Yes, of course. And so that was where their friendship rested: between the lines of hunger and opportunity. It didn't lessen their bond. Maybe it was what made it so vital.

9.

By the time Girl returned to the river, Him had made good progress on cutting up the carcass. Standing on the ice, he once again put his hands in the shallow waters to take out a hind leg for Girl to carry back. Though he worked fast and hard, his wet hands pulled heat from his body. He wouldn't usually get so cold in these circumstances; it was a sign of overwork. When Girl walked up, he was pounding his hands against his legs in an attempt to get his blood moving again.

Girl squatted on the bank and called, *"Aroo."* She preferred to squat, as it kept her body away from the cold and damp. Her broad legs and thick joints folded smoothly into a position that allowed the bones rather than the muscle to hold the weight of her body. Squatting was a comfortable resting position.

Him squatted to face Girl. She took his hands in hers and felt how cold they were. Even though he limited the time his hands were in the water, the cold had washed away the blood, and his skin was white and creased. They were both tired from the work and their sorrow. Since Him's hands were the primary tools required to finish cutting and hauling the carcass, they demanded the most care. The need to warm Him meant that all other work stopped.

Bent would have glanced at Him's hands and taken over the job of cutting the carcass. Him could be on lookout, take a rest, and chew on a piece of meat. That's what his body needed, to refuel the fire inside and make it burn brighter. As it was, the heat was withdrawing from the ends of his body to focus on the important middle. It was a first sign of danger. If a body started taking heat from the fingers, it would soon start taking heat from the head too. When the blood started to withdraw from the head in favor of warming the chest and the belly, the body would start to tire and freeze. Girl knew that a body could do unpredictable things. She believed that the reasons for acting crazy often came down to temperature.

But they were short on bodies. The family was so small that they both had to keep working. Girl had to warm Him's hands the best she could, and quickly, because they couldn't lose this bison meat. Girl took his hands in hers and pressed the palms together. She cupped them and huffed a breath of air on his skin. This didn't have much practical application—in a cold climate, his skin could be warmed effectively only by bringing his core temperature up—but her hot breath did wonders for his mind. It sent a clear signal from one body to the next. She understood that he was cold. She understood that he was working hard. Where the mind goes, the body can follow.

Girl parted his hands and brought them under her armpits. Armpits were the best way to warm hands, and her armpits were especially well suited to this task. Her broad rib cage made a great landing spot, and each hollow under the muscles could take in a large hand. A generous brush of hair provided insulation.

Him was immediately grateful. He closed his eyes and rested his head on her shoulder, their knees touching, his hands warming. There were times that he would do the same for her. He breathed in her scent as she warmed him and it reminded him of all the other times that she had helped him. With his head on her shoulder, he opened his eyes. As she was squatting, the soft, pale skin of her parted thighs was visible against the muddy bank. He saw a streak of something on her inner thigh. After killing and slaughtering a bison, this was hardly surprising, but something about it caught his attention.

He sniffed. It wasn't from a bison. It came from her. She was in heat. The smells—wet soil and the crisp mint of first shoots of fresh grass—mixed with her warmth. He leaned into her, trying to get more. He put his mouth on her shoulder and bit into the round muscle. She twitched, as if flinching, but she didn't pull back. She leaned in too. Their chests came together and he felt the strength of her arms around his neck.

He lifted her hips so that her thighs spread over his. With a grunt, he pushed in. Unsure, unsteady for a moment, there was a wobble and then she wiggled. And that was right. He felt a glow like a hot ember move up from his groin and spread out. He was filled by the heat of her body and with the rhythm of how she moved and the smell of earth around them.

The land came together inside them. Everything that his senses took in—the scents and patterns on the sand, the sound of the river water running close by, and the sway of the branches on the trees—turned inward toward her. Rather than scanning the land and listening to it, he was inside of it. Just then, just there, Girl became the land. She was what fed him and kept him alive. They moved together. It was *warm,* more than they ever knew.

That's what Girl kept feeling: *I am the body.* It was as though she were joined to the family in a way she had never been before. But she also felt full. The hunger that had been gnawing at her belly was finally sated. She found a way to satisfy the craving and there was no question that she would indulge it. She rocked and pushed in a way that was more like compulsion than choice. A year of restless chewing and pacing, and she had finally found a way to feed it. Her appetite, as always, was fierce.

And after they were done, they stayed like that, Girl's legs wrapped around Him's waist. She breathed in and his lungs inflated and let go like an answer. A peacefulness settled around them. The land seemed to acknowledge what was going on. The pinecones vibrated, the birds started to chirp, the bear stirred and cracked open one eye, and the youngest badgers chattered with curiosity.

Girl pulled back and she didn't look at Him, not directly. She looked at his shoulder and it occurred to her that she wanted to bite it. Not just a little, but to sink her teeth in deep. And then she knew she was a glutton and soon she would want more. With a sorrowful feeling, she knew that it was a drive as strong as her hunger and that the real problem was its persistence. It was already coming back.

Him held his palm up and toward her. She did the same and they pressed the skin of their hands together. It was an oddly formal gesture, given the moment.

But Girl was unnerved. For that length of time, they hadn't been watching their own backs. No upper lips had been raised to check the wind; no eyes had been scanning and no ears had been turned out. The strongest two of the family had let their guard down. They had left the others exposed. It was risky.

The hard truth was that although nothing dangerous had happened in that moment, they weren't safe. The leopard, the young male that had been slinking around the edge of their land, had climbed up to the perch he used as a lookout. He had been monitoring the crossing from there. The young leopard had taken note because he had left his mother during the spring melt. She had taught him to hunt as well as she could. She had tolerated him and his brother for an extra year to hone his skills, but when she became pregnant again, it was time for him to make his own way on the land.

With bared teeth, his mother chased the brothers away again and again. The leopard hadn't wanted to leave. Her care and scraps of meat were all he knew. For a young leopard, especially a male, the first year on his own was particularly precarious. A male had to find his own patch of land. The land had to be of a size that could sustain his body with a good source of meat. His needs were much like those of the family.

In more usual times, a leopard his size would never think of taking on the family. The fear of primates who used rocks as claws and spears as teeth was bred into him. Once, when he was with his mother, they had sensed a family coming, and she had made sure they turned and went in the other direction long before an encounter. Going near them or encroaching on their territory often ended in death for his kind.

In most species, those lower down in the hierarchy tend to be finely attuned to any shift in the upper levels. After coming across the family, he studied their habits. By that point in the spring melt, he was aware of their ways and strengths and especially their weakness. When he heard grunts and gasps from the two strongest of the bunch, he walked over to his perch to take a look.

The leopard didn't try to interpret the commotion. He only observed the scene with a cool eye and knew that they were not watching their own backs. For a young male leopard who needed to claim a territory large enough to sustain and grow his body so that he could mate, there lay a small chance.

Archie Comics

My grandpa was the first to tell me about Neanderthals. He had a log cabin on the hard slopes of the Laurentian Mountains. He and my grandma lived in Montreal but spent much of their time at the cabin. When Grandpa wanted to get my brother and me out of Terrible City (his favored name for Toronto), he asked us to visit him at the cabin.

The winter he first told me about the Neanderthals was particularly cold. A groaning woodstove heated the cabin. Grandpa stirred the fire, arranged logs, and then went out to the shed for more wood. The back door opened with a swirl of snow to announce his reentrance. I pulled my scratchy wool sweater up tight, and it chafed my cheeks, still ruddy from tobogganing. My brother shivered beside me on the couch and read a comic book. Once the flame was strong in the stove, Grandpa sat down between us.

"Do you know of these Neanderthals?" my grandpa asked in his deep rasp. His thick work shirt smelled of woodsmoke and pine. Delighted to hear that I didn't, he raised a book to show me an illustration.

My brother glanced up from his *Archie* comic just long enough to look disgusted. "Hairy like you, Rose."

Grandpa only lifted an eyebrow. "The book is by a gentleman named H. G. Wells. Listen to the description: 'An extreme hairiness, an ugliness, or a repulsive strangeness in his appearance, over and above his low forehead, his beetle brows, his ape neck, and his inferior stature'—"

"What does *stature* mean?" I asked.

"It slumped over when it walked," he answered. "Wells says that the idea for the ogre in folktales came from the Neanderthal."

"You mean it was like an ogre?"

"Except it was real."

"A real monster?"

"And maybe it ate the flesh of its own. A cannibal."

"Robert, you'll scare the daylights out of her," my grandma called from the kitchen.

"Not a chance." My grandpa torqued his torso to address her. "She's the brave one."

My brother chose that moment to pounce. He ducked around Grandpa and roared. I startled and screamed. One glare from Grandpa and my brother slunk back to his seat and hid behind his *Archie* comic.

"They ate each other?" I asked Grandpa, eyes wide.

"We don't know exactly," he said, backing off slightly, "but it had very primitive habits. We've come a long way since then."

"What part did they eat? Like a leg?"

"That's why we can look back on history with a sense of triumph. They were somewhere between the humans and the apes. An evolutionary middle point, if you will." He tapped his head. "We got smart. That's what makes us different. We control the world around us. It's no longer necessary to stoop to such vile acts."

"The arms? Or the body?"

"My point is, Rose, that the Neanderthal was driven by instinct alone."

"I hope I don't get eaten. Do any live in this forest?"

"They were animals. Not men."

"How about the female Neanderthals?" my grandma called from the kitchen. "Were they as fierce?"

"No," Grandpa called back. "And not nearly as good at the dishes, dear."

I heard my grandma's light laugh as the drain sucked the dirty water from the sink.

After Grandma tucked me into bed later that night, my eyes were still wide. Despite the cold, I hopped out from under the thick pile of blankets to press my nose against the glass and peer out into the dark. Outside, the snow-tipped trees lined the slope down to the icy river. Did the Neanderthals come out at night? In the distance, at the bottom of the hill where I'd been tobogganing earlier, something moved. It was a dark shape, furry, but it stood upright like a man. I strained my eyes to take it in. The figure stopped, as if he knew he had been seen. I'm sure I saw him turn toward the window. He must have spotted me. For a moment I was terrified, but then I remembered that Grandpa had said I was brave.

I wasn't scared of the Neanderthal. I wanted him to know that I didn't fault him for eating anyone. I pressed my palm flat on the glass in greeting. I hoped he could see me. But I couldn't see him anymore. He was gone. I watched for as long as I could keep my eyes open, but I never saw him again.

I was thinking of my grandpa when I wrote an e-mail to Tim Spalding to let him know that I was pregnant and due in three months. I needed to be brave, but all I wanted was to curl up in Grandpa's lap. I couldn't articulate exactly why I was so nervous about breaking the news to Tim. I hadn't hidden anything from him. It wasn't wrong to wait until I knew the pregnancy was progressing smoothly. By then I was six months gone and showing.

I didn't think word of my pregnancy had traveled to the museum. By that point, six students and assistants worked alongside Andy at the site. I had hired locally and through colleagues. People came and went. A museum photographer based in France visited regularly to capture our progress. The museum's shipping company brought in some things and took away others. To each person I explained that we needed to keep the project under wraps. I asked all of them not to speak of what they knew about the site. Maybe they thought my standard speech referred to my growing belly, and I dropped a few vague comments to imply this, but it was mostly about limiting the number of visitors to the site. More people brought more risk of contamination or improper procedure. I ran a tight ship.

Still, the dig was going slower than I would have liked. This was partly because the logistics were difficult but more because the site held such a wealth of artifacts. It was good news, but I could see that we weren't going to be finished by August. I had to send the e-mail now because it was clear that I would have the baby while the excavation was still under way.

Tim didn't get back to me that day, or the following week. It was late in the evening two weeks afterward when his reply slid into my in-box. I was exhausted from a hard day and had stayed up too late in an attempt to get caught up on the administrative tasks that were piling up. I was about to collapse into bed when Tim's message came.

> What a nice surprise! Congratulations to you and your partner. Lucky kid to have a mother who is so bright and energetic.
>
> We are thrilled for you and have been arranging things on this end to make sure our project can continue without interruption. Great news! Do you remember Caitlin Alfonso, the committee member you met while you were here? She is going to be project manager for the site while you are on leave. She will arrive in a week so there'll be a smooth transition.

I stopped reading and immediately hit Reply. How could they make this decision without me? It was apparent that the intended transition was mine—off the site. Barely able to contain myself, I started to type. A primatologist would take over while I was away? How on earth would someone with training in another field ensure the excavation was done correctly? It defied any reasonable explanation.

Guy clearly wanted one of his own in control of the project so that he could shape the announcement of the discovery in whatever flashy way he wanted. By then, I'd already seen warning signs. During my weekly Skype reports to the committee, there had been a few awkward conversations about the dig's progress. I couldn't keep every detail under wraps. Word about the find was filtering through the community. Some prominent people in the field were quietly questioning the evidence of a relationship between modern humans and Neanderthals. Guy wanted to lead with the image of the two skeletons and call them "the Lovers," but the idea that our species had killed off the inferior Neanderthals was deeply embedded. As humans, we are drawn to the simple story about our species: that we evolved from primitive to become perfection. The messier truth was much less in line with Guy's marketing plan.

I knew it would be difficult to figure out the politics behind their decision to put Caitlin in charge. I was an outsider. Even if I took the time to fly to New York, I would only be given the party line, and I would be on their turf. I decided the best way forward was to avoid all the unpleasantness of a power struggle and skip to the end. I hastily wrote back with a few terse words and a reminder of New York law: "It is unlawful for an employer to compel an employee who is pregnant to take leave of absence, unless the employee is prevented by such pregnancy from performing the activities involved in the job or occupation in a reasonable manner." I asked Tim to let me know if he felt that I wasn't performing in some way. If that was not the case, then I would dictate the terms of my leave from my own project.

I shut down my computer, stood up, and pushed aside the tent flap; by that time we had upgraded to the luxury of a wood platform with a large canvas over it. Andy was sitting nearby, staring into the campfire. I pulled up a lawn chair and lowered myself into it. I felt uneasy about the e-mail I had just sent. It was my usual habit to let an e-mail sit before sending, but in those final few months of my pregnancy, my blood was quick to boil. Though I had no interest in blaming hormones for my temper, my impulses had become harder to check.

"Andy?"

"Rose?"

"Am I difficult to work with?"

He stared into the fire. "My wife used to say that when she asked me a question like that, she wasn't actually asking."

"But am I?"

"She wanted me to smile and say no." He let out a quiet laugh.

"You haven't told me much about her," I said. "I'd love to hear more."

"But you're not my wife. Do you want me to answer your question?"

I nodded and poked a stick into the fire.

"Yes," he said.

I gave him a light punch on the arm. "Wrong answer."

"It's not a bad thing. You are trying to alter an entrenched way of thinking. People don't change their minds without a push."

"I don't want to be difficult."

"Rose, I'm saying I think you're brave."

10.

They buried Bent at dusk. That was the best time to transition to the other side of the dirt. Him dug a shallow hole, as deep as the frost would allow. Girl folded Bent's knees up to his chest and wrapped his arms around his legs. They placed him in the hole in the ground. His head was lowered down so that his eye sockets touched his knees. His toes were tucked in. They folded his body into the fetal shape in which he was born. They kissed Bent's cheeks and smoothed his hair. They all closed their eyes, held hands, and let their minds sink. Deadwood. Each body thought of moments with Bent and so the others also felt those moments. In this way, the family shared Bent.

The rare times that they questioned or feared death—for even such a formidable family was prone to moments of doubt about the hardship of living—a message lay in this shape. If decomposition and renewal felt too hard to grasp, if a body ever worried over what might happen to it after death, Big Mother made a shadow to show this fetal shape. Think back to that time before you were born. Did you suffer? Were you hungry? Were you cold? You were none of those things, she reminded them, casting the shape of a baby on the wall. Your body was of a different form then, as it will be again.

None of the things Bent used in life were placed in his grave. Runt would inherit his cloak and hand ax. Girl would use his drinking sack because hers had begun to crack. Him would repair his trampled spear and carry it. Honor lay in the family's using these things in their day-to-day lives. These items held the memory of Bent's work. The family would hold and use the tools he had owned. They would benefit from his effort.

Once, long ago, they had buried the body of a brother, Fat Boy, under the roots of a freshly downed tree. It was warm then, and a day before he died, the rains had soaked the land, and a fairly healthy pine tree had lost its grip and fallen over. The root ball left a large hole that was big enough to place a body in with only a little more digging. With the body curled into position under the root ball, Big Mother instructed them to right the tree again. They packed dirt around the bottom to replant the roots. In a short time, Girl could feel that the life from that body had transferred to the tree. The needles turned a deep green and the branches stretched to the sky.

Girl wished they could do the same for Bent. That way when she missed the work of his body, she could put a hand to the tree and feel the strength of his muscles, and if she placed her ear against the bark, it would sound like the blood in his veins. Every tree had a beat and she wanted one to remind her of Bent, but there were too few bodies to spend energy on doing more. A burial under a tree was only for when there were extra hands and meat.

Runt put the first handfuls of dirt onto Bent, but Girl wasn't ready. It was another sign that she wasn't accepting change as she should—a sign that trouble was to come. She stopped Runt because she wanted to look a bit longer at Bent, curled and naked as he was.

Girl knelt beside Bent's curled body and pressed the backs of her fingers against his cold skin. His heavy brow shielded his eyes. His long lashes spread against the skin of his soft cheek. His broad nose flared out. It was the same shape as hers. When he was small, she used to pretend to grab that nose from his face and put it on her own. There was always a pause as he crossed his eyes to see if his was still attached. She would pretend to throw it to Him and soon a wild chase would be under way.

She looked up to the long faces of Big Mother and Him. They didn't tell Runt to keep throwing in the dirt. Maybe they wanted to linger too. Big Mother was in charge and no one questioned what she said. Not only because her kick was swift, but because she had lived so many years and knew of all the changes. She had seen them before and had the ability to predict what might happen next. That skill was so rare, and when a body had it, respect welled up in the chests of the family. It helped them stay alive.

But now Big Mother was bent and stooped. It somehow felt like her bison horns had shrunk. She looked so sad that Girl wondered if her heavy head might roll right off into the dirt of Bent's shallow grave. Another child on the wrong side of the dirt might be one too many.

There was always change, but for one more thump of her heart, Girl wanted things to stay as they were. She climbed down into the hole with Bent. She got onto her side so that her head was level with his. With her arm draped over his shoulders, their legs intertwined, she put a finger under his chin so that she could look at his eyes. For a moment, she stayed like that and felt the warmth of her body settle onto Bent's skin. She stroked his hair and whispered, "Warm."

11.

The family crawled into their hut, into the belly of the bison, to sleep that night. Their bodies curled into one another's as they had so many times before, but it wasn't the same. Girl was no longer on the inside of the pile. Her back was exposed at the edge, the flesh bumpy, like a bird with its feathers plucked.

Runt was between Girl and the whistling nose of Big Mother. As the smallest, he needed the warmth most. Girl snuggled into him as best she could, but his bony elbow jabbed her stomach. Just as she pushed the elbow away, his pointed kneecap jutted into her thigh. She let out a small cry of protest, only to have Big Mother's broad hand come down heavy on her head with a shush. Girl was further unsettled as Wildcat stared at her. She could feel the heat of his eyes. He had snuck into the hut earlier, only to be shooed outside by Big Mother. Wildcat sat by the flap and watched, waiting until the silence was complete and Girl gave her signal. Then it would be safe to come in.

Girl turned and pulled at the hides and muttered. Another large hand came to her head to still her. This time it belonged to Him. He lay in his usual spot, the protective position above their heads. She laced her fingers through his and pressed her palm against his rough skin. She pulled on it. She wanted a warm body to line the outside of hers.

Him lifted his head for a moment and surveyed the sleeping bodies. Their breathing was still shallow. Silently, he moved beside Girl, to the spot where Bent used to sleep. He settled into the impression of the boy's body on the hide. It was nice to feel his brother in the hollow. Him put a large arm over Girl. The skin along the back of her body was cold. He moved in close to warm her.

It wasn't too long before Girl felt very warm. She broke into a slick sweat on her back. She started to move under the hides and Him couldn't help but respond. He reached out with his hand and found the thick thatch of hair between her legs. With one finger, he felt she was wet, and a signal came like a kick, sending his body into action. He found Girl's hand and pulled on it. She followed him out into the cold.

With distance between them and the hut, Him spread out their cloaks and pulled her on top of him. They tried to keep from yelling to be sure they weren't interrupted. They were led by impulse. Like hunger, their immediate need overrode any care about what might come next. Breath was heavy, fingers found skin, and bodies rubbed and twisted into each other, as rowdy as the bison during the rut.

Later, Girl crept back into the nest. Him took his place at their heads, but shame began to gnaw at him. Since the last Father had gone hunting and not returned, Him had tried to fill the older man's role. When he looked at Runt curled in the nest and listened to the whistling nose of Big Mother, he recognized that while he had been out with Girl, he hadn't been protecting them. He felt the sting of guilt. To do the work of the Father, he needed to watch the family.

Him stretched out and closed his eyes, relieved to be back in his place. He thought of Girl and what had happened, but his immediate worry was Big Mother. He knew he wasn't supposed to touch Girl like that. He ran his fingertips along the wound on his forehead from the rock that Big Mother had thrown to warn him off. But what if he fell asleep and dreamed of Girl? Would Big Mother know? Soon his body tugged at his mind too hard. He fell into a deep sleep.

When Big Mother woke, it was still dark. Her eyes flicked open, and she took a big sniff. That's what woke Girl up, the sharp intake of air. The old woman sat straight up in the nest in one swift movement. For the first time since wintersleep, she did not need to be hoisted upright. The cowlick at the back of her scalp swirled like a whirlpool in the river. The large head slowly turned toward Girl, who felt disoriented for a moment and couldn't think what had changed about the old woman, who looked too small and bare. In the next moment, she knew. The horns. Big Mother took them off to sleep but was quick to put them on each morning. It was strange to see the old woman with this big, bare head. Girl shut her eyes and pretended to sleep, but she made the mistake of squeezing her eyelids too tight. Big Mother was good at spotting a fake.

"Hum," the old woman grumbled.

More sniffing. It was loud, as though Big Mother was tracing a scent. Girl bit her lip. She had been told to stay away from Him. She knew that her job was to hold her urges. They would go to the meeting place in time for the fish run. Other families would also be there. They would see her sister, Big Girl, who had moved to another family. That alliance would give them status to take a better place along the river. The more connections a family had, the more likely they were to be welcomed and allowed to take the good spots for fish.

At the fish run, they would eat and watch one another and Girl would see which families needed breeding-age females. She would try to figure out which family she wanted and which family wanted her. There wasn't an exact process around it. Sometimes there was an obvious fit. Other times, the girls were the wrong age or the Big Mothers had a strong hold and no match was made at all. In times of peak population, when the bison herds had been large for a number of seasons, the competition could be fierce.

In the best times, when the families were full, the fights between the women for a Big Mother position could be to the death. They told stories of the legendary battles between potential Big Mothers. Though those years hadn't come in a time that any of them could remember, there was a certain kind of luxury in those stories. It was a point of pride to be well enough equipped with bodies, food, and tools to afford the risk of a fight.

At first, Girl didn't attach what she had done to Big Mother's sniffing. What Girl didn't account for was Big Mother's good nose for the smell of sex. Girl was born farther down the line and so had always known Big Mother as an older woman who mated only when absolutely necessary. Mating for her appeared to be a task, like chewing a hide, not something she did for pleasure.

In her prime, Big Mother had sought out the penises of the strongest men. They left their mark in her and lots of fluid got inside. She had all sorts of elaborate theories about the way ejaculate smelled and how strong it was, how it would add to the strength of the baby that would eventually come, how to know when a man was no good or when he might plant the best seed. Using the knowledge wisely was the reason she had managed to have so much success in life.

Big Mother turned her head to look right at Girl. There was no need to ask. She knew who owned the semen and where it had gone. She knew what this meant, too, as she had delivered enough bodies from between her own legs and seen the babies of her sisters at the fish run. She knew what was the same from one generation to the next. Sometimes it was a cowlick, sometimes a nose, and sometimes a bend in the arm. Girl and Him, who had seen only a handful of families at the meeting place and who had lived with very few relatives around them, didn't understand the taboo. In a vast land, seeing a trait one recognized filled a body with the warmth of familiarity. And this was so much part of the family's strength.

But a strength can also become a weakness. Big Mother knew that there was also great danger in things that were too much the same.

She thought she had taught her children with the shadow stories. But for fear to work inside a body, the threat had to feel tangible, and a shadow on a wall wasn't that. Girl and Him hadn't seen what she had. They broke the taboo in the way that a younger generation will.

Big Mother knew the power of sex; the overriding strength of the urge was something that she had felt many times in her earlier life. She couldn't keep her eye on these two for every moment. They were quicker and stronger than her. They sometimes needed to work away from the family. She used to wake up to wrong noises, but now she apparently slept with all the cares of a body that was already on the other side of the dirt. Until the time of the fish run when other mates could be found, one of the two would have to go.

In this case, Big Mother pushed aside her love and devotion for Girl. All the knowledge she had accumulated gave her the ability to override her instincts. The old woman saw a young version of herself in that body. She knew that the family was thin and that the other families would be struggling too. In Girl, she saw the makings of a woman who was clever and kind and quick. She would produce many babies. Where others were failing, here was a girl who would keep a family on the land. Just the thought of this girl's work made her chest puff and her heart throb.

The next thing Big Mother did was brutal, but she did it because she believed with all her being and experience that when a brother and sister got a taste for each other, as sometimes happened when a girl came into the heat at the wrong time, there was only one way to keep the body of the family safe.

Big Mother pointed a finger at Girl. She hissed and spat so hard that her cowlick bounced. Runt leaped up in surprise. He grabbed at Girl out of fear, but Big Mother reached out for his arm and pulled him to her. She looked at Him, who had woken up with a confused look, and gave a short hiss. He quickly lowered his head to show submission. And this reassured Big Mother that she made the right choice. Him was quicker to fall in line than Girl. With the success of the hunt, his strength might be enough to keep the family alive until they moved to the fishing grounds.

"Fly away," Big Mother growled at Girl in a voice so sharp that the rumble ran through the pine boughs under the nest. She meant for Girl to go. It was an absolute command. If one of the family didn't obey, it was a challenge to Big Mother's position as head of the family and would be met by force. Big Mother raised her long arm and pointed a gnarled finger. The crooked joint stretched toward the front of the hut, where the flap shook. "Fly away." Big Mother's intention was to banish Girl. "Come fish," she said next, to let Girl know when she could meet them again.

If the old woman couldn't communicate the consequences of forbidden things clearly, she could at least show the absolute seriousness of not listening to her warnings. This was one of the challenges of being an old body surrounded by young, fleshy ones that had yet to understand the ways of the land. In this case, Big Mother had only action to make herself vividly clear.

While Girl was growing and twisting in new ways, her kind and loving temperament wasn't something that would change. Her mother knew that the independent streak made it harder for Girl to submit, but it also meant that she had the disposition and resourcefulness needed to survive.

Girl scampered to the side of the hut, cowering to make herself small. Maybe if she could make one last try at submission, it would put an end to this idea of flying away. But the old woman wouldn't be swayed. The power of sex was too great. The two could not resist each other, and so one had to go for now. There was no backing down. Big Mother grabbed the horns from a hook and held them up and shrieked at the top of her lungs to assert her strength: *"Big horn!"* She pushed the flap to the side and crawled out of the hut.

Girl let out a sob. She scrambled to pull her cloak up and then grabbed her spear. She felt like she was in a dream, but one that none of the other bodies in the family could feel. She fingered the shell that she wore on a lash around her neck to make sure it was on. Him and Runt were silent as she crawled out of the hut in the morning light. The beasts outside must have sensed the change because there was not a chatter, chirp, or hiss. Big Mother had shuffled along the narrow path and now stood by the hearth. She kicked a log onto the fire and stirred up the flame from the evening before. It was the only way for Girl to go, so she followed Big Mother down toward the fire. Big Mother threw on another log. The flames jumped up, as if fueled by her anger. She bared her teeth and hissed as Girl approached. She stomped a foot in the dirt and shook her spear.

Head low, Girl tried to get close to her mother. She would never fight. She wanted to crouch down and try once more to show that she would be good, submit, and that Big Mother was still in charge, but the old woman was having none of it. That was not a solution. Girl had shown her willingness to break the taboo. Actions meant everything; gestures had little influence, and words barely registered. A wad of spit shot out from Big Mother's lips and she threw the horns down between them. The message was clear. Girl could try to take them by force and strap them onto her head to become Big Mother, or she would have to leave and meet them at the fish run.

"Fly away," the old woman snarled.

Big Mother's temper came from deep down in her belly. Looking at Girl stirred the feeling of hot fire in her chest. This beautiful, strong Girl would soon be their best hunter. Big Mother had lost so many children over the years and each loss broke her body down further. Each death felt as if it took a strip of muscle from her thigh and a few teeth, and a chunk of bone, and a large mouthful of blood from under her skin. More loss would break her body and she would fall. But she knew that Girl could use her clever mind to survive. She was a good scavenger. Of them all, she could be safe on her own.

A mother makes a child from her own blood and bones. They are attached in the first part of life, and although the connection lessens, it never goes away. Big Mother had always felt the dreams of her children more clearly than the dreams of the others in the family. She'd felt the horn in her rib when Bent was gored, and the piercing shriek of a fang through the neck when the young one, That Boy, had been snatched by a lion. She knew Girl better than the others. A girl so like herself with the potential to grow a large family. Because they were so alike, Big Mother believed deep in her heart that Girl would live. They were so much the same.

But Girl wouldn't leave, so Big Mother waved her broad head with menace; each shrunken muscle twitched under her thin skin, and the tendons in her neck stood out. Puckered lips opened to show a growling, hollowed mouth that howled with a deep fear. She shook her spear. It was time to go.

Girl shrank back in terror but saw the seriousness of her mother's command. She had her cloak and her spear in hand. She turned and slipped into the trees in the direction of the river. That was the way her feet carried her, maybe because they had walked there so many times before. She went as far as her legs would take her and then she tripped over a branch and fell. She lay in the dirt; the strength needed to get back up was something she'd left near the hearth. The trees shook with worry, and the land let out a huff of cool air. She waited for a moment to see if she could hear anything or if the smell in the air might change, but it didn't.

For the first time, Girl left the hearth of the family.

Ketchup

I stayed in France as long as I could. Once I was eight and a half months pregnant, I was not allowed on an airplane. Not that anyone was trying to shove me on one. I had made it clear to the team that it was quite normal for North American women to work to just before their due dates and that I intended to do so. I had worried that my impulsive e-mail restating the laws around maternity leave would come across as too aggressive, but apparently it had been helpful. No one said another word to challenge me.

Though Caitlin had been sent over, she was not in charge of the project. She took on a role as project manager and handled the logistics. The only conversation on the topic of my leave I had was with her, just before I left for town. Simon was flying in and I wanted to rest so that I could enjoy our visit, but my schedule felt too open-ended. I knew it would be hard for me to make decisions about the next few months with him. I sat across from Caitlin at the picnic table to go over the project timeline. She very deliberately bit her lip when we talked specifically about my schedule. She made it clear that I was in control of it.

"Just remember that the project is under the jurisdiction of New York laws," she said. "There is no paid maternity leave."

"None?" This caught me by surprise. The lack of conversation had also left me uninformed.

"The museum made a strategic decision some time ago not to pay for maternity leave. Of course, you are allowed by law to take time off."

"Aren't taking leave and getting paid inextricably linked?" I asked.

Caitlin didn't have an answer.

Simon had been teaching an intensive summer course. He had another week to go, but he kindly offered to fly over one weekend, rent a car, and drive me home to have the baby. He would arrive on Friday and we would drive to London on Sunday, but the thought of leaving the site made me sick with panic. Not only was there the bleak state of my finances to consider, but the dig wasn't nearly as far along as I'd hoped it would be. New artifacts—bone fragments, pieces of stone tools, char marks—kept coming to the surface. Our progress was painfully and necessarily slow. I had only the skull of my Neanderthal dug out to a depth that I wanted by then. The rest of her body was still to go, and, judging from my initial pass, it looked like there were more artifacts buried around her body, something by her neck and something else by the pelvis. I desperately wanted to be the one to uncover them. The pressure to finish was mounting because rumors about the site were swirling within the paleoarchaeology community. I'd had to fend off a deluge of visit requests.

Andy dropped me off in Vallon-Pont-d'Arc at the small pied-à-terre that Caitlin had rented to allow for days off, visitors, and overflow. I got there an hour early so I could rest before Simon arrived. I didn't want to look like my usual mess. The team also had a larger house in town, where many of them slept most nights. It was nicer than the pied-à-terre in some ways, but I felt the need for privacy. It would allow me to focus on Simon, and I didn't want the others to see how sluggish I'd become when I let my guard down.

When Simon arrived, I was installed on the daybed in the small main room. He came into the flat without announcing himself, eyes down and looking at his shoes. I'd usually walk to him, put a hand under his chin, and lift his eyes up to mine; it was our established greeting. This time I just sat on the daybed and looked at him. He wore a crumpled linen blazer over a striped shirt with traces of airline coffee dribbled down the front. Hands shoved into the front pockets of his jeans, he gave me a shy glance. He was not reluctant, but he always wanted to make sure that he was welcome. Though we'd been together for five years, he still held a slight formality. I'd come to understand it as a show of respect. I reached out to him to reestablish our link. He came over, shucked off his shoes, and curled up on the daybed with me.

I laced my fingers through his. Simon was so clean. His hands belonged to someone who didn't spend his days in the dirt. He raised my hand up to his cheek.

"These fingernails wouldn't look out of place on a Neanderthal," he said. He kissed the tip of each of my chapped fingers, not flinching once. I put my palm to his chest and felt his warmth. The beat of his heart alone was enough to soothe me. I lowered my cheek and rested it there and listened to him breathe.

It was not only Simon's kindness that I craved, but the comfort of silence. We stayed curled up for a long while before I finally spoke. "Are you surprised?"

"To see you sitting still?" he asked. "Yes."

"Am I bigger?"

"Beautifully so." He knew the precise kind of diplomacy that was required.

"A lot, yes?" I asked.

"Well . . . that is how pregnancy works."

"I'm that much bigger?"

He sighed. "It's more . . . you used to look like Rose with a belly. Now you are a belly with Rose attached."

"Really?"

"Like you have been hired to carry a baby bump around."

"It's heavy."

"I wish I could take it for you," he said.

I first met Simon at the dinner party of a mutual friend, Richard. He had been my lab partner in a brutal organic chemistry course years before. After asking me out one too many times, Richard and I had bonded as firm-and-fast friends. He moved to the U.S. for a while and returned to London to run a successful start-up that helped people find lost relatives. He had a new girlfriend, Nita, whom he wanted me to meet, maybe so he could get my approval, and they were throwing a party. There were two other couples invited, and Simon. Or "Single Simon," as he referred to himself in a slightly anxious voice when he first shook my hand. It was nice to know that he felt as set up as I did.

During dinner, one of the other couples started asking me questions about my work. They wanted to know about the digs I'd done and what I'd found. Soon the whole table joined in the conversation. At the time, I was up to my eyeballs in the review of the new science of Neanderthals. I enjoyed holding court while dispelling myths.

"So they were not hairy?" Nita asked.

"Not particularly. Their hair wasn't much of an insulator; it was more for protection from the sun and elements, like ours is. Mind you, they didn't shave, pluck, or wax."

"I imagine them grunting all the time," she said.

"No less than Richard, though it's likely they weren't as subtle. I talked to an expert in voice recently who thinks they probably spoke at three volumes—loud, louder, and loudest."

"They could talk?" Simon turned to me. "Really?"

I told them that Neanderthals had the FoxP2 gene, which in humans was connected to the development of speech and language, though we needed to learn more about how it functioned for them. "And they had a hyoid bone," I said, "the anchor for the muscles of the tongue. Given their squat larynx and its position in relation to their heavy frames, their voices were most likely high-pitched."

"I can't blame my grunting on my Neanderthal-like qualities?" quipped Richard.

"You can blame many of your qualities, ninety percent or more, on the substantial part of human history that our ancestors spent as hunters and gatherers. That's what your body evolved to do."

"But will you ever settle down?" Nita asked me.

The conversation stopped. Everyone looked from her to me and back again.

"Sorry?" In that first few seconds of silence, I was sure Nita had been having some ongoing conversation with Richard and had addressed the remark to him.

"Richard said that you worked all the time and didn't want to settle down." Nita tried to rescue the situation. "I don't mean that I think you hunt for a living. I mean, it's more about not staying in one place. Not having children . . ." Her voice trailed off into another uncomfortable silence that followed.

Under normal circumstances, I would have simply steered the conversation in a different direction. By then I was a single woman well into my thirties. My days were stuffed full of questions about why I wasn't with a man and why I didn't have kids. But that night, I was so deep into our conversation about Neanderthals—and my focus on my work tends to be single-minded—that I didn't realize that she'd just changed the subject. I let the silence hang in the air way too long. She and Richard had apparently talked about me. I hadn't expected Richard or Nita to understand the demands of a nomadic life or grasp the pressure this must have put on Neanderthal child-rearing. This confused me. I didn't immediately realize that her point was a much simpler one.

Simon was much quicker to catch on. "What about me?" I heard him say. "Am I going to have children?"

"I don't know." Richard's eyes darted from me to him with some relief. "Are you?"

"Well, Richard, I appreciate your concern. I would really like to, but I just haven't met the right person yet."

"I'm sure you will." Richard took a big gulp of wine.

"I worry that I'm getting on in years, that's all," said Simon.

"Perfect time for dessert," said Nita, standing and starting to collect the plates in an effort to shift the conversation.

Simon got up to help. My first impression of him remains the most enduring: he is a flexible thinker in a world that is not, and he's on the edge of defiant. He came over to retrieve my plate, and as he did, he turned his head toward me, crossed his eyes, and stuck out his tongue so that only I could see.

Now, on the daybed, Simon shifted around to look at my swollen feet and immediately saw something he could do. He pressed his palm on the soles, one at a time. My skin was puffy and hot to the touch. Gently, he rubbed my sore calves. He moved upward and eased into rubbing my back and my breasts.

We tried a few positions before sex felt possible. We were usually fairly seamless in reading each other's needs, but this time required a fair amount of conversation, giggling, and adjustment. We ended up making it work with Simon crouched over me as I lay back with my legs to the side. It must have felt like making love to a hot-water bottle for him, but he's never been picky. Between us, there was more laughing than pure pleasure. But this was also a form of release.

Afterward, Simon made me the best grilled cheese sandwich I had ever eaten. And he'd thought to bring a bottle of the kind of ketchup that I loved most; this particular brand was a delicacy that could be hard to find in rural France. The moment I clapped eyes on the bottle, I admit that I started to wrestle with my conscience. When I brought the ketchup back to camp, would I tell Andy that I had it or would I follow my instinct and hoard? My usual way was to share, but I could barely predict my own actions anymore.

As I finished eating, Simon got an uncomfortable look on his face. "I have news," he said.

"Good news?"

He cleared his throat and paused. "From the university."

"About your courses for September?"

"Yes."

There was little noise outside the flat: the angry groan of a moped in the distance, the creak of a clothesline being pulled down the cobblestoned lane, a slight breeze rattling through the trees. The stone construction of the building meant that the low, huddled windows kept it cool inside. Lavender grew in pots on the porch and the heavy smell wafted in. I usually loved the scent. In fact, the lavender was a large part of what had prompted me to approve the flat, even though it was cramped and had little storage. But just then, as I waited for Simon to speak, I regretted the lavender. The heavy stench of it pressed down on my chest and blotted out everything else. If I'd had the energy to move, I would have shut the porch door.

"They don't have courses for me this year," said Simon.

"Not one?"

"No."

"Oh."

For the previous two years, Simon had taught as an adjunct at the London School of Economics, and that's where he was currently teaching the intensive summer course. It was something he'd taken on after giving up his tenure-track position at Bristol. We had decided to make changes in our lives so that we could spend more time together. With my schedule, we agreed that we needed to be in the same city at least some of the time. His specialty was English, which wasn't ideal for a lecturer at the LSE. It mostly meant taking on students who came from abroad and helping them function in a business setting. He preferred teaching more esoteric topics, anything from writing techniques used by Igbo authors who were raised in the oral tradition to the study of hyperrealism in Margaret Atwood's speculative fiction as a tool for social critique.

We both knew that when it came to our income, Simon teaching undesirable courses was far better than his teaching none. A heat came to my face. I turned toward the wall and experienced a sensation with a detached wonder: Was I really going to cry? I could feel small hairs rise on my neck. I clenched my hands tight. I'd weathered many things in my life, and my usual reaction to getting hit by bad news was to dust myself off and work harder. But at the moment, I could barely get out of the daybed unassisted.

I'd always managed to make enough money to get by. I had turned down a tenure-track position, a decision Simon had supported. I wanted to be able to explore and follow my interests, not be forced to adhere to strict publishing and teaching schedules with the occasional sabbatical. I would never understand how a paleoarchaeologist could spend more time in a lab or classroom than out in the elements. Our subjects didn't live in test tubes. I gained insight about how people might have lived some forty thousand years ago from being outside, as they were. The problem was that while a patched-together income had once been fine for us, it suddenly became hard when living in London.

The museum grant money was generous enough, but it went into the project, not my pockets. When working on a site, I didn't have time to take on the lucrative speaking gigs or court-witness contracts interpreting burial sites that kept some of my colleagues going. And the economics of living in London had radically changed. I had been quite comfortable for a while, but now London had been swept into the swift current of a global economy. In a quick few years, living in the city had become viable only for bankers, barristers, and foreign investors. Academic salaries and grants had stalled or, in some cases, been cut altogether. My non-tenured colleagues and I were often told by the administrators in our department that we should feel grateful that we hadn't yet been axed. "Look at the sponsors of the business school," they said. "Let's try to imagine how archaeology might pay its own way."

While still on salary at Bristol, Simon had bought a modest two-bedroom flat in Islington as an investment. Because I made more money than him at the time he quit, I said that I'd cover the mortgage on the flat so that we could move in. It was partly to show that I could agree to a nest in London, though to be honest, I thought of it more along the lines of a base camp. It was the one place we could imagine both of us finding work and funding, and it had good access for travel. But many of our colleagues were migrating out of London in response to the economic pressures. Our mortgage was enormous by any standard. Like people in New York or Sydney or Vancouver, we lived hand to mouth no matter how much we tried to cut back and pare down. Keeping a roof over our heads took up much of my pay. We needed Simon's income to eat.

Now I took a deep breath, an increasingly difficult thing to do. The baby was squashing part of the space formerly used by my lungs.

"Are you okay?" asked Simon gently.

"Yes." I tried to smile, but I couldn't look at him. "I'm more worried about you. If you aren't teaching, how will we keep you entertained?"

He let out a nervous laugh of relief at my willingness to make light of the situation. But the tone of my voice masked the blackness that spread in my mind.

I had an urge to run. That was how I was accustomed to burning off stress. A hard run for an hour always set me straight and helped calm the flighty feeling I often got in my chest. But with the baby, I was a huge lump. The adrenaline had nowhere to go. It only made my heart beat harder. Could Simon hear it?

I stood up and walked stiffly around the room. "Just need a stretch."

Simon watched me closely. When my heart slowed enough that I thought the thumps were no longer audible, I leaned over and gave him a dry kiss on the cheek. "We'll be fine."

"If I'm around the university and keep showing my face, I'll pick something up."

"That's great."

"I'll do my best."

"I know."

A new feeling settled on me, mixing with the dense scent of lavender. My face and neck suddenly felt red and irritated. Did I have an allergy? And what was Simon's best? Before, there hadn't been a moment when I doubted that I could provide for us. He had said the same. But now that I couldn't was his best enough? I hated myself for thinking this, but I couldn't push the thought away.

I looked around the small flat and tried not to claw off my own skin. The tiny galley kitchen was crammed into the corner. There was one closetlike bedroom in the back, and the main room had space for only a small dining-room table and the daybed. The flat was on the second floor of a former stable, above a garage that held an ancient, dusty Peugeot. I went over to shut the door to the small porch, hoping for relief.

Simon had put his bag on one side and his running shoes on the other. To shut the double doors, I had to move both, an awkward reach down, all in the face of that ghastly lavender. My tool belt had fallen off its hook on the wall, and it dragged along the floor as I tried to wedge the doors shut. My prized trowel fell out of one of the pockets. I tried to find a place to hang the belt, but my hard hat was on one hook, and someone who had stayed in the flat the week before had left a windbreaker on the other. It was all too much. There was nowhere to put the clutter. This was the problem with France—no storage. This continent as a whole, with its narrow buildings and reluctance to bash things down and start again, was the problem. I'd made a mistake in coming here. I should have stayed in Canada or moved to the U.S. If nothing else, I'd have had a big closet. Where the risk of moving and learning new things had once felt exciting, it now overwhelmed me. And the damn lavender still stank. My breathing came hard again, my lungs fighting the baby for space. Hand to chest, I knew I had to get out.

"Simon?"

"Yes?"

"I can't live like this!"

"Like what?"

I took a hard look at the mess. "I need to go to the site today, but I'd like to fix this space. All the clutter. I can't leave it this way."

"But you are leaving it. We're going home."

"Will you help me sort it out on Sunday, before we go?"

Simon looked at his shoes on the floor and back at me. It was clear that he didn't see what I did, but he knew better than to argue. "Okay...what did you have in mind?"

"I need to go to Ikea."

12.

There was a border around the edge of the family's territory. It wasn't indicated by anything visible, but it wasn't imaginary either. It marked the land about a day's travel in every direction from the camp. A body who came to it might not know it was there unless she had a sharp nose for detecting the liberal sprinkling of badger and wolf urine around it. But Girl knew exactly where it lay. To her, it was the boundary of the family.

Girl couldn't stay on the land, but it was difficult to know what to do in the absence of the family. When she was with the others, they would wake up hungry, and each day was shaped around filling their bellies. She didn't consciously decide where to go; it was not a choice, but an instinct. Big Mother might set the course, but the seasons governed their movements, the patterns of the beasts showed them the way, and the weather dictated the speed at which they traveled. None of that would happen now. Without a family, she had no one to follow. Girl just squatted by the river and waited for the dawn.

As the gray light stretched out into the day, her grim situation sank in. The land was in a morning state; bright green shoots were starting to push through the forest floor, but the colors looked muted and the clouds were flat. The mud stuck in cold clumps to her feet. The mist blended into a light rain that touched her forehead and dampened her skin as she huddled near the rocks of the crossing. There was nothing in the way of comfort.

When the day settled in, she started to walk. The rain had stopped; the family might move out from the hut, and she couldn't risk being found so close to the camp. Big Mother would take it as a threat. Girl followed the river down and walked in the direction of the water. It was the same way they went for the fish run, so she decided to walk that way as far as the boundary of the family's land. Once she crossed it, there she would remain. It was as close as she could stay to the family without challenging Big Mother. It was as far away as she had ever been on her own.

Girl stopped often to rest. When she saw a nice round boulder or a comfortable-looking log, she would lower her large frame down and rub her feet. Her muscles were better designed for short sprints, big lunges, and powerful thrusts. Walking over an extended period wore on her.

Sitting on a rock, Girl took a foot in hand. She looked at the calf meat on her leg. It was round and curved, and the oily skin was stretched over it like the best hide. All she could think of was Big Mother, how the old woman had given Girl's thick thigh an admiring pat and said, "Chewfat," a word of encouragement that meant "Keep your leg bones inside this nice meat." Or when they were resting, how Big Mother would often give Girl a soft pat on her head and mutter, "Pitch," meaning "Keep your head attached to your body."

Girl's legs felt to her like tree trunks. Down from each bulky thigh was a thick knot of muscle, then a solid knee. Her calf curved out, and a sturdy ankle joint anchored the bottom of her frame. Rubbing her feet, Girl worried that these ankles might become thin. Her body required a tremendous amount of food to survive every day. Without the family, she wouldn't be able to hunt and eat meat. Her legs would soon become like the thinnest twigs on the trees. They could snap in a light breeze.

Girl's vanity was fundamental to her survival. Only the strongest and most impressive girls became Big Mothers. The others could stay in their families or move to other ones to breed, but they didn't have the power of a Big Mother. And one good indication of a body's strength—and therefore its worth—was its leg muscles.

Girl knew she was focusing too much on the future. This was dangerous. To survive, she needed to reset her mind to the things immediately around her. She forced her senses outward from her body. She curled her lip, felt for heat, and carefully sniffed the wind. The leopard wasn't following her, as she'd thought he might. He had tracked her progress for a short while. It would be a way for him to gain a meal, picking off a lone body, though he knew she wasn't an easy target.

When Girl sniffed the breeze and found no trace of the leopard, she was almost disappointed that he had decided to turn away. A leopard watches and waits for his best chance. He can read the patterns of prey. He anticipates where the creature will be and waits in a tree. When he leaps, it's often from at least twenty feet. He will aim for the back of its neck, and his large fangs will sink in. If he doesn't kill on first strike, he will lie on top of his prey and close off its windpipe with his powerful jaws. Suffocate the body to keep it still and then pin it down and eat. Girl knew it would have meant a swift and sure end to her life. There was some comfort in that. In a way, Girl already felt half dead. To take a body out of the family was like a severing a limb.

Near the end of the day, Girl got to the place where the river valley became steeper and rockier. A few seasons before, Big Mother had pointed to a path that went up a break in the cliff toward the setting sun. She had cupped her hands to show that it led to a small, clear tarn of water. Now Girl made her way up the rock and found what her mother had described. It was a small lake fed by springs, a sharp blue like the middle of her eye. She knelt down on a small strip of pebbled beach and took a drink with a cupped hand. It soothed her throat.

It was a rocky part of the land. The mountain flank plateaued into a large shelf that gave a wider view than she had on the family's land. She could see down through the trees and this made her feel exposed, as though the top of her head had been lifted off. Like a bird, her eyes could soar and look out over an expanse that seemed endless. And that meant the birds could see her too.

But Girl knew she couldn't go back. *Fly away* had been done, so she crouched by the clear water and looked up into the face of the hanging moon. It traveled in the sky despite the sun still hanging over the land. And that moon was large and round and full of menace. The family believed that the moon was made of the coldest kind of ice. She couldn't walk on its surface because it would freeze the soles of her feet. It would go up through her body within a few beats of her heart. The moon was a stark place that had no meadows for bison to feed. There was no river, no crossing, no thundering hooves, no sweet stink of bison shit. On the moon, a body would never feel *warm*.

She looked around to take in the sharp edges of the rock and the silky-smooth surface of the water. There was no immediate threat in the air. She supposed that this land was too barren to attract other meat-eaters. As night fell, the moon was hard against the black sky, which meant it had become the dominant force in this land. The flecks of light from the moon, the stars, stretched across the sky. Her skin shone with the grit of her journey. Her muscles burned too bright. She wanted to cool them for sleep. She pulled at the lash on her waist and let her cloak slip down.

She walked until she stood knee-deep in the water. It was cold but clear. A good spring was feeding it from a source deep in the belly of the mountain. She closed her eyes and raised her palms toward the mountain, feeling its pull on her skin.

After a deep breath, she went under. The cold pushed the breath out of her lungs. When she resurfaced, she shouted out with the thrill. She went under again, slowly this time. Underwater, it was quiet and still. She lifted up and sucked back a big gulp of fresh air.

She didn't swim, but she liked to float. It was shallow, so she laid her head back. With her bum touching sand, she put her feet up.

Toes kissing the surface, she looked up at the circle of rock around the tarn. She knew that it had existed longer than the family. The trees at this spot had also lived much longer and were wiser than her. The mountain had been here long before, and the moon and the stars had seen more than she could feel. She would change faster than the rock, and that felt right. And these were odd thoughts, but there was a reason they were coming so freely. She wasn't part of the family for now. For the first time, she didn't have a job to do. There were no bison to hunt. The boughs of the nest didn't have to be changed and she didn't need to feed the fire. But something else came over her too—an odd sense of freedom. Though it wasn't necessarily welcome. Her way of experiencing time passing had evaporated. To fill the void, new feelings and thoughts crept in. They made new paths in her mind, like worms churning through and changing the dirt.

Girl lay back and looked at this strange land of the moon. All she felt was profoundly alone. She thought of the death of the bison calf and wished that someone would take pity on her the same way.

It was only after she got out and put her cloak back on that the dark sky came down and wrapped around her. She felt scared. She had never been in the night alone. There were a few bigger boulders around the tarn that loomed like scary beasts. In the cliffs were dark cracks that looked like they wanted to swallow her whole. She wondered if eyes peered out at her from the dark. This place felt full of strange creatures that she couldn't smell or know. Unless she wanted to go to the trouble of starting a fire this late, there was no way to make the night feel smaller around her.

Only one thing looked friendly. A large pine stood about twenty feet from the tarn. It was the biggest tree around and obviously had taken advantage of the water source to grow. Maybe a body had been buried under it at one time. She crept up to the broad trunk and put her arms around it. Her hands didn't quite touch on the other side.

She closed her eyes and sniffed. The spicy smell was warm and deep. Did she sense something in the tree? She wondered if it was someone from the family. But there was...a sound. A snap of a twig in the night. What? She was not alone.

Through the dark, a warm body was creeping. It had approached from the slope as she had, probably following her trail. She stayed stock-still and curled her lip. Her impulse was to climb the tree, but it might be a beast that could follow her up. She stood beside the base, her arms wrapped around the trunk. It was hard to focus on anything in this place. Everything was new. Everything was different. Her senses were swamped.

She smelled cat breath and the sour stench of fish on whiskers; the leopard must have found her. Maybe he was above her, already in the tree and planning to pounce? She wanted to run but knew better. A predator had a strong urge to chase fleeing prey. There was no time for another plan—something soft brushed against her leg. She pulled her foot away and let out a yelp.

There was a movement by her foot, but where exactly? Her eyes searched in the night shadows. It had moved behind the tree. She looked for a rock to throw. Her spear was two strides away, close to the water. Could she grab a broken branch? She didn't know the land. Nothing was near enough. Her breath came in shaky huffs. She heard a pebble shift and a single sound in the dark. Like a chirp. From a throat smaller than a leopard's. A cat. Wildcat had come.

13.

Each day the sun climbed into the sky and then slipped back down. Girl came to know what was the same about that place. The smells settled down. The sway of the tree became familiar. Her legs didn't turn into twigs, but they did look more and more like the branches of the tree where she slept. It made her wonder if she might turn into a tree. That might be why the trees had always felt so alive: they were lone daughters standing along the ridge.

She came to know that a family had lived there. Not hers, but another. She found a stone tooth, a hand ax, that had been dropped or left behind. What body would be so careless as to leave an ax? It was a different kind of ax than she knew. The flint had been flaked in a different pattern from the stone core. She found an old hearth, a scar from a fire that had been lit many nights in a row. She found grooves on her tree from where the feet and hands of the family had worn it smooth from climbing. It was a lookout tree that had been used to scan the land. She wondered about the family, who they were and why they had left. Big Mother hadn't told their stories with her shadow. The trace of a scent from long ago barely clung to the trunk.

She didn't hunt, but Wildcat did. He offered her the limp body of a rock mouse, a kindness that she gently refused. He gave her an odd squint and settled down to chew its guts.

There were things around the tarn to nibble, but most of them were green. She didn't like green food and ate only enough to quiet her growling belly. She drank water because thirst was so sharp, but that was all she took in the way of sustenance.

Mostly she waited for what she thought might come: death. She was listless, dull, and empty. But each morning she woke to find her head still attached to her meat. "Pitch," she would spit angrily, and she meant it with none of the usual goodwill. It was more that she was horrified to see her body still in one piece.

Her bad fortune continued. The leopard didn't come to maul her and end her life quickly. The crows left her eyes in their sockets. No lightning struck her skull. Her body remained stubbornly resistant to the wrong side of the dirt. Nothing was altered. It was as if the land had stopped its constant cycle. She didn't grow older. She didn't change, which might have been what she'd wanted a few days before. But now a moment stretched out and went on forever. Away from the family, she left time behind.

And then, just as she became convinced that everything would always be still, the changes caught up. If time had been held back for a moment, it now rushed in. That morning, when she stood by the tarn, a shift entered the air. A warm ripple of heat came down the river valley. She closed her eyes, curled her top lip up, and tried to feel what it was. She tilted her head toward the meeting place farther down—maybe the families were gathering early. But it wasn't coming from there. The air in that direction was still cool and dry and undisturbed. The ice clogged the shallow parts of the river and was in only the first stages of softening its hold. The fish weren't yet able to make their run and she didn't think that any families had arrived or set up camp. She pushed her senses up and over the valley toward the next fork of the river. It was the direction her sister had gone when she became a Big Mother, but it was too far away for her to feel any changes.

Still, there was something, a thin but heavy strand in the air. It came down with the river. It tasted of iron and was thick like blood.

Eyes open, she looked up toward the land of the family. She ran to her tree. Silent, hand over hand, she climbed and pushed at the branches with soles that were as rough as bark. As she climbed up to see out, finding a place for a foot and for a hand, she could sense the bodies of the family that had lived here before. The bark held their memory, though faintly. Now she could feel the smoothed wood on the holds from the family climbing this same tree. She became the family, climbing alongside all the hands and feet that had used this tree over suns and moons. She wondered if it was their blood she sniffed, the story of what had happened to them, that had come in a dream the night before. Or maybe that was what she hoped.

She put a foot on a sturdy branch and held the trunk with arms wrapped tight. She pressed her body against it. The warm trunk pulled her in and her body melted into the trunk like softened sap. Her limbs stretched down to dirt, and sap ran in her veins as if it were blood. This was the strength of the forest. Her fear became just a tremor on the needles. Light vibrations. Listening. What?

The trees stood together like the whole body of a family lining the ridge. The swaying branches talked and told one another of what they saw. One flicked a branch. A few dead leaves that still clung after the winter storms rustled. The limbs let the secrets pass among them. Twigs snapped and the needles clattered together in discomfort. They swayed with sadness.

Meat that is alive sends pulses of heat into air. This comes from the fire inside the chest of a body. When this warmth hits the air, it moves in patterns around the trees. It pushes and pulls at the leaves in particular ways. Just as the surface water in a river tells the story of what lies underneath, the patterns in the air can tell the story of what disturbance it flows over. The trees that line the valley take up and exaggerate the movement. They pass the message down. If Girl watched and felt the patterns in the leaves, she could read them.

She cocked her head and held her breath. Only the sap ran. A bad pattern came through the leaves. Something was wrong. It was too far away to know what, but there was a disturbance. There was trauma. She pulled away from the trunk. The blood ran back in her body and around her bones.

In the sky there was a clatter of birds. Her head snapped up to look. Three birds, black crows, flapped their wings. Their shiny beaks caught the glint of the sun as they passed. Talons curled in and oiled feathers soared. The birds screeched and brayed as they noisily made their way up the valley. They were heading toward the land of her family.

She climbed down, and when she hit the ground, she clicked her teeth to let Wildcat know that she was going back. She ran to the lip of the plateau and then down the slope. Soon she picked up the faint trail by the river and made her way up to the crossing. She was breaking the rule of Big Mother, but the family numbers were too low. She would risk showing her face at the hearth. Nothing could stop her. Nothing did.

14.

Girl's longing to return to the hearth of the family was like a need. She filled it without question. She made the bison crossing by midday and then, nose to the wind and top lip curled up, turned cautiously for the camp.

Girl didn't know that when she'd left the hearth of the family, the leopard had followed her for longer than she'd thought. In her experience, leopards were fairly timid beasts. They used their superior sense of smell not for tracking the family, but for staying clear of them. When Girl left, though, the male leopard was interested to see the small group fracturing further. He followed her tracks long enough to know that she was going far away from the camp. He might have kept trailing her, his interest always drawn by what the hunters were doing, but he picked up another scent. This one was familiar.

Cautiously, he tracked the smell until he saw a body that was much like his. It had a long, slinky coat and spots that perfectly blended in with the mulch of dead leaves and downed logs in the forest. A female leopard had come onto the land. They saw each other and both crept closer. She rushed at him and they had a brief scuffle. He tore a small rip in her ear near the tip, but soon they decided it best not to test each other further. That became the beginning of a sexual interest and the accompanying hunger.

When Girl got within sight of the crossing, she had a brief thought about the leopard. She wondered where he was and if he was tracking her. But the leopard wasn't following Girl to her family's land. He and the female leopard were already there.

Girl heard a sharp shout. It echoed on the rock cliffs of the crossing, a disorienting boom and vibration, and she couldn't tell what kind of beast had made it. The hair on the ridge of her spine stood up. She lifted her top lip to feel. The disturbance of the air was strong. There had been a struggle. It came from the camp.

Approaching slowly, creeping, Girl made her way. She knew all the trees here, which to climb and where the good rocks were hidden, but it didn't feel like advantage enough. She clutched her spear; the worn groove in her armpit throbbed. The smell of blood was thick in the air. There had been a fight and there was still a warm body moving.

She crept up close. In a fight, she needed to be present with her senses turned outward. Rational actions have constraints. Instinctive actions happen fast. She tapped into the unthinking part of her mind. She was close to the camp, the fire there was still smoldering. She knew the leopard would know where she was. She couldn't see him yet, but she could feel his heat. She could smell him in too many places, like he was more than one. She strained for the slightest sound. Nothing.

To provoke a movement, Girl let out a yowl. She stamped her feet and waved her spear in the air to make her body look as big as it could. But there was no rush of air. He didn't scare. He didn't run off. Where was he? She spun on her heel in a desperate search. Before her mind could provide the answers, he burst out from a branch behind her. She turned with only enough time to catch a glimpse of flattened ears and bare fangs.

The crows startled from their branches then. They had come after the first fight to watch for the moment they could pick at the bones, but that screech let them know it was too soon. With a series of caws, they flapped hard to get some distance.

The leopard was on her chest. Girl hissed and spat and gave a screech that rushed from her lungs. The cat held fast, his claws hooked in Girl's cloak; teeth searched for purchase on her neck. She let out a low moan, the sound of fear boiling up in her blood. The fire inside her chest felt low. For a moment, the ground tugged at her. She could collapse under the weight of the cat's body. She could lie down in the dirt and slip through to the other side of it. The death would be quick. With her cheek against the cool earth, the cat would pierce her neck with his fangs. He would cut off her air and she would fall away. Her meat would go inside the cat and take his shape. She would no longer be part of the family.

"Aroo!" Her eyes snapped wide open. It was Big Mother. She wasn't on the ground, but she was somewhere nearby. The sound echoed from so many warnings through her life. It was the sound of encouragement and pride. It was the sound of the family. Girl knew that she must fight. She swerved with the large cat clinging onto her back by his claws. She turned her spear out to catch him in the ribs with the end. With a crunch, the shaft connected. The leopard yelped and fell.

With narrowed eyes, the female, who had been interrupted at the start of her feast, watched from a tree with ire. A rock whistled by and nicked her ear, so she crouched closer to the branch. She measured Girl's strength and health, afraid of the upright body. It was of a kind she had rarely seen before. Loose skin hung around the shoulders. The fur was mottled in patches. The leopard's ears flattened as she felt both attracted to and repulsed by what she saw. She pushed aside her usual fear of the unknown as a larger force swelled inside her body. She wanted to eat and mate. She hunched, flexed her claws, and waited until the upright was close enough for her to pounce.

Girl staggered, pulled her body up straight, then tucked in her spear to be ready for the next attack. Cold ran along her spine. A growl came up in her throat; eyes wild and the hair on her back erect, she signaled her intent to fight. The spear was part of her body, like an arm that extended her strength. She shrieked and spat, pulled her lips back, and grimaced at the cat.

The male leopard pounced again, trying to push Girl closer to where the female waited in the tree. He sprang. She watched the long, white fangs come toward her neck, the spotted body in the air, claws out to grab her. Girl thrust her spear sideways. The shaft caught the cat in the mouth. He clamped down and they both fell. There was hot breath. Claws raked and tore through her cloak to her skin. They swiped at her face and chest. The air was full of scowls and yelps, and a clump of fur was in her mouth and grit between her teeth. She wrenched the spear to the side and thumped the cat's head against the dirt. His jaws let go and he pulled back again.

Girl scrambled to right herself, but his fangs were almost immediately in her face, like he was intentionally driving her back. She was looking down the cat's throat now, no time to get the spear around in front of her. She threw her left forearm up and he clamped down on the bone of her arm. She thrust at his side with the pointed stone of her spear, again and again. He huffed through his nose with each stab—hot breath with the tang of blood—but the jaws stayed clamped and he snapped his head to the side. Their bodies rolled. Her shoulder strained at the joint. It felt like the gristle in her arm wouldn't hold. She curled and got both feet between them. She kicked out. It was enough to release his teeth. His eyes went wide in surprise and a loud mewl came out of his mouth. He leaped back.

All sides of Girl's body felt exposed to the air, bleeding. There was no family to watch her back. She didn't know where Big Mother was. She pulled her bloody arm close to her body. Meat hung loose; skin dangled. The thought of lying down flicked at the edges of her brain, but the blinding-hot pain felt too much like sun. The cat was hunched over and recovering and would soon be on his feet and only one quick pounce away. There was more blood on her. She knew in an instant that only one of them would live. Some meat would get to eat.

The taste of rock and fur and earth was in her mouth. The bad arm dangled. She had only one arm, one try. The cat's eyes flickered. He was fur and muscle and force. Her spear was aimed toward him. She held it strong, but too much blood dripped. Her movements were slow. The cat's eyes flashed onto the tip of her stick. The air between them thickened and their movements slowed. He jumped, but to the side of her spear. One beat of the heart and she had missed stabbing the stone tip into him. The spear glanced off his head. There was no second move.

The leopard got his claws into her cloak and dug them in. That was when Girl felt the second cat. The weight of the female cat thumped against her back and cleared up Girl's confusion. She had never known a lone leopard to fight like this. A cave lion might take on the family, but not a lesser cat on its own. There were two cats, a mating pair. They both grabbed at her cloak with their claws and hung on. One thing went through Girl's mind like a burst of light: She was the eaten.

Elastic Band

On Friday night, Simon and I joined the team sitting around the campfire. Most of them would take a break for the weekend and go into town. The next day was my last at the site; Simon and I would drive back on Sunday. He and I sat together on a bench. He rubbed my shoulders while looking around the ring of faces, the people he had heard so much about. Andy gave out beers and one of the students pulled out a flask. It was passed around, each person happy to share the spout, eyes bulging at the burn. Simon took two swigs. I waved my hand and gave the flask to Andy, who had some room in his Dr Pepper can and made a show of tipping in the whiskey. This instantly united those around the fire in a collective "Eww." He passed the flask to Caitlin. Her hand darted to cover her tea mug. "I should get to my car before I lose the light."

"I'll walk you." Simon stood up. He seemed glad to be her escort, maybe because he knew that I'd relax once she left.

"I'll see you tomorrow afternoon, Rose," she said, pressing a cold hand on my shoulder, acknowledging our final handover meeting.

I nodded good night.

Simon led Caitlin down the path from the camp to the rough parking lot. The rest of us watched them walk away. After a pause,

Michael, an intern and the youngest on the team, stifled a laugh.

"Let's just say she's not one to let up on her regime." Andy tipped his can and nodded to Michael. The others felt bold enough to giggle.

"I don't think we should laugh at Caitlin," said Anais, a postdoc whom I admired. "She's rigid for a reason."

"What's that?" Andy asked, always willing to do my dirty work.

"She had a breakdown in Kenya." Anais looked to me. "We all know that, right?"

"I know her only professionally," I answered.

"I heard about it," Michael chimed in. "Like, she was out in the field for a long time and lost her shit."

Anais put her hand on his arm and gasped in reproach. "Michael."

"What, isn't that true?" Michael swiveled his eyes around to me, the acknowledged boss. "Oh, shit, Rose. Sorry, did I piss you off?"

"I'm hardly that delicate, Michael. But thanks for your concern."

"I didn't mean to tell her secret—"

"Everyone's history is their own business."

"—or make you mad, especially when you're pregnant." Michael continued to dig himself into a hole. "I mean, it's just that I shouldn't...you're pregnant...sorry." He stumbled. "You still walk faster than me."

"Yeah." I shook my head at him. "And I have larger breasts."

"I wonder, is a breakdown why she stopped working in the field?" asked Andy. "I read her book about the gibbon study. It's out of date but really good. Before Kenya, she was at the top of her game."

Anais leaned forward awkwardly, her face filled with shame. "I feel terrible, like I just outed her mental illness or something."

"We all have a past." Andy shrugged kindly at Anais.

She raised her can. "Cheers to that."

Simon's face appeared in the ring of the fire just as the flask was going around again. "What I'd miss?"

After an hour spent on lighter subjects, the team left the camp to go back to town. Andy, Simon, and I had agreed to stay in the canvas platform tents for the night to leave enough space in the apartments for everyone else. There was some objection to a pregnant woman sleeping in the camp, but I waved it off by telling them I found the cots comfortable. They weren't, but I couldn't quite bear to leave the site.

I crawled into my cot soon after. Andy and Simon stayed up long into the night. As I fell asleep, I heard Andy's voice by the fire talking about Patricia, Patricia, Patricia. His wife. All I could think was that he barely ever mentioned her to me.

The next morning, I woke up feeling confused and thirsty. Had I been at a wild party the night before? Yes, but I hadn't been drinking. It was my last day on the site. Simon and I would drive back to London soon. Panic set in. My mind leaped into action, but my body failed to follow.

I tried to sit up but soon realized that I was stuck in the low camp cot. Simon was asleep on the other one; I would have squashed him if he had tried to wedge himself into mine. Andy must have slept in the other tent. I decided to leave Simon be so that I could check the site before he started herding me toward the car. I rubbed my left hip. My tendons were loosening to make room for the baby. And then there was the matter of my lips. They were swollen and cracked. A large, crusted flake of skin jutted up from my bottom lip to pierce the top. This area was hot in the summer, but just then conditions reminded me of my time in the Gobi. I had never felt so parched.

I didn't need a biology degree to know that I had not had enough water the day before. The issue was that each mouthful of water reminded my bladder that a small infant was sitting on it. And since I couldn't pee near the site, I had to spend precious time lumbering out to the latrine. My solution was to limit my water intake—not too much, as I was aware of what the baby needed, but enough. Low on water, my body had diverted resources to the baby to ensure it was healthy, which was a good decision. Or so I tried to tell myself. My body had a clear purpose—to grow a child—but it suddenly seemed at odds with the rest of me. Weren't we, my body and me, one and the same?

I grabbed the metal edges of the cot with both hands, pulled my knees over, and rolled off carefully so that I wouldn't wake Simon. As I stood, the weight of the baby moved along a nerve with a sharp pinch. My breath caught, but I'd managed to relieve the pressure on my left hip. All my things were in their proper places—my work clothes hung on nails banged into the wood tent frame, my trusty laptop sat under a dust cover on top of my cluttered desk, my tool belt with the waist extension waited for me on the floor—but there was a difference. I wouldn't be using these things anymore.

There was a wooden crate beside my cot with a water bottle, still cold, judging by the droplets of condensation. It was evidence of Andy. I reached out an aching arm, grabbed it, and chugged. If I hadn't fully appreciated him before, I was completely devoted to him by the time I drained the last of it. Also on the crate was a plastic Tupperware container, sealed to keep out rodents. It held an apple, a granola bar, and a small square of chocolate. Andy's long marriage had trained him well. He had a wonderful way of sensing and anticipating my needs. I looked to the bed at Simon, rumpled in sleep. Though our relationship was close and comfortable, we had each stayed fairly self-sufficient. If I was hungry, I got food and ate. I expected him to do the same. Neither of us wanted it to be any other way. But chocolate? Andy had a nice touch.

I couldn't hear the clink of breakfast dishes or smell the coffee warming on the camp stove, but I soon remembered it was Saturday. I sat and rubbed my hair, which was thick with dust and seemed to have flattened on one side during my sleep. I glanced at my phone. It was 9:00 a.m. After eating, I heaved into action. Was it possible to dig just a little more today? I had marked a specific plot around the cervical vertebrae, where there was the imprint of an object that might have been handmade. I was burning with curiosity about it. I knew one more day of digging was not enough to make much progress, but nothing in my career so far had felt possible. My willingness to trample whatever doubts lay in my path had brought me this far. I wanted to know what the object might be. In a stiff waddle, I made my way to where my clean trousers were folded and waiting.

How had I become so pregnant overnight? I stuffed my sausage legs into my work trousers and tugged on the elastic that I used to secure the rivet on the fly. I had rigged the band to bring the two sides as close together as possible. As I stood to pull the pants closed, the elastic band snapped against my fingers and flew off. I looked around for another band but couldn't find one. The fly of my trousers gaped open.

I had made a decision long ago that I would never cry at work. While tears are a natural reaction to adversity, I believed crying played into negative assumptions about a woman's ability to cope with difficult situations. Through all the trials and tribulations that came with an academic career, I had not shed a tear. Not when I was at a site in Turkey and a large pallet slipped from a truck and broke my foot. Not when one of the outside examiners on my dissertation tried to set me back two years by refusing to accept new dating methods. Not when I was publicly mocked at a big conference by a prominent academic ("You sound like you would like to get up close and personal with one of your Neanderthals," he had remarked during the Q&A session), and not when the room had erupted with nervous laughter and the comment achieved its intended effect of discrediting everything I had said. I took it all on the chin.

I did not cry at work until I was unable to find a second elastic band to fasten my trousers. That triggered the silent sobs. I managed to bite my lip and not wake Simon, and I hoped the tears would go unnoticed, but then I heard footsteps outside.

"Rose?"

I paused, sniffed, and bit down harder on my lip.

"Rose?"

Andy. At least it was Andy.

"Hello. I'm looking for one Dr. Rosamund Gale?"

"Hi, Andy," I said weakly.

"Wha..." Simon rolled over.

"Are you up?" Andy asked.

"Yes," I said.

"Did you eat?"

"Yes, Mom."

"Don't get me started about your mom. She's called twice."

"Where am I?" Simon sat up, startled.

I didn't want Simon to stop me from digging, and I quickly set myself straight, wiped my eyes on my sleeve, and jammed my feet into my boots. I grabbed my tool belt with one hand, bunched the fly of my trousers with the other, pushed through the tent flap, and launched outside to see Andy. He looked surprised by the sudden burst of activity and instinctively stepped back. "Rose?"

"Got any bungee cord?"

"Somewhere."

"I'm going to need it. I just have one more thing to do at the site."

"I was coming to get you, Rose. Caitlin's here."

"Where?"

"I know—surprise!" He pointed toward the site. "She went up already."

"Without me?"

"She assumed...you were asleep, judging by the snoring."

"That was Simon," I said.

"Hey, I don't snore!" came a muffled cry from inside the tent.

"Caitlin is at the site?" I started up the trail. "You should have got me right away."

"Caitlin said you should rest," he said.

"Meet me up there." It came out as a bark. The thought of anyone at the site without me made my skin crawl. A primatologist! Caitlin's job was to be a representative of the museum first and a project manager second. She was at the site sporadically and had spent a total of only a few weeks there. She seemed much more interested in schedules and logistics than in the actual dig. Though I didn't know Caitlin all that well, she didn't have the background to appreciate my interpretation of our find. The person who controlled the site could influence how it was seen by experts and, eventually, interpreted by the public.

"Bring extra chocolate," I called back as I hiked, already panting.

"You should know—" Andy hollered.

I stopped and turned.

"She has a reporter with her."

"Grab a bungee!"

"From *National Geographic,* I think . . ."

"Maybe bring a pair of your pants," I yelled back.

Before I turned up the path, I saw Simon stick his head out of the tent and give Andy a bewildered look. Then I heard him mutter to Andy, "She wants your pants?"

My stomach dropped as I rounded the last bend of the trail and saw the plastic cover that hung over the opening of the cave had been pushed to the side. They had gone in, which was bad enough, but they also had not put the plastic back in place. This left room for all kinds of impurities to get into the excavation area, and I took it as a sign of things to come. Without the most careful protocol to prevent contamination, the evidence could be deemed inconclusive. My find would be seen as tainted in some way or used as proof *against* what I knew, not as confirmation of the answers I was sure I had found.

"What the hell are you doing?" I yelled.

I could see Caitlin and a man standing inside the cave. I wanted to push in and clear them out, but I didn't dare. There wasn't room for my belly. If I knocked them to the side, they could break an artifact. Caitlin's gray ponytail wiggled as if she was startled. I hoped she was.

Caitlin backed out first, looking slightly skittish and blinking in the morning light.

"I need to have control of the site," I said to her, my hands clenched into fists. "Of both the physical space and how we tell the story."

"You made that clear." Caitlin held up her hands as if in surrender. She obviously didn't want to have the conversation just then. "I'm trying to help."

"Help by mishandling the site?"

She glanced back apologetically at the man who emerged from the cave behind her. "I know you are scheduled to leave tomorrow, Rose. I hope to have our funding in place so you can leave knowing all is well." She nodded to the man beside her. "Fred is a good friend, a trusted one. I've brought him to vouch for us."

"To leak the news?"

"The museum values Fred's opinion on the site's newsworthiness."

"I'm sure they do."

"We've worked this way together in the past. The gibbons in Zanzibar? Fred's coverage in his magazine is how I got enough support to find more funding."

"You are putting the show before the science."

"If only this were just about the science, Rose. We both know it's also about optics. The pinch in funding happened to us first in primate conservation, but now the same thing is happening in archaeology."

"These aren't gibbons," I spat.

She flinched and gave the journalist a tight smile. "Excuse us, Fred?"

When he stepped away, Caitlin pulled on my arm. "I ask that we keep this professional."

"I am professional."

"You appear to be slightly out of control. You're shaking."

It was the first moment I noticed that my hands were vibrating. I was so mad, it felt like I had a motor inside me. "With all due respect, Caitlin, I'd prefer not to be told what my body is doing. I happen to be in it."

"Pregnancy stirs up instincts, Rose."

"If you were talking about gibbons, I'd be interested."

I heard throat clearing and glanced over. Andy stood at the top of the path. He looked worried, or maybe shocked, I couldn't tell which. He held a bungee cord and a pair of pants in his hand and for a moment I couldn't think why. I became very aware that there was a man, a journalist, in our midst. I doubted that a raging pregnant lady swearing at an older woman with gray hair would come off well in the press.

Caitlin felt the shift. "Perhaps you would like to meet Fred Long?" She gestured to the man. I pressed a ridiculous smile on my face, which probably only confirmed to him that I was a maniac.

"He's from *National Geographic*," said Caitlin.

"Hello."

"Dr. Gale, it's an honor to be here."

He looked vaguely familiar. I was usually excellent with names and faces, but I couldn't place him. "Have we met?"

"I wouldn't expect you to remember." Fred gave me a warm smile. "At the archaeological society conference in San Diego last year."

"Nice to meet you again, then," I said, extending my hand. I was pregnant and crazy, but at least I still had a firm handshake.

As I reached, I let go of my trousers. I tried to catch them, but my belly got in the way. They fell around my ankles. My face crumpled up. I couldn't keep it in. For the second time that day, I broke my no-crying rule.

PART III

15.

The male leopard rose up on his hind legs to swipe at Girl with his front paws. He tried to knock her back, pin her down, and hold her still with his powerful shoulders so that he could sink his teeth in. The female tried to do the same, swiping and then digging her claws into the back of Girl's cloak; the sharp points bit into her skin. The land turned into a blur of fear and mud and struggle. Girl heard a snarl and a tear, and one side of her cloak ripped from the armhole to the neck. It started to slip from her body. Without the cloak, her vulnerable skin would be exposed to sharp claws that would rake her open to bone. Girl let out a terrible moan. The leopards heard the sound of distress as a sign of progress. They both closed in.

Something awoke in Girl. It wasn't an idea—it happened too fast to be described that way—it was more like when the sun suddenly breaks through the clouds. A body that can see the sun knows the way. Girl ducked down and to the side and out of her torn cloak. Both leopards felt her body fall. They pounced on the fur cloak. Saliva filled the mouth of the male; strings of spit flew to the sides. He had Girl's neck while the female pushed sharp teeth into the shoulder. Once they got hold, they both bit down with force to search for flesh and make the kill. They dug in their claws to cut deep and to hold tight. And under them, the fur flopped and fell in a flat way. The male didn't hit flesh, muscle, or bone. Instead, dirt pushed up into his nostrils.

The female sensed the male's failure to make the kill and wanted to show her strength. She pinned the fur in with a paw and stabbed her fangs in. They sank down with great force. She hit hide and then punched through to find blood. The male leopard let out a howl. He jumped back with his paw pulled into his body. It was his foot she had bitten. The leopards soon realized that the fur was now empty. They weren't familiar with a kind of prey that had the ability to shed its hide. This was the first time one of the family had done such a thing.

Their confusion gave Girl time to swing her spear hard enough to knock the male back. The wounded cat scurried off a few steps. Girl came after him, driving him back toward a thick stand of trees. He retreated farther, but then flinched with a yowl. A dull thud. Sensing danger, he twisted around to look. What?

A shout from behind: *"Aroo!"*

Girl saw the male's concentration slip and she took that moment to bring her spear down. She clubbed his head hard with a crack. But as she did, the female came for Girl. Another shout and a crack, a squeal, a whimper, and the female fell back. Limp on the dirt, she was in a daze, her tongue out and bleeding from her head. Girl didn't know what had hit her, but she didn't wait to find out. She jumped up, lunged, and with her good arm plunged her spear deep into the side of the female. Stab after stab, she gored both cats.

Girl watched for long enough to know that the leopards would never get up again. She fell down on her knees, still stunned from the fight. She rolled onto her back, breath heaving, trying to get her lungs to take in air. The scent of dead cat filled her nose. All she could think was that she hated the smell of cat meat. And she had a flash of a thought that maybe that's why she and Wildcat were such great friends: she never had the urge to eat him. It was a waste to kill a beast and not eat the meat, but cats were stringy and lacked fat. And she knew that she would think of Wildcat if she licked the bones of these leopards, even though he had no particular affiliation with them. Her nose wrinkled. Eating cat meat was a sign of weakness.

When she'd caught her breath, Girl stood up and checked for blood. Her arm was the most damaged. She would need to clean it, but not yet. She didn't smell or feel anything of a threat, but what had struck the female leopard? She saw a rock the size of her fist close to the body. It had hit the female's skull hard enough to crack the bone just above the eye. The rock had been perfectly aimed and it had given Girl the chance to kill both beasts.

Girl walked carefully in the direction that the rock must have come from. It took ten more steps to find Him. His body lay facedown. A large foot and calf stuck out from the brush. She put a hand down to feel the muscle. There was little heat in his body. He was already of the dirt. She glanced up to see that the leopards must have only just started eating. She had interrupted them right after their kill. Girl took a breath and felt the loss of Him settle into her. She couldn't let her mind go back in time or forward to grief. She needed it to stay with her.

Where were the others? Girl sniffed something in the air, trying not to be distracted by the scent of Him's own blood. She caught a movement in the air up ahead. She pushed the dense brush aside with an arm and crept forward. What?

"Aroo." It came in a gentle tone.

Girl moved toward the stand of trees. The branches swayed and there was a bulge in the tree—it was Big Mother and Runt. They clutched each other in one of the branches higher up. Though a leopard could have come up a tree after them, they were high enough to make it hesitate. Claws that were busied with climbing were not available to fight.

The old woman wobbled back down the length of the trunk, hands reaching down and thin arms lowering her shaking body. There was no satisfaction for Big Mother in her perfect throw. Her face told only the story of loss. Runt lowered himself next, quiet and pale. When they got to the bottom, Girl took them both into her arms and they sank down to the ground. The three of them stayed like that, at the edge of the clearing by the base of the looking tree. They were silent.

It was Runt who broke the huddle. When no words of comfort came from Girl or Big Mother, he found his lungs were filling up with air. He couldn't be quiet any longer. Only the sound of Big Mother's whistling nose cut the stillness. She was sniffing like it might be a way to express her thoughts. He tried to do the same, a big inhale. He didn't smell anything in particular. The scent of the pine tree, the hind-end breath of Big Mother, Girl's sweat stuck to her matted hair, the earthy mix of blood and flesh. He knew that there was an injury, but the smells told him little else, so Runt kept his ear to Girl's chest and felt it rise and fall. It wasn't enough. He needed to get rid of the bad feelings in his chest and make a sound for the sorrow. His own voice surprised him, thin and shaking. "Bearden."

As Girl shifted to tighten her arm around Runt for comfort, Big Mother gasped. That was the first moment she let on about her own injury. Her face was draining of blood. Girl's mind had been turned too far inward to notice the smell, but now she kicked into action. She lay Big Mother down and lifted her cloak, which the old woman had pulled up to cover the wound. There were two long gashes in her side. A sharp claw had cut through to expose her rib. From the sliced skin came a stem of gut. Severed intestines bloomed out from the wound.

Girl quickly checked Runt's skin. There was one puncture in his leg, a claw from a leopard who had tried to stop him from climbing. It was clear that the leopards had gone after the weaker ones before Him interfered. They must have surrounded Him, or clawed him down when he tried to escape up the tree. Together the leopards overpowered the young man. Runt's wound would need care, but his life would continue. She turned her attention to Big Mother. She was bleeding. The climb down from the tree had probably opened the wound and increased the bleeding under her cloak. They would have to get her into the cave for protection. Other predators would come sniffing. Girl leaned in to pick up Big Mother in her arms, but one tug and the woman shook her large head. *"Ne."* She didn't want to be moved.

Runt dribbled some water from his leather sack onto Big Mother's lips. Girl put a hand on the old head and they looked into each other's eyes, something they rarely did. Direct eye contact could be perceived as hostile. Two bodies who knew each other well might do it to look for the direction of a gaze or to check for health, strength, or sanity. Since all these were flowing out the large wound in Big Mother's side, the look was Girl's way of offering comfort.

Big Mother knew that she no longer had health or strength, only sanity, and even that was slipping. She let the air out of her lungs and gave in to the change. She had spent many restless years in the constant quest to get enough meat for herself and her dependents. With her remaining energy, she could think only of the pleasure in a sustained rest. Rather than fighting it, as she had been, she looked forward to a long dirt nap. *"Ye,* deadwood," she said with a sniff as she pointed to her nose, as if to say, *I can smell the earth.*

Big Mother looked at Girl, at the shock of red hair, the pale skin flecked with mud and blood, and she sniffed again. There was something new. Under more regular circumstances, she would have noticed right away. Girl was pregnant. A mother was often the first to smell it on her daughter's breath.

Big Mother slipped the horns from her head and passed them to Girl without a whiff of blame or bitterness. In that moment, her pain was replaced by pride. "Pitch," she said. The word meant much more than "Keep your head attached to your meat." It was Girl who would keep their family attached to the land.

Girl dipped her head as a sign of acceptance. Big Mother's chest swelled with breath once more. She took in a big sniff of the pregnancy. The girl was fertile. The family might live. The old woman turned her head to Runt and opened her mouth. She knew that the stench of her old breath wafted into his small nose before he heard any words. She let it. They would remember her by that. Smells took the mind to a place like none of the other senses could. Anytime he caught the stink of bison meat in his nose, he would think of the way she had taken him in and kept him alive.

Big Mother let out one last long, slow breath. "Deadwood." Both she and Girl knew how much had changed in a short time. Their lives together had slipped away as the ice breaks from the river in the spring. It does not melt off in a slow thaw. Instead, a series of deep cracks destabilizes the structure. When it goes, large chunks get pulled away all at once. And in the span of a day, before disbelieving eyes, the ice is gone. But underneath the river is the same, just as it always was.

16.

Girl woke just before the sun, stepped out of the hut, and walked in silence to the hearth. She squatted down by it with open palms, feeling the warmth from the night before. She leaned in and blew on the hottest of the ash-covered embers, and a glowing piece of charred wood in the middle throbbed with heat, a chest-aching red. She steadied her breath and blew once more. A flame jumped up to bite the twigs and bark she piled on. The flicker crackled and caught. The warmth licked at her skin and ruddy cheeks. Another day had started.

Soon the yolk of the sun cracked into the sky and color bled. She watched as it climbed along the line of the cliff and disappeared behind it. In a few days, as the sun rose, it would kiss the top of the cliff. That meant it would be time to go to the fish run. Her mouth watered at the thought of orange flesh. With that feeling, there wasn't a decision to make, only the urge to go. She would travel to the meeting place. She would gorge on fish. Her belly would be full.

Girl heated water in a cured sack to open a new cache of bison meat. By pouring hot water into the frozen cache, she could access some of the slabs of meat they had saved after the hunt. There was more than enough food for the short term. Rather than getting distracted by sadness, she worked the saliva around in her mouth. She could double her portions and eat when she was hungry, something she had rarely been able to do before.

She gently flexed her hand and was relieved to see the muscles work. The leopard had taken a deep bite and some of her flesh was gone, but the ripping hadn't been as bad as she'd first thought. Before crawling into the hut the night before, Girl had forced herself to stay up and tend to her wounds. She soaked and boiled mustard seeds. She chewed these until they were mashed and then spat out the fine paste. Next she put water in an emptied turtle shell and rinsed her wound. She sliced off the loose flesh with a sharp stone. This she did with a piece of meat between her teeth to muffle her cries of pain. She stanched the blood by holding the smooth side of a folded hide over it. Then she packed the wound with the mustard-seed paste until her arm looked whole again. It stung enough to make her moan. She took a piece of hide that was scraped thin and wrapped this tight, like a second skin, around her forearm. Her fingers were working well. They showed no sign of getting puffy, which was the first sign of dying rot.

Then, squatting, moving her fingers slowly, chewing by the fire, Girl ate her fill. She would build her legs back up. Soon they would be muscled limbs the size of tree trunks with thick knotted knees. She would be the Big Mother that everyone wanted.

Girl had an odd thought: Maybe Big Mother was looking after her. She dismissed it right away. As Big Mother always said, the dead can't see a body from the other side of the dirt. But there was a feeling that lingered. Maybe because she could no longer feel her mother in sleep, she needed to feel connected when she was awake.

Wildcat came up, rubbed against Girl's legs, and squinted his eyes to ask for meat. His timing was always perfect. She laughed and gave him a large chunk. His pupils dilated at the size. Still wary of the many pairs of feet belonging to the family that had kicked him over the years, he snatched it and darted off to eat under the cover of brush.

Soon, Wildcat had finished eating and was back at the woodpile by the hearth hoping to catch a red squirrel. Though Girl was sure he registered the absence of bodies, nothing changed his instincts. He approached this day exactly as he had the one before.

It was only then that Girl thought about the one body that was still in the hut, Runt. She climbed back up and pushed aside the flap of hide that hung over the door. For a minute, she couldn't see in the dark and could only hear the boy's breath. After a restless night, he was still sleeping off the terrors of the day before. He had a funny way of sleeping: on his stomach with his legs pulled up so that his bum waved in the air. She had never seen a child sleep this odd way. Slowly her eyes adjusted, and she could make out the edges of his body. His back looked soft and small. His skin was surprisingly bare; only the finest of hairs were visible in a crack of light from the door. She wondered if more hair would grow in along his back. For his sake and the lovers he might want to attract later on, she hoped it would.

Runt sighed in sleep. She hadn't given too much thought to the boy before beyond the practical steps of caring for him. She had taken part in raising him, the way they all did. Whoever was cooking would make sure he ate; whoever was sleeping would pull him in; they would all tuck him somewhere safe while they went hunting and make sure he got instruction through the year. The family knew that their children were different from the babies of the beasts around them. While the badgers could leave a baby in the nest while they went to forage for food, a child of the family could rarely be left unattended. The red deer's fawn could walk within hours of birth, whereas the family had to strap a baby to someone's back for more than a year. It was a lot of work to raise such slow-growing offspring, but the effort they put in eventually came to good. Now, though, there were no other hands to care for Runt. It was all on Girl's back.

Girl only foggily remembered the day Runt had been found wandering by the river at the meeting place. None of them could guess whom he belonged to. The family who brought him lived far up one of the forks of the river. They pointed back to show they had found him on the way. Perhaps he had been traveling with an adult who was taken by some kind of disease, beast, or misfortune. Big Mother had searched and sniffed as best she could. She never found any clue.

Runt's limbs were oddly slim. His chest was as narrow as a leg. Girl had got more used to his looks, but at first she'd worried that his bulging eyeballs might pop out of his head. His forehead was flat and his chin protruding. With such poor looks and physique, she doubted that he would ever mate. As he grew, he made up for his weakness by his willingness to work. Though he seemed slow to develop, when he figured out a task, he would take it on. This was the reason he was fed by the family. Runt's desire to be useful had kept him alive.

The boy sighed again and lowered his bottom down to the hide on which he slept. Girl heard it then—a shallow rattle like beans that had dried in a pod. She froze on the spot. It was the unmistakable rattle of a snake. Waiting, she scanned the dim hut to see where it was. If she stepped on the long body, it would bite.

The crisp mornings meant it was a dangerous time of year for snake encounters. The snake bodies cooled overnight and it was only the touch of later morning sun that woke them. Once, when Girl and Him were small, Him had found a poisonous snake with a rattle, and he took it for dead because it was so still. He had wrapped it around his neck, pretended it was twine to tie his toy spear, and kissed its scaly nose. When he tired of it, he dropped the long body on a rock. It soon warmed. Girl remembered watching Him's jaw go slack as the warmed snake slithered off into the brush.

But Girl's problem was that this snake had woken up—the rattling sound told her as much. Slowly, she pushed aside the flap of the hide for more light. For all she knew, the snake could be curled up by her own foot. She might have narrowly missed stepping on it when she entered. But it wasn't there or on the floor around her. She looked up to the boughs and scanned slowly, carefully. That kind of snake was colored to look like bark and could be hard to spot in the branches of the hut. They weren't usually longer than her arm, but size meant nothing when it came to the strength of their poison. One fang-full from an adult was enough to take a body down.

The boy was on his stomach. For a moment, Girl's eyes played tricks on her. She wondered if Big Mother had made Runt a necklace while Girl was away, for there was something on his neck. She knew it was the snake draped across him, but her mind grappled for anything else. If Girl rushed forward, the snake might strike him in defense. If he sat up, it would do the same. She opened her lips to warn him, but even that could set the snake off. It had already given them a first warning with its rattle. Snakes rarely gave two.

Girl did the only thing she could think to do: She held her breath. In doing only that, she felt weak and inept. This small boy had no one but her, and she could think only of not breathing. And seeing him lying in the nest, bare back exposed to the snake, his helplessness transferred to her. A snakebite was a horrible way to die. It took days of agony, skin turning black, and the body blowing up big because it was already rotting from the inside. Her heart thumped with dread because she knew that if he suffered, it was her fault alone. It was one last change and she wouldn't recover. She was acutely aware of her failing and fragility.

Waiting, watching. The snake lay over Runt's back as it nosed at the hide. It looked as if it wanted to crawl under the covers to find the dark places beneath, but the hide was folded and there was no way in. It slithered farther, and Girl bit back a gasp. The sliding might wake Runt. But the boy didn't stir. His soft, dark eyelashes touched his cheeks. The snake nosed and poked and decided it didn't have time for the hide. It slithered forward and soon the rattle was clear of Runt's back. It pushed into the thick wall of branches.

Girl quickly backed out of the hut and picked up her spear. She took two steps over to the small hole to see that the snake had come out the other side. It wriggled on the rocks in a curve as the tip of

Girl's spear slammed down. In one stab, she pinned the back of its head to the rock. With a stone, she smashed its head.

Later, when Runt wriggled out from the hut rubbing his eyes from sleep, Girl called him down to the fire. She sat with a stick in her hand, the meat of a snake curled around it and cooking. He barely looked at Girl, just came and pushed her torso back so that he could sit on her lap. He laid his head on her chest and breathed deeply, like this was a usual thing. He seemed to transfer his affection from Big Mother to Girl without much effort. Maybe it was her age, maybe he saw the two women as one and the same, or maybe it was this thing about Runt that she could never quite put her finger on. He was different in many ways.

Runt reached his hand up. He flapped his fingers twice and waited. Girl placed a piece of cooled meat in his palm. His fingers curled and she heard the good sounds of sucking and chewing. Part of her admired his ease. Runt knew where his meat would come from. He knew who would keep him safe. She wished for the same.

Girl told Runt to play for a while so that she could take stock of what they needed in order to make the migration to the meeting place. She could choose the best sacks for water and the best spears for protection. She could wrap extra meat in a soft hide and carry it on her back. They would take an extra fur for warmth. Once there, she would build a shelter out of fresh pine boughs.

Runt squatted in the dirt, playing with something. She absent-mindedly looked over and was surprised to see it was her shell. Hand to throat, she realized it must have come off her neck. How did she not notice this before? She leaped forward. Maybe she lunged at Runt too quickly, but there was anger in her action. It wasn't his shell. She wondered if he had stolen it while she slept.

"*Ne.*" She grabbed it back.

The movement and the sharp word surprised Runt. His eyes went wide. He stared at her, shocked for one beat of his heart. And then in the next, his face cracked and melted into tears. She had suddenly become so important to him, like the sun. The anger in her face filled Runt with heat. He wailed and screeched in a way that she could barely stand. She put her hands over her ears and pressed to muffle the noise.

"Ssshh," she said to silence him, but it had no effect. "Crowthroat," she said, placing her fingers against her thumb to show him he was making too much noise, like an awful crow. He kept wailing and shouting unintelligible sounds. The force from his throat filled up the camp. There was no space left for her words.

Girl sat heavily on one of the logs near the hearth. She kept her hands over her ears and lowered her head, waiting for the sound to stop. How had Big Mother kept him quiet? She had never heard the boy cry like this. After a while, the wailing stopped. She slumped with relief and took her hands away from her ears.

She felt a soft hand on her back and startled. It was only then that she realized how vulnerable they had just been. With her senses turned inward, any beast could have staked its claim. With only two in the family, it was only a matter of time before another one tried.

But it was only Runt with red, bulging eyes and hiccups. His small cheeks were puffed out. He lowered his eyes for a moment. She gave him a soft click. He took this as a chance to push onto her lap again. She sighed and let him. He had something else in his hands now—the horns. She had forgotten to put them on when she woke. Or maybe *forgotten* wasn't quite it. It was more that she had never thought to put them on. She nodded to let him know this was good. He put the horns up to her forehead. She tied the thin tendon, chewed soft by Big Mother, under the thick plait of hair that hung down her back.

Girl lifted her head and Runt looked at her admiringly. With thin fingers, he tucked in a loose strand of hair. He adjusted one horn so that it stood straight. A look of strength and pride came onto his face. He held up a palm to her. She held up her hand and their skin pressed, his fingers reaching only the middle joints on hers. His skin dark and soft like shale; her skin light and rough like granite. They pressed their palms together harder. He gestured toward her neck and the shell to ask if she wanted help tying it. Big Mother had given it to Girl when she was about Runt's age.

The shell was the size of a walnut and large enough to make sounds when held to an ear. Big Mother had held the shell for Girl to listen. That was how Girl knew that it matched the shadow stories. She knew that the woman had traveled far away to where the water tastes like sweaty skin. There were bad stories about the sea, but good ones too: It goes on for a long time until it drops off into a land that belongs to the biggest fish. Those fish dive and send ripples through the water in a wave. These continue from the land of the big fish and they come to the shore to pound and play on the sand. Sometimes the pounding makes the water froth like in the rapids of a river.

Girl showed Runt how to put his ear to the shell. He listened to the sound of the waves as they crashed in the sea. He closed his eyes and maybe he felt the tumble of the surf, the fine dirt in his teeth, and the smell of wet rocks. It wasn't just the sound; maybe he could taste, smell, and feel the ocean, an echo from his past. It was something that rumbled deep in his blood. With the shell to his ear, he looked like he was there.

Later that night, Runt tossed and turned and waved his bottom in the air in his sleep. With her eyes open a crack, she could see his swirl of hair—the color of black moss—and his broad mouth and white teeth. Then he woke and leaned in close to her, trying to see if she was asleep, unsure if he would get in trouble for waking her. His soft breath brushed her cheek. It smelled like mint. He had a strange habit of eating things that were green. Wildcat did too. She sometimes caught the cat chewing blades of grass. But Runt's appetite for it was larger. He would sniff strange plants, lick his lips, and stuff them into his mouth before she had a chance to stop him. She worried that one of these times he would end up nipples to the sky. It hadn't happened yet.

Girl rubbed the boy's back and soon he was tired again. She told him to pee in the tree boughs by the door; a little pee to mark their place went a long way to warning off beasts in the night. After that, he ate a small strip of meat, sipped some water, and yawned. He curled into her, ready for sleep. She watched the rise and fall of his belly slow. Small hands curled beneath a soft cheek. His lips went slack. Girl couldn't settle back down. She lay back and blinked in the dark. Tomorrow would be a hard day of preparation for the fish run. She squeezed her eyes shut but found it hard to sleep. Despite Runt by her side, the body of the family was missing.

17.

Girl got up before the sun to start the fire. She squatted back on her heels to watch. As the sun rose, it kissed the top of the cliff. The fish would start their journey soon. It was time to go to the meeting place.

Girl didn't put on her horns. She tucked them into a fold of the hide that she would carry on her back as a pack. Her belly wasn't showing, but she knew that she was pregnant. She could tell by taking one sniff of her morning pee. The awareness made her feel unsure about what their reception at the meeting place might be. If other families had had a lean year, then, as an unknown adult, she could be seen as competition for food. They might drive her off and expect her to fight her way back to show her strength. Her fertility could mark her as a threat. However, if times had been good, the families might happily welcome her in. They might see her resemblance to Big Sister or remember that her family had good land. There were as many possibilities for her reception as there were forks in the river. She didn't have the experience to know how the water might flow.

Not wearing her horns was a signal that she would submit, but it was also a sign of what was happening inside her. The pregnancy seemed to be altering how she felt. The brave swell that once came so often to her chest had melted back as the ice and snow receded. She was now strangely timid and undecided. And that was why she tucked the horns away. She would enter the meeting place as a girl. That much would stay the same. She could slip in as a girl and watch the others before she made a move.

All the times she had been at the fish run were one big picture in her mind: how she would smell the matted fur of the bears long before seeing them, the spreading green of the needles on the trees lower down, the stimulating combination of new families and foods. She longed for the days when she could youthfully mix in with the strange, new bodies and sniff while knowing that she still had a firm place at the hearth of Big Mother.

Girl let Runt have a last long sleep in the hut while she ate. She buried the best bowls and tools that they didn't need to bring along. When Runt was up, she settled him in to eat meat and drink. She piled the sleeping hides in the middle of the hut to keep them protected. She put rocks around the edge of the hut to hold it firm if the wind grew fierce. She pulled their cached packs out of the tree and lashed sacks for water onto the outside.

Runt stood nervously by the hearth. She walked up to him with the shell and tied the lash around his neck. His lips spread back in a huge grimace and he let the tips of his fingers run across the shell. For strength on the journey, she gave him the Sea.

Ready, he turned his back to her, and she looped the straps over his shoulders. She kept a hand on the pack to hold him steady. He bent his knobby knees, braced himself, and nodded that he was ready. She let go of the pack. His legs quivered like green boughs, but they held. Girl heaved her own pack onto her back. It was heavier than she liked, but she didn't know how long they would be gone. She would be responsible for setting up their camp at the meeting place. Everything they needed would take a year to make by herself, so she had to bring sacks, foot covers, lashes, and stone teeth. Those things, along with a spare spearhead, sleeping hides, an extra cloak, and dried meat for the journey, made for full loads. With so few bodies, they had lost the indulgence of traveling light.

Girl let Runt go first so she could keep watch. He staggered in the direction of the river, and she chewed on her lip as she wondered if he was traveling more sideways than forward. He stepped over a branch on the ground and this seemed to be his undoing. He lost his balance and his knee buckled. The pack lurched to the side and pulled the boy's body down.

In three strides she was beside him. On his back, arms and legs thrashing, he looked like a turtle flipped onto its shell. She bent to grab him by the pack and hoist him up.

"*Ne, ne,*" he said.

He pushed at the air with his hands to tell her not to help him. He was determined to get up on his own. Finally, he caught onto a root with one hand. He pulled to roll his body around so that the pack was on his back. On hands and knees, he fought for balance. The strain showed in his face, his teeth bared like the most frightening beast. Girl had to cover her mouth for fear she would laugh.

Runt got one foot up and pressed. With a roar, he pushed with the other leg, and he was up. A wobble to the front and a lurch to the side; his feet darted around as he tried to find a stance that would allow him to balance. Eventually, he got it. Arms out, fingers splayed wide, he stopped for long enough to still the pack. Holding his breath, he took a cautious step and then one more. Slowly, he made his way toward the river. Girl felt proud that he was trying so hard as she ambled behind him. She also felt that it would be a long day. Wildcat seemed to think the same. He was in no hurry as he took to the brush and followed.

As Runt shuffled along under his heavy pack, Girl felt increasingly antsy. The last two days of their journey were especially hard. When the sun was this high, it was strong enough to make large cracks in the river ice. Once the ice had melted, the fish would run and the games would begin. Girl worried that the action might be starting without them. If a sturdy young Big Mother appeared, she might claim the best family before Girl even had a chance.

It ended up taking three suns rising for them to make it to the meeting place. They traveled down to a lusher flank of the mountain. The river ice had broken by the time they arrived. The bush was dense, and the bugs swarmed around their heads in a cloud. The water ran fast and wide.

When the season was right, all the families came together at this spot where the forks of the rivers met. Girl could remember when as many as five families had gathered. Last year only two other families had appeared. There were stories of many more, though that hadn't happened in her lifetime. Big Girl, her sister, had become a Big Mother and now headed up one of the other families. When Big Girl left the meeting place last season, her belly had just been starting to round out with a child. Girl wondered if there might now be a plump baby to hold. She remembered the soft skin and downy hair of infants she had snuggled at the meeting place, and she put her hand on her own belly. Until that moment, she had only worried that she was growing bigger. She wondered if she should feel proud.

In Girl's mind they were late, but she guessed not in the minds of the others. She rounded the last bend and looked out at the broad riverbed, a yawning slice of silt, rocks, and sand through which the heavy spring waters ran. She felt glad to be there again. The air carried the heavy southern oils in the pine, the scent of berry buds, and cool whiffs of the very slightly salty water. It brought back all the feelings she had had here before. Like a cluster, the families crowded into her head. While she gave them little thought at other times, now she could see each one of their bodies in her mind.

Those smells and sights brought back other things. She quickly remembered where the biggest berries hung. She eyed her favorite blackberry bush, often among the first to release its fruit. The stone platform that Big Mother preferred to stand on in the rapids might be less slimy this year. It was a good steady base, the perfect spot to stand

and catch fish as they lunged by. Girl's mouth watered in anticipation.

But when Girl and Runt came down the last rocky slope to the place where the river spread out, she was surprised to see that there were no shelters along the edge of the brush. Usually the families built temporary shelters in a row near a band of rock. In front of that lay the pebble beach, which stretched a long way to the river. This was like an open field where all the action took place: the sniffing, the circling, the fighting, the choosing of mates, and sometimes the mating too. Everyone knew what was happening and took a keen interest. This wasn't seen as snooping in the least. The speculation and gossip that spread among them had a purpose. They might throw support behind one Big Mother and feed her. Or throw small rocks at another to discourage her bid. It was rowdy and bold and brutal action. And it was important to them all. Their fates hung on the outcomes.

Girl picked a spot against the band of rock, a good one, but not the best. She didn't want to send a silent challenge to the Big Mother who arrived next. But the patch of land she chose jutted toward the river with the rock at their backs and gave a wide view of everything around them. She tied green branches to make a frame. Over this, she spread a thin hide. Using twine made of vines, she tied the hide to the branches. The vines would constrict as they dried and tighten the bind. The inner hide was so tight that when Girl gave it a smack, it bounced under her palm. Over this, she and Runt heaved a thick hide, still full of bison oil to keep out the rain. Inside, she spread boughs and placed the sleeping hides on top.

Wildcat poked his nose out from behind a bush and chirped. Girl stuck her head outside of the flap to see. He gave Girl a slow blink, signaling his approval of their chosen spot and letting her know that he would be back for scraps of fish. With that done, he dashed off, likely in search of a mouse.

Runt made a place by the door for their spears. He put flat rocks by the nest for their water sacks, horns, and his shell. He made a ledge in the middle for the lamp, a lump of bison fat with a wick made of twine sitting on a flat stone with a depression in the middle. The lamp was good to have, a sign of their relative strength, though they wouldn't need it much. The sun stayed up to watch the fun at this time of year. They would have more than enough in the way of light.

They would cook outside on the pebbles along the river, as the clouds were high and dry. Girl dug a shallow hearth. They both collected an ample supply of wood. And by the time this moving-in was done, they were tired and happy. They were ready. They sat by the fire and waited for the others.

The first to come weren't the ones they'd expected. A family of brown bears pushed through the thickets on the other side of the river. It was their usual pattern to come after all the families had arrived. They liked the families to find their places first, as it was long established that the upright walkers could be skittish and defensive little beasts. If the families were settled, then it was easier for the bears to give them adequate space. That, in turn, kept everyone out of trouble. The bears' willingness to come to the fish feed second was a show of their strength. With their powerful muscles, large teeth, and sharp claws, the bears had little need to worry about getting enough fish.

Girl and Runt sat and watched the bears come. To Girl, they felt like old friends, as she saw the same ones year after year. They were great, lumbering beasts when compared to the family. Though they did somehow remind Girl of Big Mother in her later years. Maybe it was the way they rolled on their hips as they walked. Their heads and their snouts were much larger, though. It was strange that the bears had come before the other families. Girl lifted her lip to the wind, but sensed nothing new.

The bears' side of the river also had a stretch of pebbled beach with ample space. Girl saw a female who now looked to be a Big Mother. A pair of young cubs scampered by her heels and chewed at her legs as she tried to walk. Runt was the same kind of pest—if only he had such fuzzy ears. With her hand, Girl felt the slight curve of her own belly.

A large male stood farther off. If Girl was right about who he was, he had been much smaller the year before. He wasn't the father of these cubs, as he hadn't been big enough to win the right to mate the year before. Now a great hump of fat sat on top of his shoulders and neck to show his success. It was easy to admire.

The mother bear caught the scent of the big male too. She eyed him suspiciously. Girl knew that the male bear might kill the cubs for the chance to mate. She had seen it happen with her own eyes. Big Mother had sounded a call when the trouble across the river started a few years before. They had all scampered up looking trees to watch and make it clear that they would stay out of the way. That was how the two groups lived easily together. They made sure to give each other space.

At a time like this, with plenty of fish to go around, the male might not go for the cubs. Especially if the numbers of fish were up, he might focus on keeping his coat glossy and putting on fat. But it was always hard to know what he would do next. He had his own life equation that needed to be constantly adjusted for balance. The mother would need to watch her cubs, just as Girl would watch Runt.

While they waited for the families and for the fish, Girl showed Runt how to make a net. They waded upriver into the shallows where the riverbed bent like an elbow. Inside the crook, the still waters allowed for reeds to grow. They used their stone teeth to slice them off at the base. They brought these to the hearth, where Girl had set the frames they'd made from green branches. She placed the first reed across the frame, doubled it over the edge, and brought it back. Then she did the same on the other side. When one row was complete, she wove the next row of reeds at a right angle to it. Soon, she had a large, flat basket with slits to let the water run through. It would last just long enough to catch all the fish they could eat.

The first fish showed up a few days later. It was the bears that alerted them. A lone fin wiggled its way upstream toward the falls. A few of the younger bears leaped and pounced after the fish, trying to pin it to the riverbed with their claws. Girl was dozing on her back in the sun. Runt punched her arm and pointed excitedly. He started to chatter and chirp about the fish and begged her to run over. He wanted to join in too.

Girl looked across at the older bears. They also lay in the sun. The mother gave her belly an absent-minded scratch. They knew what Girl knew, that a lone fish was very difficult to catch. It wasn't worth the energy. They needed to wait until the river became thick with the bodies of fish.

A heavy rain came the next day and Girl and Runt stayed in the hut to wait it out. Wildcat preferred to hang back from the river, as he didn't like cavorting with bears, but he joined them inside the hut to save himself a soaking. Girl struck a flint rock to make a spark. She blew on a handful of dry twigs to coax a flame and lit the fat lamp on the ledge. Big Mother had told Girl stories about the fish with her shadows. Now Girl used the shadows cast by her hands to tell Runt: After collecting the salts of the sea, the Big Mother fish brought her eggs back to her part of the river. The fish of the same family followed the mother home. The Big Mother fish decided it was the right time and spread her eggs. She died soon after that, and the rest of the family died too. The dead bodies of the family became the food for the babies. In that way, the fish were like the family. They gave everything they had to feed and grow their young.

As Girl told stories that day, it rained and rained. The water level rose quickly, enough to allow the fish to make their way through and up the shallows lower down the river. When the sun rose the next day, the river came alive. The first few fish took a leap at the falls. The bears got up and started to pace back and forth along their side of the bank. Girl was glad to see the fish; she felt as though they were old friends. The anticipation of food and *warm* flooded her, and she sprang to her feet. She grabbed the reed basket and prodded Runt to come.

Girl took one last look up the valley. She curled her lip up to feel for anything she might have missed and watched the leaves on the trees. There was no warm meat making its way to the meeting place. The run was starting and they were the only ones who had arrived. This gave her chest a feeling of emptiness, like the fire had gone out.

The bears had lined up on their side of the falls. The fish that had made it this far looked big. A fish body leaped, a band of muscle that used its tail to push up through the air in flight. The fish knew the game with the bears. The thinking ones did small jumps first. They would eye the bears and aim to jump past the snapping jaws.

But the sheer number of jumping fish meant that the bears quickly started to catch them. Girl knew it was time. She sat Runt on the rocks with a large stone in his hand. She eased out onto the slick ledge. Big Mother had earned this spot through years of snarling, spitting, and beating. With the old woman gone, Girl had expected to have to fight for it again, but no challengers were there to step up. She gained the ledge and held up her reed basket to catch the fish.

A few fish jumped, but Girl didn't lean out for them. There was no need to risk feeding the hungry river with her own meat. She would wait and time it just so. And soon, a fish as large as her arm jumped close by. She placed the basket underneath in a neat sweep. The fish landed, and the water it brought with its body ran through the reeds. Still, it was heavy. Girl said, "Oomph."

She turned and dumped the fish out beside Runt, who put a foot and a hand on the large body. He lifted the rock and brought it down, but his muscles were too small. The rock only glanced off the large fish head. The gaping jaws with long saber fangs came perilously close to his thin arm. So Girl took the rock and gave it a knock in just the right spot. The rock cracked the fish's skull and smashed its spine in one swift move. Runt threw up his hands and cheered.

When Girl turned back for the next fish, she was surprised to see that the mother bear had moved quite near to her ledge. It was a new thing for the bears to come so close. The mother raised her snout and caught Girl's scent over the water. Girl did the same and in this way they compared news. Girl felt the mother was doing well and nodded in a show of respect. She hoped this might avoid any sort of challenge of position. While it was clear that Girl would never win in a fight, they both respected the dangers of breaking their truce.

The mother bear also sniffed curiously. She held up her nose and lingered in a way that reminded Girl of Big Mother. Had this bear eaten her mother's meat? Was the old woman inside? It was rare for the bears to pass by the land of the family on their way to the fish run, but they might have. Rather than feeling disturbed at the thought of the family being meat, Girl hung on to the idea. Her feelings about death and the way that a body died were flexible depending on the circumstances. In the best times, when there were lots of living bodies available, she would have buried Big Mother, maybe under a tree if one had come down. But after the leopard attack, Girl had only dragged the bodies of Him and Big Mother farther into the brush. To find the right tree and dig a hole took a lot of work. It was a job that would occupy the only adult pair of hands, which needed to be busy with getting food and keeping Runt safe. She didn't have such luxury.

The idea of this bear bringing part of Big Mother to the meeting place in her belly felt efficient, since Girl couldn't have carried the body. She found herself trying to feel Big Mother in this bear. The bear dipped her head and seemed to eye Girl's belly. Balancing the basket on a knee, Girl put a hand to her own belly.

"*Ye.*"

It was the first time she had acknowledged that the baby might be something separate from herself. It was more than a belly. This baby would come out from between her legs and become a body that could later walk away.

By nighttime, they had caught more fish than they could eat. They gorged on the sweet orange flesh. They found the sacs of eggs and popped the globes between their teeth. Wildcat came for a piece. As she was cautious, Girl put a few strips of fish by the fire to dry. Later she would cache them in a tree just in case, but food was in abundance. There were no other hungry mouths on their side of the river. They could eat until their bellies were round and their limbs as wide as the river itself.

Girl lay back in the hut that night, held Runt's sleeping body, and tried to connect to his dreams. There was nothing. She couldn't feel any other body with her mind. Despite the baby growing inside her, she was alone.

Pressed Particleboard

By Sunday, I had calmed down enough about Caitlin and the management of the site to start worrying about more important things again, like storage. Simon agreed to one last act before we left for home. He would drive me to the Ikea box store outside of Avignon.

On the drive, Caitlin's voice kept playing in my mind. She had mentioned there would be a videoconference with the museum committee the next day. I was filled with dread at the thought of not being part of it.

"Bringing a journalist to the site?" I couldn't keep my thoughts in. "It shows her lack of judgment about the scope of this project. I doubt she has any idea how controversial my interpretations of the findings might be. People resist the idea of being close cousins to Neanderthals because of how the species has been characterized in the past. No one wants to think of himself as a hairy beast."

"Rose?"

"Simon?"

"I wonder, given your state, how much sense does it make for us to be going to Ikea right now?"

"My state?"

"You are pregnant. We are broke."

"I'll expense the purchase to the project."

"Can we expense meatballs too?"

"I wish you could have the baby." I looked out at the blur of landscape speeding by. "You'd be much better suited to it, don't you think?"

"Oh yes, I'd be great." Simon gripped the wheel. "I'd be barefoot, pregnant, and alone in our flat wondering when my husband might come home."

"Why barefoot?"

"Since you have turned into a ferocious beast, Rose, you will have eaten my slippers for breakfast."

"At least I'm not hairy."

We passed a lavender field in bloom, clutches of fragrant purple plants in obedient rows. A stone cottage was nestled in the midst of it, looking squat and solid, like it had spent all its years refusing to budge.

"Caitlin is a reputable scientist, though. Am I right?" Simon asked.

"When it comes to gibbons, she's the best."

"Wouldn't the museum appoint someone capable?"

"Maybe not."

"Do you doubt her because she's a woman?" He flashed a triumphant smile.

"I'm too evolved to take that bait." I sighed. "Though, to be honest, it's an important thing to ask. I do think Guy has purposely appointed a nonexpert in order to leave a gap. It's a power grab. That gap leaves room for experts to weigh in and for Guy to decide what he wants to do based on how it will affect visitor numbers or his private funders' hearts. There is a videoconference planned for tomorrow. One of the expert consultants they hired will be on it. Isn't that convenient?"

"Do you know what the expert will say?"

"He hasn't shared his results, but I know he's being paid by Guy. He will say whatever Guy pressures him to say."

"Guy?"

"Guy Henri."

"That curator from the museum in Arles? I didn't know you were working with him."

"Caitlin won't know how to interpret the expert's opinion. The science will get left behind. And so will my reputation over the long term."

"I see."

"That's why, Simon . . . I . . ."

"Yes?"

"I'm thinking I should have the baby here."

"Where? In Ikea?"

"In France."

Simon was silent. I saw a spot of bright blue on the horizon. The Ikea had been permitted to sprout only outside the stone ramparts of Avignon.

"I want to be able to keep an eye on the project," I said.

A small muscle in his jaw twitched. "Rose?"

"Simon?"

"We live in London. I"—he pointed his finger to his chest—"live in London."

"I know."

"Fuck. You are such a handful."

"I'll assume you are referring to my breasts."

Simon bit back whatever he was about to say as he guided the car into a parking spot in the enormous yet crowded lot. "Let's just go in," he said through clenched teeth. "We'll talk about it later."

The store was turned in on itself with no view outside and no sense of its surroundings. Once we got inside, I realized that was exactly the point. I was free to close my eyes, sit on an overstuffed sofa with too many pillows, and inhale the scent of spray-on fabric protector. I could have been anywhere in the world. Simon seemed to relax as well. And I suppose Ikea was a more straightforward adventure for him than most of the ones I had suggested. Having grown up in what

I would call the suburbs of Bournemouth, he was naturally forgiving of big-box stores and sprawl. And he quite liked the meatballs they served.

He led the way along the yellow line through the displays of rooms that belonged to pretend people in my mind. I made up the life story of each imaginary occupant.

"You see how she's laid out the table for dinner and it's only ten in the morning?" I said with a *tsk*. "She's having trouble relaxing. Can't live in the moment. And it puts him on edge when she sets it like that because all he wants to do is watch the game with a bowl of pasta in his lap."

"Do you think they'll make it as a couple?" Simon straightened their napkins while looking at their credenza with concern.

"Not a chance," I said. We strolled toward the next display in the dining section. "They won't last the year, poor things."

"This looks suspiciously organized, doesn't it?" Simon gestured to a table in another room. The place settings used more utensils than needed. The plates were all odd angles and points.

"Control issues." I nodded.

"Perfectionism is a flaw disguised as control." Simon rubbed his chin thoughtfully. He was quite worried for them.

When we got to the bedroom displays, we saw one with a particularly puffy arrangement of pillows on the king-size bed. Simon sprawled out and pretended to snore. A little girl snuck up to see the spectacle. I'm not sure if he knew she was there, but when she got close, he suddenly rolled over and let out a growl of a yawn. All I saw were the soles of the girl's sneakers as she screamed and sprinted off.

Soon afterward, we settled in for meatballs, salad, and those strangely yummy wafer cookies that no one else in Europe makes the same way.

"Do you ever wonder"—my eyes darted as I ate—"why you were put on this planet?"

"I feared this would happen." Simon gave me a weary smile. "You're attracted to this kind of big-box store, but once inside, you have an existential crisis."

"Seriously, Simon. Why do we bother?"

"Many great philosophers have asked the same question."

"All this disposable furniture. It's flat-packed. It will cause fights between couples as they assemble it. And then it will end up in land-fill. Why do we have to struggle this way?"

"It's pointless."

"I know why," I said.

Simon stopped, meatball speared on his fork, eyebrows up toward the glow of the fluorescent lights overhead. "You do?"

We'd had this conversation many times before. I asked him the same question at least once a year, if not more. Simon's answer was that he didn't believe there was a point. He just got up each morning. Removing the need for a larger meaning made the small things more important. He loved tea in the morning, especially blistering-hot tea. For him, tea and an unread newspaper were point enough. I, however, had been driven by a constant search for the meaning of life since the day I was born, it seemed. I talked about it often. The first time I asked Simon if he thought there was a reason he had been put on the planet, he had taken the question completely seriously. He stopped, sat down in a chair, and considered the issue in silence. He thought until he came to a conclusion. It wasn't his answer that got me. It was that Simon saw thinking as an activity that had to be done separately from other things. And once he'd thought it through, he came up with a firm answer.

"No," he had said.

"Then there is no point to getting out of bed every day?" I asked.

"I don't think about it. I never have."

"Will you?"

He looked at me and I realized that he already assumed we would be together for life. "I won't have a choice, because you'll keep ask-ing."

I fell in love with him then.

This new turn in our conversation—that after all our years to-gether, I had an answer to why we were here, and one that had appeared at the same time as a plate of meatballs in Ikea—caught Si-mon off guard. He seemed to brace himself, realizing that he now had to contend with whatever the answer might be. He ate the meatball on his fork and stabbed another one. "You know why we were put on this planet?" He waved the meatball at me. "All this time, the answer was here?"

"I don't wonder anymore."

"I was going to say the same. That I suddenly do see a larger point to all this." He smiled broadly.

"I found her." I grinned back.

"The baby."

"The Neanderthal."

"Oh."

"I have this feeling, Simon. Once I've excavated her completely, she's going to show that my theories are exactly right."

"Oh yeah?" Simon plopped the meatball into his mouth, looked away, and bit down hard. "I'm sure that's true."

We found the perfect shelving system that could be customized for the cramped nook by the double doors in the flat. I worried that it might not fit in the car, but Simon waved his hand. It was all flat-pack, no problem. I didn't think so, but I had nodded because I was getting tired. We spent a long time making sure that we had all the little shelves, drawers, and braces that would make it complete. You'd think it was a task that two PhDs could accomplish easily, but it was ridiculously complex. I had a stubby brown pencil to tick off the items as Simon loaded them onto the dolly. He had to run back in twice to get the last few parts. We had a small disagreement over the pronunciation of a Swedish name and another one on how the aisles were numbered. Why did they skip numbers, and what was the ra-tionale for aisle 11 being in the back corner across from aisle 4? Then there were the screws. I was sure they were included and Simon was convinced we had to buy them separately. The answer turned out to be both.

We were finally set but had to wait in the checkout line for the better part of an hour. Our cart with the bad wheel and I finally wobbled back to the rental car. Simon pushed all the shelves into the passenger-side footwell. He didn't have much concern for where my feet might go, but they were so sore I would have been willing to leave them behind anyway. I took the small wire baskets to hold on my lap—or the small slice of my lap that was left. The back braces that supported the shelves slid into the gap between the front seats.

"Are we all done nesting, then?" asked Simon. His back ached too.

"I need a nap," I said.

The last thing to go in was the backboard of the shelving unit. I stood out of the way while Simon wrestled it in on top of everything else. He got the front in and pushed. The end stuck too far out of the rented hatchback, so he pushed again. It wouldn't go in any farther. I quickly saw it wasn't going to fit and something inside me turned. I'd told him as much in the store. I couldn't stand the thought of going back in and standing in the delivery line, which seemed to snake for miles and miles.

"I warned you," I snarled.

"You said we should try."

"You never think ahead."

"You're always running off to different countries."

"I can't run. I'm the size of a large chair."

"I move to London and you take off for France," he snapped. "How do I plan for that?"

"You could start by renting a car that is big enough for me to fit inside."

"I'm trying to save money."

"Because you aren't making any."

Simon stepped back from the car. His face hardened and he almost looked like he might run, but then he abruptly let out an anguished moan. A sound I'd never heard from him. He was suddenly large and fierce, his lips pulled back to show his teeth, eyes wide. Whatever despair and helplessness he felt came out as rage. The small girl whom he had accidentally frightened earlier was just walking to her car with her parents. She froze in fear, her mouth agape, and then gave a terrified yelp.

I turned my back to Simon. My feet ached and I was exhausted. I was worried about my Neanderthal lying in the dirt. I wanted Simon to step up. I didn't want him to be upset about the pieces not fitting. I wanted him to fix it. I wanted him to fix me because by this point I felt broken in ways I never had before. My body was no longer mine. I couldn't will it to behave as I wanted it to. I slumped down with my bottom on the bumper and listened to Simon wail.

Finally, he took a breath and came around to my side of the car.

"Rose?" He spoke in an exaggerated calm.

"Yes?"

"Get in."

"Now we've got two things that will barely fit."

"We are driving to London."

"Now?"

"Right now. I've had enough. This baby is coming. I will have the shelves delivered. We are going home."

"I'm not. I can't."

"You care more about that Neanderthal than you do about me."

"I've worked my whole life for this."

"Well, me too." He stomped off toward the store.

Simon came back after an extended stay in the delivery line. I had wedged myself into the passenger seat to wait. He got in and put his head on the steering wheel. If the purpose of customer service is to beat a person down until he agrees to pay any amount asked, it had worked. He looked utterly defeated. "You want me to stay in the village?" he asked.

"No."

"I can't miss this week of teaching. It will ruin any chance of picking up more courses in the future."

"I know."

"Where will I work here? I can't even speak the language. You know all this?"

"I do," I said.

"We need to feed this baby." His voice was low and sad. "I can only do that by making money."

Since meeting Simon, I had been stronger, braver, and I had taken more professional risks than I ever had previously. He watched my back and that made it feel safe to take chances. His flexible mind made my thinking even more so. But I suppose having a baby with someone is the ultimate risk. And just then, I was terrified. Simon wasn't watching my back. Or if he was, he didn't know what to look out for. The baby was inside me. He had no idea how that felt.

"We are the only primates who delegate the gathering of food," I muttered, trying my best to explain.

"Sorry?" He looked at me, exasperated.

"That's what Caitlin said to me the other day. All the other female primates can resume gathering food just hours after they give birth. Their babies can cling to their mothers and nurse while the females work to feed themselves. Humans can't. We have to rely on others to forage. It leaves a woman very vulnerable."

"Sounds mildly threatening."

"Yes. Caitlin wants me gone—"

"Are you sure?"

"—and I need to stay."

"Rose," he said in a low voice. "The baby is coming."

"In two weeks." I tried to force a smile.

When we got back to the village, I stepped out of the car. "I'm sorry, Rose," Simon said, his voice breaking, "that you don't feel I'm fit to forage. I'll do better. I'll get a post for September, I promise." He drove off to find parking so that he could come back to the apartment to get his things. But to me, it felt like he was leaving for good.

I stood watching the tiny car disappear. The unease pulsed from my chest and ran through me to every part of my body. I tried to decide whether I felt guilty, angry, or mad, but I was too physically uncomfortable to settle on one. There were no words that could counter the feeling that took hold of me. Even if Simon said he wanted to be with me, there were no guarantees. Life and jobs were unpredictable, as were loyalties. It didn't matter if he tried to convince me otherwise. I was the one carrying the baby. For him, there was a choice. For me, there was none.

18.

Girl and Runt spent the short summer season gorging on fish and growing. With only the bears for company, Girl tried not to let Runt see how lonely she had become. For his part, Runt didn't mind the lack of other families in the least. His belly was full. He felt no more alone than he had before. In fact, he thrived. He had no reason to worry about being kicked by a foot that belonged to one of the family; his place by Girl's side felt firm, and watching the bears on the other side of the river provided endless entertainment. The air was warm. They slept with the flap of the hut open and he loved hearing the rush of the river as he drifted off.

In the morning, the sun shone down on them. They stretched and yawned and wondered what might happen next. All the beasts along the river were thriving—Girl and the bears and Runt. The large amounts of food opened up possibilities. Good health sometimes allowed a beast to take a wider view than it had the day before. It also brought restlessness.

Girl sniffed the air and realized that the big male bear was stirring up trouble. She watched him snapping at the fish in a careless way. He had eaten so much that he was only trying to show off by clipping their fins as they soared by the tip of his nose. He wrestled with a younger male bear in the shallows, but the youth was clearly no match. He chased other bears away from the falls, and even that was too easy. Girl pulled Runt back from the river. If there was trouble, it was better not to be in its way. She sent Runt off in search of hazelnuts. Best to keep him busy.

So Girl was already alert and watching when the big male bear started in on the mother of the cubs. He lifted his nose in the female's direction and gave her a meaningful sniff. She pretended to ignore the interest and started to round up her young ones. She stopped their wrestling, pried them apart with her muzzle, and nosed them in the direction of the brush. But the male bear wouldn't be shaken off so easily. He sniffed even more pointedly in the mother's direction.

Girl knew he was checking to see if the mother was fertile. Her cubs had only been born that spring, her milk glands were still full, and although the cubs were feeding on fish, they still got most of their nutrition from her. When strong cubs were feeding that way, the mother wouldn't be able to get pregnant. All the energy in her body would go toward making sure the cubs would live. When they were big enough, she would move on. She might have an interest in mating with the male bear then.

It didn't take more than a sniff for the big male to know the whole story. But he didn't want to wait any longer. With a gnash of his teeth, he let out a great huff. He charged at the mother bear, butted her hard with his head, and shoved her to the ground. From that position, he tried to climb on top of her. She was as fierce as every mother has ever been. She raked her claws on his glossy coat and snapped her teeth at his neck. She managed to connect her sharpest incisor with his nose and bit down. He yelped and jumped back in surprise.

There was a momentary truce, but no one thought it would hold. While the mother bear made a panicked dash for her babies, Girl had a similar instinct.

"*Aroo!*" She gave a sharp call to Runt to tell him to get in a tree.

If the bears were fighting, the family moved away. It was part of the agreement that kept the long-standing peace between the two groups. Both had a security in their strength to the extent that they could allow the others to dominate for a time. If the family had a fight, the bears would slink back into the brush. Now, it was up to the family to clear out.

The family did this by taking to the trees. Being up high in the branches wouldn't necessarily keep them out of danger. It was more about making a show of conceding the ground to the bears.

Girl quickly jumped up to the first branch of the looking tree nearest her. She climbed, feet and hands on limbs, and there was an excitement in her climbing. Even with her belly in the way, she bounced up from branch to branch.

The summer had held much drama for the fish. They had risked everything they had to get up the river; their hearts, scales, and lives had been thrown on the rocks. But Girl's time at the meeting place had been sadly still. While she was glad not to be challenged—or, worse, killed—for the family's land, the quiet came at a great cost. There was no posturing, strutting, or flexing of muscles. There wasn't a great display of urges or the satisfaction of a public copulation that had been a few days in the making. There were no dances or moans or fights. Her heart had not throbbed longingly once.

So although the unfolding drama did not belong to the families, it was better than the calm comfort that had settled in at the meeting place. She reached a high branch that had a good sight line. Tucking her bum onto a crook, she snapped off a few leafy branches for a better view. She could see the male bear was charging at the female. He was doing this with a clear purpose: to separate the mother from her cubs. If successful, he would kill them.

Girl knew this without needing to be told. She had many things in common with the bears. She knew their ways much as she knew the ways of her own family. The bears felt hunger, as she did, and thirst. They ate and pooped like she did. And they wanted to mate, just as she did. They shared the basic drives of life, and without those drives, both the bears and the family would cease to be.

Girl knew this game and that it was in her interest to stay clear. This male bear had satisfied his needs for water, food, and rest. And now he wanted to mate. There was one viable female at the meeting place that day. By killing the cubs, he could hope that the mother would turn her attention to him.

The mother bear was strong and a good fighter, which only convinced the male bear that his efforts were worth the trouble. The harder she fought, the clearer it was that his potential offspring would stand a good chance under her care, and the more determined he became to win his prize. While he wasn't mortally injuring the mother, he was hurting her. They both reared up on their hindquarters and pushed against each other's paws. She swung her large head around and caught him in the jaw. He took advantage of her waver in balance and checked her with a rounded shoulder. They went sprawling across the sand and into the shallows.

The smells and the sounds thrilled Girl, the mother's great roars and the male's snarling growls. There was a huff of milk and the stench of fear and fighting. Soon their coats were matted with spit. Their muscles were tiring and they rolled and stumbled along the shallow shore. There was blood on the teeth of one and sand in the eyes of the other. An ear was torn. A claw split. There would be some kind of resolution soon.

They rolled into the river with a huge splash. The male came down on top of the mother with all his weight. She was pushed sideways and into the deeper waters. She paddled and pushed, but her body was dragged downriver with the current. The male knew this was his chance. He sprang out of the water and lunged for the cubs. Having anxiously followed their mother into the shallows, they scattered in different directions.

There was another roar. And it came from the brush.

At first Girl thought the roar was from another bear—the sound was that well-developed low tone in the throat. She strained forward to see if the mother had made it back already, but she had been swept far down the river by the current. While the sow paddled hard, Girl saw that she had only just made it to an eddy and still struggled to pull herself out. If it wasn't her roaring in the bushes, then had another bear taken up her cause? It would be the first time Girl had seen such a thing. Bears usually lived solitary lives. One didn't get caught up in the business of another.

So what was this in the brush, roaring and disturbing the leaves? Girl squinted and leaned from her branch for a better look. She saw a stick waving and then the bushes were pushed to the side. Out popped Runt.

Runt waved his stick and yelled at the two cubs. He barked at them as though he were their mother telling them to stay away. And then he lifted his stick and pointed it at the charging male bear. He bared his teeth, and his bulging eyes were open wide. He made a fierce face and waved his arms over his head while marching toward the bear.

Girl's heart seemed to fall out of the tree and roll toward the river. She wanted to be right there to grab the boy, but she knew she could never get to him in time. The male bear was charging fast at the cubs. With each stride, Runt screamed and yelled more, as though in a fury. Girl's first thought was that one of the green plants he had eaten must have turned his mind mad. She wondered if it had given him a deluded belief in his own strength.

The male bear still had his eyes on the cubs. The two little things had run to separate trees. One got a paw on the bark and the other started to climb, and it was just then that the large bear's head snapped around and he set his sights on Runt. He lurched in the boy's direction. With her heart now in the icy waters of the river, Girl watched. If Runt made it through this charge, she would do her best to grab the boy, or what might be left of him. Girl had to force herself to keep looking.

The male bear charged for another two strides and then stopped dead. His front paws jammed into the mud of the shallows and he halted his momentum with his heavily muscled shoulders. Runt continued to wave and yell. The bear sniffed the air and stood up on his hind legs to look at Runt. He tilted his head and kept his nose to the wind. Then he dropped to all fours, nodded to the wind, and turned.

Mouth agape, Girl watched as the bear loped into the brush and disappeared. Soon the mother made it back up the bank to her cubs. After she'd finished licking her wounds, the two small bodies curled up to nurse.

The air settled slowly around the river, but it took Girl longer to do the same. She sat by the hearth and turned the strips of fish that smoked on racks to dry, as she was starting to feel the cooler press of summer's end on her skin. Runt was gone for some time but later came striding to the hearth like it was any other evening. He had the reed basket on his hip, but it was lined with leaves and filled with hazelnuts instead of fish. The branches were starting to let them go. She had almost forgotten that she had asked him to collect them.

Runt placed the basket on the ground. Hazelnuts spoiled quickly in the heat. They had to be roasted or the worms would find their way in. She had taught Runt how to do this. When she put the hazelnuts in coals long enough to get hot, she could crack them and pour their hot oil into a turtle shell. This was good to drink or for curing a hide before winter; the pores were closed with a bone tool and oil worked into the hide to repel water. They would also pound the meat of the nuts to make into cakes with fish and berries. Girl looked at Runt long and hard. He avoided her eyes and started to tuck the nuts around the edge of the coals.

For Runt, it was like many other evenings. For Girl, it was like none before. Maybe the altercation with the bear had ended peacefully this time, but she believed that bears had long memories. A truce was a delicate balance. It had been held for as long as her memories went back; that way their energy wasn't wasted on needless fights. It kept their numbers up. If there was enough fish for all, the family had no interest in changing anything. The truce wasn't something that was discussed or debated. It just was.

And now Runt had gone and tilted it by provoking the male bear. The bear might now see Runt and others like him in a new way and remember the frustration of being unsuccessful when attempting to mate. Though it was hard to know when or where that frustration would spring, it would come with the deepest roar. There had been a disturbance in the order of things.

Girl had an urge that bubbled up in her throat. She couldn't just shout at Runt or scold him. She searched for a word that might speak of the delicate equation of fear and respect that went into their truce with the bears, but her lips hung slack. The task felt too difficult; it would be like walking up to a bear cub, tapping him on the shoulder, and trying to explain to him. Runt was young. His behavior was sometimes unpredictable and he was an odd boy.

For a mother bear, there was no point in trying to convey her wishes to her offspring through subtle means. There was a way to do things and the methods weren't up for question. She might push him toward food and warn him away from danger. If a cub did something foolish, the mother bear might bat him with a paw. But in the long run, a young cub either learned and did things right or died. And Girl was at a loss about what to do for similar reasons. The gulf that lay between her and the bear felt as vast as that between her and Runt.

She looked down at the fire. The shells of the hazelnuts were starting to char, and the smells met her as memories. When her sister was still with their family the year before, they had made dough from mush and the meat of nuts when it had hardened just enough. Big Girl handed her berries to stick in the dough. Then they wrapped it around a stick and held it over the fire; the aroma rose up like heat from the flames. Once it was baked, she and her sister ate the bread straight from the stick, the glow of the fire on their skin, basking in the warmth of each other's companionship.

With no words to convey the complexity of her thoughts, Girl focused on what she could do. She wanted to eat warm bread by the fire as she had before. She handed Runt a small tool that she had shaped out of a shard of stone. He had proved himself especially good at cracking the nuts with it, making a small puncture first on one side and then the other. Carefully, he poured out the oil without burning his skin. While his thin hands lacked strength, they were very good for this kind of work. She pounded the cooked nuts on a depression in a rock to make a paste while Runt continued making the oil.

Beside her, Runt started to hum. It was a lower pitch than his usual one and it seemed to flow over her. Soon she joined in. Her nasal sounds were like the rocks that made bumps and turns in the river, while his smooth water flowed over the top. Wildcat ate a nut and listened and let his eyelids fall. They worked the nuts until the basket was empty.

The dark wrapped in tight around them as the light from the fire lit up their faces. They sang and worked. They didn't speak of bears and the order of things. There were no words.

19.

Girl stood in ankle-deep water in the river. She planted her spear in the soft sand and leaned on it. Her feet were swollen and sore and the water did wonders to cool them. Her belly was heavier. She spent much of her time feeling uncomfortably hot. She had found a favorite spot beside the river under the broad shade of a leafy tree. Runt played with rocks in the shallows for long spells.

Given how scrawny Runt was, he could throw rocks surprisingly long distances. He was already rivaling some of Big Mother's best throws, and Girl wished the woman were alive to see. There was something about the way Runt's arm was hinged onto his body— perhaps the lack of heavy muscle—that let it swing in a wide arc. And his arm was long in relation to his body, which allowed for great force behind each fling. He might turn out to be among the best throwers of the families. She was glad for this, or perhaps relieved. While he was no longer ugly to her, his looks certainly weren't conventional. He would need to prove himself more than most others did.

A battered fish nosed around in the shallow water in front of her. Its scaly skin had turned a bright orange, which happened just before they died. This told her that the fish were almost finished with their journey, and it would soon be time for her and Runt to go. The bears would stay on and gorge on the dead fish bodies, as was their way, but the families took their dried fish and turned back toward their lands.

This spoke of the vital difference in how the two groups weathered the winter. The bears ate the live fish as well as the dead. They ate anything and everything in order to bulk up their bodies. The goal was to get their coats as glossy and full of oil as possible for warmth, with a broad covering of fat underneath. The bears would then dig themselves into a pit and sleep safe and snug through the worst of the storms. All the nourishment they required was right on their own bear backs. They could rest without worry.

Over the years, the families had developed a different tactic. While they also fattened up during the fish run, their bodies were smaller than the bears', their hides thinner, and they couldn't store as much fat. They couldn't afford to go into a deep, months-long sleep. Their bodies simply couldn't sustain them in the same way. To compensate, they had to dry fish with smoke during the summer. They carried it back to their camp, and it became their fuel through the autumn bison hunt. They also collected nuts and berries, made pastes, and boiled fat for lamps.

However, the family did some things the bears did—they hunkered down for the winter. They dug into their huts and used snow for insulation. Their heart rates decreased and their bodies became slow. They called the state they went into wintersleep. That's how they knew they were in it: when a body could barely slur out the word. Each of them chewed on a piece of meat only once a day and took a few mouthfuls of water. It was just enough to keep things in the body ticking but use very little energy.

Every now and then, they would wake more fully. The timing was decided by Big Mother and depended on complex factors such as the ferocity of the storms that year, the state of their food supply, and the health of the bodies inside the hut. Many other things were involved—the weight of the clouds, the composition of the snow, and reports through the trees of what was going on elsewhere. When it was time, Big Mother would light a fat lamp and wake everyone to eat a more varied meal, make repairs to the hut as needed, dig out, and clear their bowels.

Traditionally this was a time when some deliberate mating would take place. If a Big Mother hadn't got pregnant at the meeting place, she would save face by feeding herself slightly more to stay tuned to her cycle. She would know the right time and wake the man she chose with a nice piece of meat. While the others were sunk into wintersleep, the couple would mate. These were the more private moments to copulate, as opposed to the rather spectacular and often public displays at the meeting grounds.

Babies conceived during wintersleep were born in late summer. It was considered optimal timing, because the baby could suckle during the autumn hunt while the mother was full of fish. The infant would be big enough to remain alive through the next wintersleep. Similar good timing was a baby conceived at the meeting grounds. A baby would usually be born when spring took hold, food became more abundant, and the dangers of early spring were past. While some babies were born during the height of winter, as Girl's would be, the older Big Mothers often greeted the news that a baby would arrive in the leanest months of the winter with scowls. It was a risk. The mother, having weathered the worst of wintersleep while pregnant, would then have to enter the starving months of early spring with a newborn baby. Her milk and energy would be low. It could be managed, but the already slim chances of an infant's survival became even lower.

Girl's belly had grown bigger. Her breasts grew, as the flesh of the best fish was now plumping them up. Her body fed on their oil and it spread across her skin like the smoothest scales from the fish's bellies. Her hair took on the color of their flesh and became the brightest red. The line of freckles across her nose looked like the spots on their fins. She was bursting with the beauty of the fish, but she felt none of it.

She looked up to the sky. The sun was already staying awake for a shorter time. The clouds overhead gave a rumble. It wasn't thunder but a small pulse that she could feel on the skin under her lip. She gave the air a sniff. Soon the weather would turn. Lifting a wet foot, leaning more on her spear, she closed her eyes. With the fine bones of her foot, she could feel that the pressure in the air was dropping. The winter storms were a way off, but the first hints of them had already arrived.

Maybe it was that—a heavy, pressing cloud—that made her look up to where the middle fork of the river split the trees. She hadn't smelled the scent on the air, but a small movement caught her eye— the twitch of a branch. It rattled just slightly and she knew something was there, high on a rocky perch above the river. It was a known lookout, the best place to see what was happening at the meeting place if approaching from the middle fork of the river.

Soon fine ripples of heat wafted out from the spot. It was the heat of live meat. From there she was able to define the shape, which clung to the trunk of the tree, using it for cover and peeking around. It watched them. And one more thing: the shape of the body was long and tall. It was upright. That meant it was from one of the families.

Girl's heart thumped hard, but she didn't move. She only watched, not wanting to scare the body. It might be someone who didn't recognize her with a pregnant belly. Girl waited for the body to catch her scent. A body that belonged to the family would have good eyes and would be able to see her even from such a distance. She lowered her spear. She didn't want to drop it in the water, so she tucked it between her knees to show the body that she meant no harm. Slowly, she spread the fingers on her left hand. She raised her palm in a greeting.

She waited like that to make sure the signal was clear. The body seemed to take her in for a moment, then it ducked back behind the tree. She watched as the ripples from its heat faded. She had no doubt that it had marked her and seen her greeting and that it would now come down and find her here. If it was coming from near the middle fork, it was probably someone from the family Big Girl had taken over. Her sister would welcome Girl and Runt.

Though Girl waited, the body didn't come to return her greeting. Runt got tired of playing and went back to the hearth to stir the fire. He called for her to come, but Girl found her feet unable to move. Much later, she went up to eat and sleep, but she came back to the river early the next morning to keep watch for the body. She did the same thing the next day.

On that third day, as Girl stood and watched from the same place, a dying fish nosed listlessly in front of her feet. Its skin was punctured and torn. Its eyes, once black, were clouded. The trauma of following its kin up the river had taken its toll. It was almost dead. But still, the broken fish pointed its nose upstream and muscled on with a weary tail. She knew it would continue that way until it died. She didn't have to ask why. The fish followed an instinct that pushed it to the end. Her instincts did the same.

By then, she felt the pull of the family. It was so strong that she didn't need to make a decision. The family was just as powerful for her as the upstream direction was for that fish. If the family did not come down to the meeting place, there must be a reason. She would go and find them.

20.

Girl and Runt left the meeting place when they had the largest bundle of dried fish, hackberries, and hazelnuts that they could carry. Runt was stronger after the fish run. His legs had gained length and muscle. He walked with a new, elegant stride. He seemed abruptly older. Girl guessed he had lived to about seven fish runs by then, though his odd size made it hard to say. She plopped his pack, much heavier this time, on his back, and he swayed only slightly with a smile on his face. Girl took a heavier load on her back too, but she carried nothing else. Her rounder belly and breasts were heavy, too, and took up all the room on the front of her body.

Under her breath, so Runt couldn't hear, Girl cursed those breasts and that belly. Her hips and ankles ached. She resented her own body and muttered at it.

Wildcat's coat was thick from all the fish he had eaten and he was very proud of it. He spent countless hours grooming and licking it to be just right. When Girl and Runt passed by the rock where he sat, he looked up at them lazily. Girl knew from his glance that he was full of himself, and, yes, he would join them, even though he was so beautiful that he would be welcomed anywhere.

When they started up the slope, Runt headed in the direction they had come, toward the land of the family. But Girl clicked her tongue, moved ahead of him, and turned to wade across the shallows toward the land of Big Girl's new family. She hadn't told him a story about what they would do, or drawn out the plan in the sand, or used ocher to make marks on a flat rock. She knew he would follow where she led. A body needed to be part of a family. And so they would go. They would cross the water where the river was wide and shallow and then follow the trail past where the middle fork climbed into the valley. They would go up to the tree where she had seen the body. Once there, she knew she could pick up the scent of the trail.

As Girl walked, she could hear Runt's breath in steady puffs behind her. He followed without question. Soon enough he started chattering, as was his way. He made sounds in his throat, including clicks and chirps, and they reminded her somewhat of Wildcat. He stopped once or twice to point at a flower or a bug he saw on a leaf. She paid little attention because it was time for moving, not for searching for bugs to eat. She glanced around at one point but couldn't see Wildcat. He liked to keep in the cover of the trees as he walked, but she knew he could smell them. To keep their bodies moving forward, she chanted in time to her steps, *"Cu-cu-cling, cu-cu-cling, cu-cu-cling."* My *head is a bison.*

Girl kept a good pace. After a hard climb up and one stop for Runt to pee, they gained the ledge where she had seen the body on the perch. Girl settled Runt and gave him something to eat. Wildcat curled up beside him and purred. Girl knew that the cat did this in hopes of scraps, but Runt took it as a gesture of affection. He spent some time running his hand along the cat's back and ended the pat with a piece of fish. This went to show why affection and scraps were one and the same to the cat. Runt lifted his left leg and let out a fart that was longer than any he'd had before. Delighted, he threw his head back and poked Wildcat to make sure he'd heard. The cat wrinkled his nose and looked unimpressed but didn't get up or walk away. It was very typical of their exchanges. The cat thought the boy was strange and the boy thought the cat was unnecessarily serious, but each tolerated the other's peculiarities.

From the lookout, Girl glanced down at the broad plain of the meeting place, where the water spread like fingers through the knots of rocks. The pool where she had stood when she saw the body was clearly visible. She sidled up to the tree where the body had been and put her nose up to the spot where it had placed its palm. The fresh scent was there, though fading. Her eyes had not been playing tricks. Excitedly, she took it in.

Girl's excitement soon turned to confusion. What was it? Though it was fading, the sour scent in the tree was that of a scavenger. They would eat anything and everything they could find. Their breath was a swampy mix of fear and nerves that she associated with a lack of control over the land. She caught some of what this body had consumed, the dry and dusty whiff of a mushroom from land not familiar to her. Maybe the body had crunched on beetles too. This made slightly more sense. Beetles could make the belly feel satisfied and full when not enough meat was available. There was something else too—a hint of marrow? The smells reminded her of hyenas in a way.

The creature's smells were different than the families', and that could mean as many things as there were pricks of light in the sky. The possibilities yawned open around her. Last year at the fish run, Big Sister had shown a shadow story. She made the shape of a body and indicated that it smelled bad, like one that was not of the family. It walked upright and her sister gave it fangs in the shadow to show the terror it held. A deep fear, like vertigo, sank into Girl's neck and pushed down her spine. The land around her felt too large and too empty.

Girl had to put her hand out and touch the tree to steady her shaking limbs. She knew she had to steady her thoughts and pull them in. To gain control, she fixed her attention in a way that her people had done for eons. She looked at a piece of bark on the tree and observed that it was the same as it had been before. She saw a blade of grass near the trunk. Maybe it had been dormant over the winter, but it had grown again. She focused on what was the same.

That had the settling effect that it always had on the family. Girl's thoughts narrowed and she focused on what she knew. She caught the faintest trace of hide near the footprint. Maybe the body had scratched at a bug under the cloak. This body wore hide over its skin in the same way she did. From the handprint, she knew the body was smaller, but from the partial imprint of the foot, she could tell it was an upright and had walked on two feet. With that information, she followed how a leg might step forward, given the terrain. Another step would turn the body and move it toward the clearing. Another few steps, and in the clearing was a patch of mud where a pool had formed in the last heavy rain and later dried up. The sandy area held a precious thing: one clear footprint was pressed into the dirt. She leaped forward and put a hand on either side of it. She put her nose right down and sniffed and felt a flood of relief.

The footprint was surprisingly small and narrow, and it curved up on the inside. The imprint showed the weight shifting from the back to the front, rather than spreading through the width of the foot. It might have been the footprint of a child. They had funny prints that were more likely to show twists and sways, as they were often caught up in the new things around them. Children were not as concerned with conserving energy or traveling the most efficient path.

If it was the print of a child, it went some way to explaining why the body had not greeted them or come down from the perch to the river. A child from her sister's family must have been sent to the lookout to see what was happening at the fish run. The child had not recognized Girl's scent, especially not with her pregnant. That's why he or she had not returned the greeting nor come down to say hello.

If Girl were to send Runt on a scouting trip, she would give him similar cautious instructions. She had no explanation for why the family hadn't come to the fish run, but she no longer needed one. She had only to follow these tracks back to her sister's camp. She would be of the family once again.

Girl began to crave the *warm* of a family. And she could feel it. Her bones ached for a sound sleep. She began to salivate as well. The fall season brought the crossing of the bison to their winter grounds, the beasts that would sustain the family for the winter. She started in the direction of that feeling.

Even with their heavy load of fish, the two made good time as Girl traced the scent. Runt was strong enough that he could hop from rock to rock as they followed the gentle slope up the river. For four days, Girl was able to find the tracks of the child and follow them. There had been a light rain since the child had passed by, but Girl had the vivid smell fixed in her mind. She found other things as they went. There was a small turd that had a terrible mix of mushrooms, green stalks, and flowers. One closer whiff and she turned her head in disgust. Another one a little way down had the shells of roaches scattered through it. This was clearly from the same body.

Maybe the child hadn't carried enough food on his journey and had turned to scavenging as a means to stay strong? Rather than imagining a small, stinky body, she pictured a resourceful child. By eating things that were usually beneath the family and not worth the effort of gathering, he didn't have to carry such a heavy load. The compromise meant he could travel farther at a faster pace. Girl felt something like pride, the same feeling she got when she held a large piece of meat in her hand.

"Eagle-see," Runt called from behind.

To get her attention, he had used a rarely spoken family word. At some point in the summer, Runt had asked her for a word and pointed to his own eye. Did he mean that he wanted the word for good eyesight? Girl would have just pointed to her eye and nodded to describe the trait of good vision, rather than having the word scrape along her throat. *Aroo* was an easier noise to make and the preferable way to get the attention of another. "Eagle-see," she had said in answer to what she thought his question was.

He had started to use the word and bend it in different ways. Now, it had become his way of calling to her. "Eagle-see," he would say when he noticed the bears doing something new. When she looked over at him, he would tap his eye and point at the bears and wait for her to explain. Of course, she never did. Her way was to show him what to do next.

But Runt was persistent. A child of the family grew slowly and had many needs. His way of surviving, of diverting resources in his direction, was to be demanding. Runt, who as a foundling could easily have been left behind in the dirt, was especially well versed in the art of demanding. It could be argued that this was the very reason he was still alive.

Eagle-see very quickly turned into his way of calling Girl to do his bidding. "Eagle-see," he would say when he wanted her to help him clean the bones from his fish. "Eagle-see," he would tell her when he wanted help reaching through the prickles to get a ripe berry. So when Girl heard Runt call "Eagle-see" from behind, she assumed it was a call for food or attention of some kind. She sighed wearily and pretended not to hear. The boy kept chattering and she kept walking. Soon she realized that he wasn't following along as he should.

Big Mother would never have stood for such disobedience. When Girl was young, the children walked in a line behind the big woman. If one stopped or got distracted, the line of bodies would keep moving and leave that one behind. As a result, the children learned to keep up.

But as Runt was the lone young one, he had somehow managed to gain more sway with Girl. She turned and saw that he stood with his feet planted near a black mark on a broad, flat rock. She could smell that the scavenger child had been here, but he had left no footprints behind. She looked more closely and realized that it was a strange fire pit. Three sticks stood up over the hearth and came together in a point at the top. The burn marks were shallow. A few unused pieces of firewood sat to the side, as though they had been collected and left. There was a rock ring around the fire and some flat ones built up on the side. It seemed like a lot of effort for a fire that might have been used only once or twice. Runt chattered excitedly, but she held up her hand to silence him. She wanted her ears clear of sound so that she could focus on the smells.

This hearth had many similarities to the fires she made. The child had used a two-hand spindle for friction to make a flame in the same way she did and had used a small bundle of dried grasses as tinder and left them to the side. He had used the inner strips of birch bark to get the flame licking higher. As there weren't any birch trees in this area, it meant he had collected the soft bark, kept it dry, and saved it. The family used the same practice when on the move.

Girl pushed aside the differences in this hearth. The three standing sticks did not mean anything to her, so she noted them and put her mind elsewhere. Runt held up a small sliver of bone and she felt more confused. On one end was a hole, like an eye. Runt smiled wide in recognition. He pretended to clean his teeth with it. Clearly he agreed that it was a tool, though there was skill in its making and it had to be for more than picking teeth. A stick snapped in the right way was good enough for that. He then pretended to poke it into his cloak and pull it back out. She took the tool from him and looked at it closely. One end had a perfect, slim hole through it, and the other end of the bone was shaped into a fine point. It didn't look immediately useful to Girl, but she could use it to puncture hides. She was interested in what her sister's family used it for, though that was crowded out by a greater concern: Why had the child dropped it? Her sister would have taught her children the importance of caring for tools. What was going on at the camp that could account for such inattention?

Girl sniffed long and hard. She climbed a tree and looked out. She started to pick up traces of the heat from meat moving in the leaves, or maybe the memory of it moving. A family had been here. Other beasts had been in the area too and the scents were confused. But the trees helped her see where a family might have gone. She was certain that she and Runt were getting close.

Conference Call

I got out of my tent on Monday and waddled up to the site. My presence was met with a few gasps and a confused "Oh, hey, hi!" from Michael. Caitlin shook her head ever so slightly. But no one said anything out loud. I assumed they had been advised to refrain from commenting on my physical state. My willingness to quote New York laws had assured a silence around me, though it was a nest of my own making without any paid maternity leave to line it. I planned to be in on the videoconference with the museum that day. My belly was heavy and my feet were sore, but I would be uncomfortable no matter where I was. I might as well get paid for one more day and keep my mind occupied with what interested me.

By then lab results and second opinions had confirmed what I'd already felt, that the Neanderthal skeleton was a female. The modern human was male. Now we could see very clearly that her skull sat in an easterly orientation and pointed toward the other one as if she were looking directly into his empty sockets. This suggested eye contact and possibly communication between the bodies. Though I didn't know anything with certainty yet, I sometimes imagined a kind of scene like Pompeii, where a pyroclastic surge—a mix of hot gas and ash—asphyxiated those who were alive after the volcano erupted. My mind lingered on what I had read about the disaster as I brushed dirt from her skull. Other times, I imagined that the positioning of the two skeletons was deliberate. Maybe they were placed that way by someone else. Looking at them, I found it impossible not to think of myself on my own deathbed. Where would my eyes turn if I were about to die?

A few weeks before, I had uncovered a delicate object using a fine-tipped paintbrush and became convinced that it was a bead because of a hole that seemed deliberately punched through the top. It was shaped like a shell. Given that it was situated in the dirt by the vertebrae, I guessed that it had fallen by her neck under her chin. Perhaps it was a bead on a string that the Neanderthal was wearing when she died. Andy and others agreed with my theory, especially as it appeared that there was a hole in the appropriate place. The excitement on the site grew, as everyone acknowledged that finding ornamentation on a Neanderthal would help lend support to my theory that they were cognitively as capable as modern humans. Those who disagreed with that hypothesis often pointed to the lack of Neanderthal jewelry and painting to make the case that they didn't engage in abstract thought. We had sent the object to the museum for the opinion of a few experts. The videoconference that day would be about their conclusions.

Until the time came for the call, I wanted to continue to work on the layer around the vertebrae to see if I could find more artifacts. In more usual circumstances I would have lain down on my tummy to work, but as I was nearly due, that option was out. Andy and I had rigged a contraption so I could continue to be productive. We had made a kind of stretcher out of two long planks and raised them on short legs to the height of my belly. Straps tied between the planks allowed me to lie facedown where I was working; the one under my forehead was cushioned with a towel. My belly hung down, but it rested in a crate and was cradled in a blanket to protect it while I worked. When perfectly positioned, I was able to hover over the spot where I brushed while my baby was comfortably supported.

I knew I looked ridiculous like this and didn't try to argue otherwise. When we got the stretcher into position, Andy could barely stop laughing long enough to help me get situated. Caitlin merely rolled her eyes and pressed her dry lips together even tighter. But soon the laughter died away as I got to work. It seemed like only a few minutes had passed when I realized that it was time for the videoconference, but I was stuck in place. I would need help getting up.

"Should I go rent a hoist?" Andy said with a sigh as he came over to help me.

A few minutes later, under the shade of a tree, I sat on the bench of the picnic table beside Caitlin, the laptop propped up in front of us. My ample hind end spread far enough that she had to squish a bony hip into me to stay on camera.

I didn't have my usual confidence going into the videoconference. The screen showed people gathering in a boardroom at the museum. I could see Tim shaking people's hands and Guy leaning back, legs crossed and watching. There was a small square in the corner of the screen showing Caitlin and me. My puffy cheeks made me look as though I were storing nuts for the winter. I tried to take pride in a healthy appearance, but it is hard to get used to your own reflection when it changes as abruptly as it does in pregnancy. I was careful to keep the screen tilted so that my breasts and belly were off-camera. No one said a word about the fact that I was supposed to be on leave. Caitlin had obviously reported in before the call. I gave her a slight nudge with my rump. I'm sure she had to dig her toes into the ground to keep her place in the frame.

Dr. Lawton was an expert on dating carbon found in the bones of early hominids. His field was fast-moving, and techniques were constantly being refined, but he had been able to date the two skeletons to the same period by measuring traces of carbon-14, a radioactive isotope that decays at a steady rate. I had had no doubt that the two had lived at the same time, but there had been some talk about how the Neanderthal bones could have been found and positioned with a newer skeleton in a kind of ritual. This idea defied any kind of logic. Archaeological finds that don't fit neatly within a theory are always explained away as a "ritual," but I knew it would be impossible to prove that a ritual didn't exist. It was good to hear the confirmation of dates from Dr. Lawton. While he could give only a wide range because we can't assume that the amount of carbon in the atmosphere is constant, he did assure us with certainty that the bones of the Neanderthal and the modern human were from the same period. Concrete dates gave me the kind of evidence that people of our time need in order to believe.

Next, an ornamental mollusk expert, Dr. Shinkoda, told us that she had evaluated a sample from the shell hoping to find traces of calcium carbonate that could be used to date it. She'd had trouble turning up much material and her results were inconclusive. "It's difficult to date the shell in other ways, as it's not definitively linked to human or animal bones," she said.

"It is linked," I corrected her quickly, "to the Neanderthal bones. It's on the same level in the site: B seven. You saw the photos I sent?"

"I don't consider a similar level on a dig site to be a definitive link," she said.

"We may have a trace of a lash or a necklace of some kind below the vertebrae. There is a pattern in the dirt."

"I saw that squiggle." She nodded. "Hardly conclusive. A worm or something that came along much later could have made the pattern. The shell could have been placed by the body after death. It certainly doesn't mean that a Neanderthal wore a necklace."

I cleared my throat. "I disagree based on what I'm seeing from the layers of sediment. You aren't able to see the context from there, so I understand your reluctance to confirm that it looks like jewelry." I knew I had to be careful not to show a trace of emotion.

"I'm not sure what evidence I could see that would convince me. It's a fantastical claim."

"A necklace?" A rumble of anger formed in my chest. "I've shown in my research that Neanderthals possessed the capacity for a symbolic intellectual life, and the use of beads demonstrates that."

"A piece of shell by the bones tells you how a brain thinks?" Dr. Shinkoda sounded almost insulted.

"The link between jewelry, or any kind of adornment, and cognitive ability has been clearly shown in anthropological research. People wear ornaments in order to convey who or what they are. The larger the group, the more need for ornaments."

"Of course I am aware of that discussion," Dr. Shinkoda said. "I was asked to evaluate the mollusk. I've done that. I can't establish a link to the bodies through dating or physical evidence." She looked over to Tim and Guy.

"Rose?" Guy's head came in closer to the screen. "Perhaps it's a good moment to bring this up. I don't mean to question your research." He made a downward motion with both hands, a patronizing way of telling me to calm down. "We've heard this, Rose, from quite a few of the experts who have come through to look at the artifacts. You know that there is resistance to your ideas. Many see the Neanderthals as inferior to us. How do you explain that their culture was essentially static for some two hundred thousand years? It shows a distinct lack of innovation."

"Innovation comes when one person passes an idea to the next," I said. "The Neanderthals lived at very low population densities. New ideas most likely came and went before they could be passed on, but they were perfectly capable of them."

"We aren't finding brilliant ideas in the dirt, though, are we?" Guy asked.

I adopted an equally disparaging tone. "We are finding that Neanderthals and modern humans were developing the same techniques at the time—the use of ocher for ornamentation is one example."

"I need the museum to have a clear and credible message."

Guy might just as well have sunk his fangs through the screen and bitten me. Caitlin could feel my tension. Under the table, she put a hand on my leg. Her hip bone dug into mine as she leaned forward. "The necklace theory is inconclusive and it may be for some time until we uncover more, but it's the wrong thing to focus on."

"What do you mean, Caitlin?" asked Tim. "If we open a big exhibit making grand statements that we can't back up, we'll have egg on our faces," he said. "The media will pick up on it."

"To be honest," said Caitlin, "we are stuck in our own heads. I'm not an expert on this topic, but maybe that comes in handy. It gives me the necessary distance."

I lowered my eyes, trying to listen.

"I had a journalist here recently. Fred Long."

"*National Geographic*?" Tim raised his eyebrows.

"Despite a press ban," I whispered to myself.

"He signed a nondisclosure agreement." Caitlin acknowledged my comment. "But his point was refreshing. And I apologize that I didn't have a chance to talk this over with you, Rose. But he felt that we were all too involved in the dig to really see the story that's right under our noses. The two skeletons looking into each other's eyes will stop people dead in their tracks. All we need to say is that one is a modern human and the other is Neanderthal. We don't need grand claims or theories beyond it. He thinks his editor will want to put it on the cover. It's absolutely iconic."

"But what about the science?" My authority seemed to be slipping through my fingers.

"With that introduction, we can tell a story that leaves room for interpretation," said Caitlin.

"A strong endorsement from a publication like *National Geographic*?" Tim beamed.

Guy let his lips slide into a smile. "A picture means more than words."

Caitlin's comments seemed to smooth over the disagreements that had come before. My theories could be put forward as just that, but the two skeletons suggested a deeper relationship that could live in the realm of everyone's imagination.

When we finished up a few minutes later, I was drained. "Thank you," I muttered to Caitlin, not having the energy to say anything else. She had gone behind my back, and all she had managed to do was open the gates for the museum trustees to present my work any way they liked. A rush of sentiment and an invitation into the realm of the imagination would do little for scientific understanding. It would likely send the public in the wrong direction. But I didn't have a countermove left in me. All I could do was heave myself off the bench and go back to the protected walls of my cave to work.

A few hours later, I slumped at the picnic table with a mug of peppermint tea. Caitlin sat on the bench across from me, her low, loose ponytail falling to the side. She gave me a long look and passed me one of the dry biscuits that she always kept in a roll in her pack. "Are you going to sleep in the village tonight?"

"I'll just curl up on the cot again," I answered. "If I can get an early start, I might be able to find more evidence of a lash. I am convinced that she wore the shell."

"You think that will settle their questions?"

I didn't answer.

"I know only one thing for certain," she said. "There is going to come a day when you have to leave the site and have your baby. In, what, a week at most?"

"Maybe two."

"You will need to focus on caring for the baby."

"Hmm." I nibbled on the biscuit.

"I want to assure you that I'll be in regular communication, Rose. I'm happy to make a call schedule. As we both know, I'm not an expert. My job is to ensure that your processes are carried out."

"The world doesn't stop when the baby is born," I said. "But my life does."

"I can come to London if need be. It's a short flight."

"I might be here," I said.

"Where?"

"The village. I'll stay in the flat."

"Oh, Rose."

"Babies are born in France too. Many, in fact."

"Yes, but Rose...babies. Don't underestimate the work," Caitlin said. "They are incredibly intensive things to care for."

"As opposed to?"

Caitlin shifted uncomfortably before she spoke. "Well, honestly, gibbons, but you already know that."

"Gibbons," I repeated. "Have you seen those carrier slings that all the moms use?" I joked. "I can get one of those. That way I can still forage with a newborn."

Caitlin didn't smile.

I have long judged people by their willingness to laugh at the absurdity of life. Caitlin rarely did. Enjoying anything seemed to be out of her reach. She drank weak tea, she ate only plain biscuits, and her idea of colorful clothing was varying shades of beige. She reacted to my observations the same way she did to my jokes: with slightly pursed lips and a long stare. She let silences hang in the air until I found myself chattering just to fill the void.

"I'll hang the little chap in a sling, a pretty floral fabric," I went on now. "That leaves my big paws free to forage in the fridge."

She kept her expression steady.

"I have opposable thumbs too." I wiggled my fingers. "Good for grabbing cake."

"The first months of life leave us extremely vulnerable," she said. "The human infant is undeveloped and extremely needy. The mother becomes equally exposed."

"Vulnerable," I repeated darkly. Simon was right—it sounded vaguely like a threat. The hair on the back of my neck pricked.

"Caitlin?"

"Yes."

"I'm pregnant, not sick."

"That's not what I'm saying."

"You make me sound like an animal."

Caitlin pressed her lips into a dry smile. "You are."

I let out a laugh, which had the intended effect of making Caitlin stop talking. The awkward silence that followed started me giggling, which turned into another laugh. I started to wheeze when I realized that my bladder control was minimal and that I might well pee my pants while Caitlin stared. The absurd situation of my professional life combined with my lack of sleep to create a hopeless brew of hysteria. I kept laughing and trying not to pee for so long that Caitlin finally stood up and muttered, "Perhaps I'll get Andy."

I calmed down when the team gathered around the picnic table for the daily meeting. I was in the habit of debriefing and assigning tasks in the evening; that way I didn't need to interrupt my work when the team trickled in each morning. Andy tried to pass around some Dr Peppers, but no one could stomach another can. I quietly apologized to Caitlin for my giggling fit, blaming my lack of sleep. She accepted my apology with a curt nod. I was truly sorry if I had offended her, but I didn't have time to dwell on it. My thoughts turned back to the team and the work we had to do.

I gave a brief overview of the videoconference. I said that the museum was happy to make the two skeletons the centerpiece of the exhibit and put forward our theories. It was all technically true and when I said it out loud, I saw the smiles on their faces. For a moment, I had trouble remembering why I had felt so threatened. But I did, because of who had said what, and I didn't have enough energy to get into that. Instead I said that I was sure that our site would make a mark on science. "I'm absolutely confident."

"Of that, Rose, we have no doubt," said Andy.

Maybe Andy meant it kindly, but someone laughed too hard. I snapped my head around to see who it was. What exactly did Andy mean, and what was so funny? The team all pulled their faces straight at once.

"You've brought us a long way, Rose." Caitlin stepped in. "We are all proud of what you've accomplished." She spoke of my work in the past tense. There were nods all around and a few murmurs of agreement that were intended to dispel the tension. I felt the balance of power in the group tilt, as though the dirt under our feet slanted toward Caitlin. Instincts drive people to huddle around the strong. The authority had shifted. The change in me now felt complete. I had turned into a vessel for the baby.

21.

Girl and Runt arrived at the camp of Big Girl, and the signs of Girl's sister were unmistakable. There was a large hearth at the center; a leather sack and a stone tooth lay forgotten, or perhaps they had been left behind while the body that made them went on a hunt, and a hut roughly in the shape of a bison was tucked against a low cliff.

"*Aroo,*" called Girl, her palm held up.

They walked toward the hearth, hearing only the sounds of their own soft feet on the dirt, and Runt skipped in wide-eyed anticipation. Though they had spent a happy enough summer, they both craved the company of others. Wildcat gave the camp one sniff and scampered into the brush.

"*Aroo!*"

There was no answer.

Girl closed her eyes, cupped her hand over one ear, and curled her top lip up. She stood still and let the currents of air drift around her. She let her mind glide over the land and felt for vibrations from the roots of the trees. If there was a family nearby, she would be able to feel them. The emptiness that clouded her body would break open and the rays of warmth would pour in for the first time since spring.

No feelings came.

Girl decided to second-guess her senses. She tried to block out the new smells and focus on what used to be. Maybe because Girl had been away for such a long time, her nose no longer held the family's smell. After some searching and rustling around, Runt and Girl established that the camp was empty of any body who might respond. The family who lived there had been gone for some time. Still, Girl was certain that this was a temporary state. She didn't know this land. Living on it might require different patterns. The family might be waiting at their crossing for the first sign of the bison. Or maybe they had made a large kill, big enough that hauling the meat back to the camp didn't make sense. It must be that they had killed two or three beasts and were camped at the carcasses having a feast. The memory of blood dripping on her chin felt fresh. The heavy feel of winter was in the air. It was the time for filling the belly and caching meat for wintersleep.

Runt called out, "Eagle-see." He had wandered to the back of the camp to inspect the hut. It was solidly built and tucked in for protection, but it looked partially broken down. All that was left was the frame and brittle branches over the top. The thickest fur hides, the ones that kept the weather at bay, were gone. The family must have taken them to another camp. They were heavy things to lug, not moved without a deliberate destination. The thick hide was always treated with the best care, as it took time and effort to cure, something usually done in high summer when the sun and heat aided the scraping, soaking, and drying. Curing another with the temperature dropping was difficult. There wasn't enough time before the winter storms.

A crow flapped its wings overhead and drew Girl's attention. *Caw-caw-caw,* said the bird who thrived on death and blood.

"Eagle-see," Runt said again. This time there was no discovery or wonder in his voice. He was out past the hut, just beyond the natural bounds of the camp. He had found a body, Girl knew, more because of the crow than anything Runt's voice told her. For a moment her thoughts turned inward. How had she not caught the scent of a body on the ground and the flat, damp air that always lies over one? As she walked toward Runt, she came across a slight mound of dirt. It sloped upward and had a healthy cover of plants, more so than the area around it. The canopy allowed some light through, but not enough to account for the extra growth. The source of nutrients was probably coming from below.

As Girl approached Runt, she saw his troubled look. He'd found the body using his eyes, not his nose. He stood back, hand to mouth, unable to take in what he saw, but also unable to look away. Girl's first thought was that she had never missed such an obvious thing before. It was not hidden but out in the open. It had been chewed and pawed by scavengers and had long before started on its way to the other side of the dirt. But it had not been buried or disposed of in any way. Either it was alone when it died or it was left in place because the others were too weak to drag it farther. Or maybe they simply did not want to.

Girl didn't register who the body might belong to because she saw the foot coverings first. Big Mother had told stories in the shadows about families that didn't go to the meeting place, but Girl had never seen one of them. Maybe they put these strange things on their feet, because no other beast, bison, bear, or wildcat would ever do such a thing. The covers on the feet were made from a finely crafted hide, something that was lighter than bison hide; perhaps it was from a deer. The covers had delicate tendons pulled through the edges to wrap them tight around the foot and up the leg. There was a hard resin like sap on the soles, maybe to reinforce the feet as they walked. They looked like awkward things to wear, too hot and tight. Girl much preferred to keep her body open to the breeze. Perhaps this body died from overheating, or from suffocation of the skin?

Girl flipped the remains of the body over. It took a moment for what she saw to settle in. The blowflies had left little of the corpse. There was a cavity for a broad nose, and a red shock of hair that slipped from the skull as it turned. The crawling bugs and flies had chewed away much of the flesh, but there was enough around the jaw to see pocks on the flattened skin.

"Sunbite." She pointed.

The shape of the bison cloak around the remaining bones made Girl sure it was one of the family. In a slow turn of her mind, she came to see that the body looked like her. For two beats of her heart, she didn't know where she was. Maybe she had died and was half in the dirt, looking back up at herself. In that moment, anything felt possible, but her thoughts caught up. And then there was the gap where the two front teeth had not managed to stay attached to the head. She saw the bison horns on this body's head, whereas there were none on Girl's. The sight clicked into place then. Girl was looking into the face of her dead sister.

Feeling like she had received a kick to her gut, Girl dropped to her knees, and the air rushed out of her body in one gasp. Here was one change too many. The careful equation of Girl's life tilted. Her balance was lost. Too few things kept her feet rooted to the ground, as a tree that becomes vulnerable when the one next to it falls after a strong gust of wind. Her senses shut down. She could no longer see. She lost track of the land around her. Noise filled her head and she clutched her ears. They were her screams, although she barely recognized the sound.

If the sunbite came, the body was buried to get it away from the burning sun. This was the only way to put out the fire that burned the flesh. Leaving the body close to the camp meant either that her sister was the last to die or that the others had left her body because they had to. Girl fell back and closed her eyes and lay still for a long time. If her whole family was on the other side of the dirt, she wanted to go too. She felt the sun on her face and willed it to take her.

But after a long time, she opened her eyes and saw feet. These were furry and there were four. They belonged to Wildcat, who touched her nose with the wet tip of his and then twisted up his face to say,

Could I have some dried fish? Girl was busy leaving the land and had no time for such physical demands. She closed her eyes again.

The next time she opened them, she again saw feet. These were not as furry. In fact, they were remarkably free of hair and there were two. They belonged to Runt. His face was long and sad, and he put his cheek down to hers and gave her the same kind of cat kiss on her nose. Even though they weren't cats, they had learned from Wildcat that it was sometimes nice to kiss each other with their noses. Runt meant it as a way to cheer her up. She knew it also meant that he was hungry. It was these two mouths that made it impossible to stay on the other side of the dirt. The baby in her belly joined in, kicking enough to make her stomach rumble. She didn't have enough energy to ignore the needs of all the small bodies around her. It felt easier to stand up.

Runt built up a large fire in the hearth. Girl knew she had to first clear the danger of sunbite. She paced the outside edge of the camp and found a larger mound of earth with fresh growth on the top. She dug down with a flat stone far enough to find the bone of a finger. One scoop more and she found the bone of an arm. Given this shape of the mound of earth and how easy it was to turn, she knew her sister had buried the bodies to get them away from the sun.

She dug down at the side and made a place for her sister. The bones weren't easy to carry over. Each time she picked up part of the carcass, some of it would fall away. It took several trips to get the body into the shallow grave. She didn't say good-bye to her sister as she pushed the earth over the bones and the last strands of red hair. She did place her finger at the front of her sister's jaw briefly, letting the tip rest in the front gap where her teeth had fallen out.

As it grew dark, the fire became a sort of company. The association of the fire with the warm feeling it had brought over the years soothed Girl. She stared into the flames and strained to see the shapes of the family dancing and swaying inside. She pointed out shapes to Runt. She knew he couldn't see them, but he nodded anyway. He sat close to her and she put her arm around him while Wildcat snuggled into Runt's other side. With these three bodies together, she could imagine that the shadows were the family dancing inside of the fire. At least they would always be warm and safe in there.

When she missed the family, as she did then and many times afterward, she would lean in to encourage the flame. The warmth of the fire reminded her of the warmth of the family, which was not just that of bodies but of being connected to so many beating hearts, to ears that listen, and to all those extra pairs of eyes that would watch each other's backs. It was how a body stayed alive. She had to find a new way. But just then she could only stare into the flame and remember. *Warm.*

22.

Girl tucked her spear under her arm. She waited for the bison at a river crossing below her sister's land, where the water spread out in a broad, swallow pool. The hoofprints were clearly marked from the spring crossing. There was no narrow channel or strip of rock to push the beasts into a single line, so there was no way to use the shape of the land to her advantage.

At this kind of crossing, the hunters must herd and corner the beasts. It was a dangerous way to hunt and one that needed many more than two bodies. She knew for certain that this was one of her sister's hunting grounds. But her sister must have hunted bison the autumn before with her new family. Falling into the same pattern gave Girl comfort and a way to keep moving forward. Somehow she had to get them meat to sustain them through the winter. It took at least one large bison to feed an adult for that long.

Girl watched. To hunt was to wait. She had carefully sniffed and followed all the tracks around the camp, but they told her only a story of confusion. There were so many prints that they moved in circles and didn't show a particular direction. It was hard to know when or if the bodies that had made the tracks might come back. But still she and Runt lived in her sister's camp. The traces of live bodies, prints, scorched rock, hand-worn tools, were like an encouragement. The family had been here recently enough, whereas she knew there was no family left alive on the land of Big Mother. If she brought Runt back there, the journey would take a toll and would not necessarily give them better chances. No one would return there, while maybe someone would here. Her instincts kept her focused on that possibility, as a cold face turns toward the sun.

Girl had kept up Runt's education for that time of year and showed him how to find small pieces of meat and how to gather things that weren't meat. She took him on a walk along the river and kicked at the downed logs as they went. After a few tries, she heard a satisfying scuttling and scurrying. In seconds, she was down on her knees with the log turned up. She stuck a length of branch down into the opening, waited for a moment, then pulled it up. The branch was crawling with black, shiny bugs. She held it up to show Runt, who gave her a broad smile. The bugs wore small plates like turtle shells on their backs. Their antennae brushed along the stick and they wiggled into each other. She put her lips around the stick and pulled it through her mouth, using her tongue to scoop the black bodies inside. She bit down with a satisfying crunch, then chewed. While they tasted good, there was also the sour taste of shame in each bite. Between her teeth, she broke the bodies of the scavengers. And in so doing, that's what she became.

The morning before, Girl and Runt ate and then dozed in a tree. After the sun moved a finger's width or so in the sky, she woke Runt and they started foraging again. Girl was good at foraging. Even though she was on strange land, the skills that Big Mother had taught her served them well. But to feed their bodies this way, especially with her large frame and pregnant belly, she had to work all the moments she was awake. If she had a large hunk of meat to chew, she would have more energy to build a strong shelter, make lamps for the winter, and round out their tool kit to make it complete. As it was, she fell over exhausted at the end of each day. Food that was foraged came at a high cost compared to the energy she gained from it.

At night, there were no dreams from the family to fill in the long, silent stretches of darkness between her sleeps. Instead of the comfort of family, her thoughts turned to meat. She wanted to sink her teeth into the pumping heart of a bison. She would put her mouth to a vein and drink her strength back. But like joy, meat was for the strong. She wasn't the apex predator of this land.

And even the season was turning against her. The fall colors tinted the trees and they released their leaves to the ground, like an exhale. The air turned a harder blue against her skin. The dirt started to pack down under her feet in preparation for the winter storms. And this reminded her of bison meat all the more.

So on this day, Girl found herself behind a boulder at the crossing on her sister's land. With Runt safely up a branch of a looking tree, she waited. Her luck turned. *Snap.* A sound. Where? Girl curled her top lip to feel the heat in the air. She twitched her head to the right, one ear out. In the distance, she saw a bison nose out of the brush. Then the beast spooked and cantered across the shallow opening of the crossing, the water only reaching its knees at the deepest point. The mud was thick and sucked at its hooves, but the passage was easy. There were many spots across the wide stretch of water for an animal to enter and leave. From the crossing, it could gallop off into the broad expanse of the plains, where she had no chance of running it down.

Girl felt a thumping on the land in the distance. Air billowed and hooves thundered. The familiar stink of bison shit came forward in a cloud. A herd of beasts was running for the crossing. It was a thin group—there were as many beasts as she could count on two hands— but it was a herd nonetheless.

A clutch of Girl's favorite food on legs was coming her way, but the problem was its speed. A beast that size expends the large amount of energy it takes to run only if it must. That many bodies taking flight meant one thing. Something, a predator, was chasing them. The beasts started to cross the river, and it didn't take long before she caught the scent: wolves.

"*Aroo,*" she called to let Runt know of the danger.

The wolves tended to roam the lands where the families were not. Her family's land had been too steep and broken for wolves. Though she didn't have much experience of them, she had inherited a dislike. The family found that wolves were too loud and barked too much, crowthroats. They rarely challenged the family, but they would go after smaller beasts that the family sometimes hunted. The family had little respect for wolves and assumed that they hunted in such large packs because their jaws were weak. If they managed to down larger prey, it was only because they had used all the teeth in the pack to slowly rip and tear at a beast's hide. Wolves were not strong enough to hold on to their own territory. Instead of staying put and commanding a piece of land, they were filled with distress and always on the move. From where she crouched, she could smell on their breath the persistent dread they lived with.

Girl's nose wrinkled up when she saw the leader dart toward the crossing. He was gray with patchy, mottled fur and eyes that slanted with distrust. She gave a click of her tongue but Wildcat was already long gone. He had tucked himself into the hollow crook of a tree.

"*Aroo,*" she growled.

She wasn't filled with fear of the wolves, but with her large belly, she knew it was wise to stay out of their way. She went to the looking tree, and Runt began to climb higher to make room for her. She quickly caught up with him and had to wait for him to pull up to the next branch. His movements were slow, and for a moment she questioned his health. But that concern was soon replaced by another. Her pride sank down as she climbed up. The wolves were weaker animals, but they might glance over and feel satisfaction that they had caused the family to flee.

The true insult was still to come. The wolves didn't bother with

Runt and Girl. The two of them apparently presented no threat at all. The wolves had eyes only for the bison. They ran around and around and nipped at hocks to drive the small herd into a tight bunch. They drove the beasts in a clump through the water at the crossing. The wolves had enough numbers that they were able to herd the group and easily select the weaker beasts. A few of the slower bison got separated from the back of the pack. The wolves soon isolated an older female bison. She was gray around the muzzle and moved as though her shoulders were stiff. Runt tapped Girl's arm and pointed to the old cow. He touched his nose knowingly.

Twelve snapping jaws worked together. They nipped at the old cow's hocks three at a time to stop her from rejoining the others. Girl could imagine her own family doing the same to the bison. She knew that they shared certain traits with the wolves. A grudging kind of respect was due, though it took these weaker beasts twelve bodies to do something that the family could do with fewer.

When it came to the kill, there were differences too. The wolves lacked large spears to make the dying more peaceful and quicker. Instead they tore and ripped at hand-size clutches of flesh, all the while yipping, barking, and carrying on in a frenzy that made Girl put her hands over her ears. Although she didn't dwell on it, she could see that the death scene in front of her was slow and tortured, and the cow bellowed in fear and dismay. Girl found it hard to watch.

When it was over, the wolves continued to bark and yip in their noisy scrum. They chewed and bit one another as they fought to take a turn at the carcass. It was a mess of a way to eat, but it got the job done. In time, the wolves had their fill and retreated into the shade of trees and brush to rest. They would stay near the carcass and feed again if they could, but a large bison was too much meat for a pack this size. They didn't cache their food. Instead, they would sit and pant and digest while they watched the weaker beasts feed. Girl knew the feeling well. She had once done the same.

The crows cawed in anticipation overhead. A vulture swooped

down and landed nearby. A small coyote darted behind a far-off bush. One by one, they all took a cautious peek at the carcass, testing to see if it was their turn.

After time passed, with red-faced shame, Girl climbed down from the tree. She motioned for Runt to climb down and onto her back, as she didn't want his thin legs tempting any jaws. Slowly, they walked up to the carcass. Eyes were all around, and she could feel the heat of the wolves' eyes on her skin. She kept her lip curled up to feel for any change in their pulses, but the throb stayed even and she knew they weren't about to pounce.

She carefully put Runt down next to her, making it clear that he was with her, not a part of the carcass. She removed her stone tooth from her belt and cut a chunk of bison meat that was left dangling from the ribs. It was not the fatty meat from the heart or the large stretch of flesh that comes from the hindquarters. Those were long gone. She looked for the parts that had the most fat. Those creatures farther down the line must take a lesser cut, full of gristle. She cut meat and cracked bone, taking as much as she dared. She would use her stone tooth to get into the middle of the bone and suck at the marrow, like a hyena. She kept her head lowered and her eyes down to show respect as she did it, and the wolves let her.

After she left, the other solitary carnivores would approach, the striped hyena and the jackals. After that, the raccoon-dogs and even badgers might have a try.

With meat and two leg bones in hand, Girl swung Runt onto her back again and pulled him close. She slowly returned to the camp. There was no triumph in the small victory. Their place in the order of things settled on her. Instead of facing forward to pinpoint prey, her eyes kept darting behind to watch her own back. Everything had changed.

23.

The next morning, Girl looked over to see Runt's bottom waving in the air. He breathed heavily and huddled up so close that she was reluctant to get up. It was later than she usually woke. Runt had begged for the bison meat the previous night, but she did not want to eat it yet. She saved it for a few days by curing it on the fire and storing it in a tree cache. She doubted that they would come across another carcass soon and they would need the energy of the meat to gather pieces of smaller meat and as many roots, berries, and nuts as they could. For food that day, she had killed a few red squirrels with rocks in the way of Big Mother. She stuck them on a stick to roast.

Girl nudged Runt and rolled her own body off the hide they'd slept on. The air was colder that morning and nipped at her nose. Her lips were dry, as her body required large amounts of water to keep it happy. She also worried about their shelter. She heaved her body out of the broken hut and turned an eye up to the sky. A thin layer of rippled clouds stretched over the trees. They were the same pattern as the sand at the bottom of the river shallows. The weather was about to change. The storms were coming.

The days would be spent making this hut smaller. That way she could use the hides they had brought to provide better cover. She started the fire and melted water to chug. She called to Runt to wake up, then sized up the poles that had been used in the broken hut. The problem was one of heat. If she made it a quarter of the size it currently was, they could keep warm with just two bodies. She could then double the thin hides and stuff in as much insulation as possible. She reached through to nudge Runt to get him up, then pulled up a small hide that had been left behind. There was something odd about it. She tugged at an end, assuming it would come off in two pieces, but though it was ripped in the middle, something held it together.

Girl examined the seam. It was like the foot coverings her sister had worn. Two pieces of hide were attached with sinew that had been punched through holes and pulled in and out. She wrinkled her nose. There was something slightly revolting about it. She imagined two bison bodies tied together this way. They would resist and struggle to pull themselves apart. It was a change of state; the animal had a form it had not had before. One life tied up with another. Her stomach gave a small heave.

At the same time, Girl could see that this attachment was practical. It made a small hide useful on a larger structure.

"*Runt.*" Never one for volume control, she hollered at him to wake him; she knew he would be interested in what she'd found. But the boy didn't sit up. He lifted his head sluggishly and his eyelids drooped. Something was wrong with him.

Girl picked the boy up. His body felt smaller than it had even the day before. She thought of her sister and the sunbite and a panic hit her. Leaning in, she smelled his breath. There were no red spots or blisters and no whiff of the disease, not yet. She checked his back, neck, and arms. What was wrong? She sat him up, put a hand on each shoulder, and looked into his eyes. He licked his lips and put his hand on his small belly to say he was hungry.

Hungry? It didn't make sense. She was hungry, but she had a much larger body. He had eaten almost more than she had the night before. She gave him water and thought back to what they had eaten. Was there anything risky that could have made him sick? They had eaten all the same things—bugs, chanterelles, red squirrel that was cooked, that sour-tasting badger a few days before. She could only think his cloudy eyes and listlessness were signs of the fat sickness. Their bodies relied on protein, but fat was just as important.

Girl bundled up Runt in a hide to fend off the cold and sat him by the fire while she built it up and heated water to drink. She pulled the foreleg of the bison from the cache and put it in the fire. Runt's eyes bulged at the sight of it. She cut off the cooked meat and stuck the stripped leg back into the flames. Once the bone was hot through, she placed the foreleg on a rock, turned it on end, and hit it at an angle with a splitting stone. The force sent a perfect crack down half the length of it. She did this again from the other side and pried the two halves apart.

The animal's best fat stores were inside the bone. Even if a beast has died of starvation and the fat stores on the carcass are all but gone, it will still have nutritious marrow in the bones. Girl had seen it herself during a time that she didn't like to remember, but it was one of the secrets of how Big Mother kept them all alive.

Girl settled Runt on her lap and held him while he ate. He scooped along the bone's length and brought the jellied fat to his lips. Then he licked each piece three times over. She could tell by the way he was devouring the marrow that he probably did have the fat sickness. That's why he got listless and dull. She was surprised that he felt this way because she was fine, but then she ate some too and immediately felt better. Still, it led her to believe that their bodies were using the food they ate in very different ways.

Runt licked the bone clean so quickly that she made him another. He sucked that up and then, eyes shining, gave her a huge greasy kiss on the cheek. He burrowed down into the hide and soon fell asleep. All she could do was watch his quivering eyelids, soft breathing, and cheeks as smooth as the belly of a fish. He nuzzled into the crook of her arm. Holding the warmth of his body, she couldn't bear to move.

She used her foot to kick a log on the fire and settled back to let him sleep. For a little while, she felt at one with him in her arms.

When Runt woke, it was like an eruption. One moment he was snoring and the next he was bursting with life. The fat sickness seemed to be cured. He jumped and hooted and ran around the hearth. He laughed and wanted to play. She did for a while, but then she glanced at the sky. The clouds were closing in and growing heavier.

Girl sent Runt out to look for green poles that might help them repair the hut. To get to a stand of trees that were the right size, he had to go far out. She had him yell every few minutes so she could keep track of him. It allowed her to continue working, as she didn't want to take the time to follow him around.

Soon enough, Runt came bounding through the brush. "Eagle-see." He chattered excitedly and asked Girl to follow him back into the trees. She had just set the spine pole of the hut and didn't want to stop working. He insisted and pulled her deep into the brush toward a clearing with a large boulder and from there to a tree. It occurred to her that he must have been suffering for longer than she knew, as he suddenly seemed ten times as strong as he had been just yesterday. His grip on her wrist was tight and he wouldn't let go.

Runt tugged her arm until she was facing a tree. It was familiar— a large pine with bark that flaked off and a distinctive twist to its growth that told of extreme weather while it was still young and supple. She nodded hello to the tree to be polite but wasn't sure what business Runt had with it. He put his finger into a mark that had been made on the bark: two slashes cut diagonally downward. Runt traced them with two fingers. They were made at an angle that followed the direction of the land away from the camp. He pointed in the same direction. "Eagle-see."

Girl didn't know what he meant by that word this time. She followed his gaze down the rolling slope. After a long walk that way, a body would end up on the plains. She wrinkled her nose as she remembered the stories she had heard from Big Mother about them. The plains were dry and full of dust. A body would always be thirsty out there. There would be no crossing, no bison, no hooves, no sweet stink of shit. The family didn't go there because there were no trees for protection. How could a body live without at least some trees to hide in? On the plains, the sky felt so large it could lean down and swallow a body up. The sun was free to beat on a head or burn the skin and make it bubble. Some thought that was how the sunbite came, from the harshest sun of the plains. It was almost impossible to hunt on the flat land, with few trees or natural barriers to help corner the beasts.

Girl wanted a big drink of water after just looking in that direction.

"Eagle-see."

"Ne," she grunted.

"Eagle-see!" He put his finger in the slashes.

"Ne."

Girl didn't know why the slashes were on the tree, but they weren't from an animal claw. They looked as though a body had been testing a stone tooth to see if it was sharp enough. But it was odd to cut into live bark. It hurt the tree, just like cutting skin. Its sap had bled and bubbled up from the wound. To Girl it was a kind of senseless violence. Why wouldn't a body test a tool on a downed log instead? The family injured bodies all the time, but only for food or fuel. This seemed to be neither.

Girl used her fingers to spread the sap into the wound and stanch the bleeding. Runt quickly batted her hand away to stop her. She looked at him and gave him a piercing growl. His renewed energy had turned into something more scratchy and difficult, as though a bug had bitten him under the cloak.

"Eagle-see!"

"Ne."

Their conversation didn't get much further. And Girl didn't see the need for discussion. What she believed had been passed on to her through the short generations of her family through experience, shared attention, and shadow stories on the cave wall. The things she believed felt as essential as the blood that flowed through her veins. There was stillness to her culture. There were few points of contact between families. Changes rarely had a chance to spread. There were no other ways to live. Other words weren't needed. The family knew how things were done.

But none of that solidity of the past stopped Runt. He chattered, flailed his arms, and filled the air with words to the point of exhaustion. Girl thought about trying to remove the marrow from his stomach, although she didn't consider it in a serious way. But it was clear that a dull and listless Runt was an easier Runt to manage. She took a deep breath and tried to be patient with the boy. She wished for a sister or a brother that she could pass the problem child to.

Finally she put her hands over her ears. It wasn't so much to blot out Runt; more that her head ached from his chatter. Just thinking of the scrape from saying all those unnecessary words made her throat uncomfortable. She turned away from Runt and walked back to the remnants of the hut. All the while, the clouds overhead darkened. Girl could feel them pressing in and making the air on her back heavy. It wouldn't be long, two suns at most, before the first winter storms of the season came. There was nothing more important than shelter to keep them alive.

"Eagle-see!"

The boy followed her and shouted, not just that word but a stream of noises and clicks and trills. There were too many words for Girl's ears. The sound chafed against the craving in her belly and the weight of the baby in it. She scowled and continued walking. "Crowthroat," she barked.

Girl headed for the broken hut and didn't look back. Runt would follow, as children always did. Wildcat would too. They both knew where their meat came from. It was the kind of loyalty she knew. She rested heavily in the hut for a moment and watched the clouds curling overhead. This side of the mountain was drier than the other, as the clouds raked over the top before riding down the slope. It meant that she couldn't see how fast the storm was heading their way, but she could feel it.

Wildcat came under the branches of the hut and sat under the new, smaller spine that she had just built. Because there were only two bodies and they still had to gather food, it would take several days to finish the shelter. The cat rubbed along Girl's back. She reached for a small piece of dried squirrel and gave it to him. She took another from her pouch and held it out. It hung in the air, waiting. She expected Runt's round face to show up at the side of the hut.

"Eagle-see," she said. The effort of saying the word was meant as a concession to the boy, a peace offering. There was no answer.

Girl crawled out to look. The camp was empty. She stood. She sniffed. She even shouted. The boy was gone.

Birth

Excavating a spinal column is a finicky job. I worked with one of my smallest brushes and felt as if I were removing one speck of dust at a time. The vertebrae have many divots and curves. Hers were large, solid. I left enough dirt to support her found position while uncovering enough bone for us to see.

By the next evening, I was working on the C7 vertebra. I had staked it out in a square long before, marked with string and wooden pegs, and it corresponded precisely with Andy's master map. I marked what I saw before I started brushing. I used an especially large scale, nine squares on the graph paper for each staked meter. I photographed each angle as I brushed, to capture every detail. Anais and Andy took out the dirt I removed and sifted it through a mesh screen to make sure there was nothing that I'd missed. A calm had settled over the site. Luckily, my baby seemed to enjoy the quiet as well. A boy, the ultrasound had said. He sat snug in my belly, showing no sign of making an appearance. I knew many first babies were late and used every moment like it was borrowed time.

"Andy!"

He pushed through the plastic. "How's the baby?"

"Which one?"

"Your Neanderthal." He laughed.

"Could you help me up?"

My joints were all loose and wobbly. My body was getting ready for the challenge of pushing out an infant with a big skull.

Andy held out his hand. We had developed a technique for getting me off the ground: he would crouch behind me and wrap his arms under my arms and over my belly, and then we would stand up together. Caitlin entered just as we were mid-hoist.

"Evolution is clearly a tinkerer, not an engineer," she said, looking down her nose at us.

"If only Rose were a gibbon." Andy sighed.

"Precisely," said Caitlin. Andy was the only one who dared to tease her, but she took many of his attempted jokes seriously. "The smaller head and the broader canal of a gibbon makes for a much easier birth."

"Yes." He nodded solemnly. "But if Rose were a gibbon, wouldn't she throw her own feces all over the place?"

Andy gave a last heave to help me stand. As soon as I was on my feet, I heard a crunch. The sound was terrifying, like a breaking bone. I was standing outside the string border, but I immediately assumed that I had stepped on and broken some part of my Neanderthal.

"What was it?" I shrieked.

"My back," Andy said, gasping.

I turned around to find him hunched over, his breathing uneven.

"Did I break it?"

"It went out."

Caitlin helped Andy lie down on the ground. I later learned that he had an old injury that had been aggravated, but I still felt as though I had broken him. Caitlin pushed the plastic aside to say, "Call an ambulance please, Michael."

Everyone had assumed that I was about to give birth, so they all looked shocked to see Andy emerge from the cave on a stretcher. The attendants brought one with wheels. To get back to the parking lot, they popped the wheels down for the flat stretches on the trail and flipped them up to carry the stretcher over the roots and rocks. They gave Andy a shot to help with the pain, but I could still see the agony in his face.

Once he was in the ambulance, I squeezed in and gently took his hand. I was crying again, although this time I didn't care who saw.

"Rose?"

"Andy?"

"Go home," he said. "And tell Simon I wish him the best of luck."

"He'll be a great parent, I'm sure."

"Not with the baby." Andy grimaced. "I mean with you."

I got out of the ambulance, and Caitlin got in to accompany him to the hospital. I watched them drive away.

Without Andy, I couldn't continue working. No one else would be crazy enough to lower and raise me without a crane. Or at least, no one offered. All I could do was worry about Andy and hover around the others. They all eventually settled down and went back to their jobs. No one touched my Neanderthal, but they worked on the artifacts around her. Two students cleaned and packed the finds that we had extracted. Anais cataloged the tag number, measurements, and description of each artifact with perfect accuracy. I had tried to catch her out more than once, but she seemed born for the job. I attempted to help with lunch and succeeded only in burning my wrist on a pan. After a few hours, I knew that I was in the way. Andy had said it: Go home.

I announced my departure with a wave. Anais started to organize a visiting schedule, but I asked her to stop. I really wanted to be alone and get some rest. Simon would come on the weekend, when his course was over. The hospital was close to the flat. I would be fine. No one said much more than a quick good-bye. They assumed I wouldn't be able to stay away and would probably reappear in a day or so. I drove to the flat in Vallon-Pont-d'Arc and put my work belt and keys on the Ikea shelves, which had been delivered and set up by an expensive man-with-a-van. I sat on the daybed and blinked.

It was Tuesday and I had promised Simon that I would have the baby on the weekend. I was left to wonder what I should do with my free time—not something I was accustomed to having. I had declined a birthing course, as it was nothing I couldn't learn from a book. Maybe the following day I could help Anais with cataloging. It would be good for me to get into the nitty-gritty. I wanted to check in on Andy too. But just then I felt exhausted.

I put my hands on my belly when the baby kicked. I had been around enough of my friends' babies to know that although it took a while for them to be able to express themselves, they emerged with their personalities fully formed. Who was this baby? I didn't know him, even though I was clearly half responsible for making him. I ate a bowl of ice cream and decided there was only one logical step after that. I napped.

The first contraction woke me up with a jolt. In the daze of sleep, my mind developed a complicated rationale. I was quite sure that I had fallen asleep for so long that storm clouds had gathered. Lightning must have hit the olive tree outside, been conducted through the frame of the daybed, and wrapped around my belly. I stood up and felt around clumsily. My daybed was wet. Had I knocked over my glass? It took me a minute to realize that my water had broken and was now dripping by my feet. I felt as though I were in some kind of comedy act, but then I imagined the horror I might have inflicted on the excavation site. Why hadn't anyone warned me how much water there could be? I was glad to be near a toilet.

Another contraction caught me by surprise. I put my hand on my belly, almost laughing at the pain. It was as if my body had started on a journey without me. It took a while for my mind to catch up. I cleaned up and changed and realized that I had to call Simon.

He picked up the phone right away.

"The contractions have started."

"Oh, shit." He sounded panicked.

"I know. It's early. First babies are supposed to be late!"

"You mean the baby is not following your schedule?" I couldn't tell if he was joking. "Why do I ever listen to you?"

"Can someone cover your class tomorrow?" I asked, all business again.

"Argh!"

"At least first babies are slow. We'll wait for you."

"Gah." Simon dropped the phone. I could hear him scrambling around and swearing, and then a door slammed.

"Simon?"

I guessed he was on his way.

I knew giving birth could be traumatic, but as I sat on the daybed and felt the contractions contort and pull at my muscles, I felt only calm. With my prepacked bag in hand, I walked down the cobble-stoned street to the small village hospital, thinking the exercise might help me relax and keep my breath even. I pushed through the doors.

"Je vais avoir un bébé," I said to the nurse at the front desk.

"Comment vous sentez-vous?"

"Bien," I said. Meaning "I'm fine." And I was.

The nurse got me settled in a room. There was some clucking about whom I should call. I had done Andy enough harm, and even though he was in a different wing of this same hospital, I knew I needed to leave him to heal, so I assured them that Simon was on his way. I didn't say that he was coming from England, nor did they think to ask.

I lay on a bed in a scratchy gown with the sharp smell of antiseptic all around me. I understood the expression *waves of pain* for the first time. Each contraction came as a submersion. If I could go with it and try to relax, I knew I would've been spat out the other side. I adjusted the bed with the remote. There was a strange popping sound, like a bubble had burst my serene state of mind. I wasn't sure what had made the noise, but the next contraction felt like a vise around my middle, gripping with a power I'd never felt before. I wanted to stop the contractions just for a moment, but they kept coming. My mind clouded over with the darkest thoughts. I tried to will in more light.

Between contractions, I gave myself pep talks. A nurse came in to check on me. I didn't want an epidural. She rubbed my back. I knew that anticipation of pain could make it worse, so I kept trying to clear my head. And then the next contraction would roll in, and it felt like two large hands taking the length of my body and wringing it.

The doctor came in to check on me and said something, but *rapide* was the only word I could make out.

Labor progressed until I felt like I was brushing up to the edge of death. At some point, that baby changed the way I thought about my body. I no longer worried about getting hurt, being turned inside out, or dying. All I wanted was for my baby to get outside of my body. It didn't matter how. I can't describe this as love. It was so different from what I've felt for my own mother or Simon. It was desperation.

A fetal heart monitor was stuck to my belly and I could hear the regular beats. I started to imagine that I was a bomb. By that time, I would have happily exploded if it got the baby out. Before that moment, I'd assumed that fear was only a sensation that protected my body from harm. As the contractions climbed, death became more than just a possibility. It was a likely truth. The statistical probability that I would survive childbirth meant nothing to me. I knew a fear so deep that it opened its gaping mouth and swallowed me up.

But at some point, I moved through that too. After a particularly strong contraction, my outlook changed. My fear no longer took root in my body. I was unafraid of my death. Instead, I twisted deeper into it. Maybe like all those women who had given birth before me, I welcomed it.

There was a panic in the room. It seemed to be in response to the sounds of the heart monitor, which was beeping more slowly. A ring of people in scrubs stood around my bed. Suddenly, the heart monitor crackled and went silent. Had the heartbeat stopped, or was the monitor just not picking it up? I didn't know, but a nurse pointed at the screen.

I turned my head to look, my wild eyes scanning for a blip that would give a sign of life. Many things were happening, but I took in only a few. Another nurse came rushing in with a contraption that had a hose at one end and a cord dangling out the back, and all I could think of was my grandmother's old vacuum. The doctor rushed to my side, ripped the monitor off, and put his head right in my face. We stared at each other, chests puffing, eyes open wide and unblinking. He could see that I was alert. He knew I spoke enough French to understand him, but I don't think it mattered. In that moment, we had a direct line of communication.

He thumped his chest. *"Le cœur a cessé de battre."* The heart is not beating.

I nodded—the heart, the heart.

"Vous avez un essai." One try. One push.

I knew exactly what was happening. The doctor's words matched what I felt; the darkness that had crept up. My baby's heart had slowed or stopped. With an infant that small, it took only a few moments for brain damage to set in. I looked at the circle of faces around me. One nurse held a hose with a cup at the top, and another had her hands on the top of my belly, as though getting ready to push from the outside.

"Dites-moi," the doctor said. "When the contraction, it comes, tell me. And you push."

A new contraction started to build. I nodded my head to let all the people who stood around me know that it was on the way. They took the cue and prepared. A well-trained staff, a well-equipped hospital, all the modern advantages in the world, and it still came down to what I felt at the core of my body.

It was silent as we waited. No tick of the monitor. No cry. No gasp.

I had left my fear of death behind. It could take me or not. I was the bravest I had ever been.

The contraction became stronger. A nurse spoke into my ear in accented English: "Close your eyes, hands under knees, work from your chest down." Two pairs of hands prodded the top of my belly. I could hear that there was a hose and suction involved. I curled up, gritted my teeth, and pushed.

I heard a loud roar; orange and red mixed with blinding lights. The colors bled before my eyes. I pushed and felt him move and I kept going, finding the muscles and going past any kind of physical strength I'd ever had before. I growled and yelled and didn't stop, and time didn't move in a linear way. Every body that had come before mine, every change in our species' structure over millennia, every flex of my ancestors' muscles came into play. I pushed and pushed through more years than I knew there were.

My baby came out with a face that was bright, like a blue moon. The umbilical cord was wrapped around his neck. The doctor unwound it once and then twice.

More silence and a long pause, a moment as endless as every birth, then a wail, and cheers from the staff. A swell of relief flooded the room. The nurse to my left leaned in and kissed my cheek. The doctor held my baby, whose legs were kicking, arms flailing. He put the thing down on my chest and I started to cry. It wasn't joy. It was only gratitude that it was over.

I was stitched up in places that I didn't realize had ripped. We were wheeled out, first my baby, in a crib, then me. He was taken the other way. I wanted to ask where, but I couldn't find the words. The adrenaline ran thick in my veins. My hands shook and I looked at them, lying on my lap like nervous claws. The colors of the hospital were sharp—a vibrant red fire extinguisher, the yellow glow of a line on the floor, and, when we reached my room, the violent green swirls on the curtain around my bed. They transferred me onto the mattress. I panted. A hand gave me orange juice and crackers. Another hand patted me on the back and stroked my hair. I could hear water drip from a distant tap.

My baby was brought to me and placed in my arms. I managed to stop shaking enough to hold him. We had made a perfect body, with a brain and a complex nervous system, a little penis, soft gums, and a tiny yowling mouth. All I could feel was wonder. Simon and I had made him, but my body had done the construction. And how? Not with my conscious mind. Before that moment, I had thought I knew many things about how life worked. Looking at him, I realized I knew nothing.

A lactation specialist came to help me nurse. For a small, soft-looking thing, my baby had gums that felt like razors. He clasped onto my nipple so hard that I started in pain. The specialist gave me a *tsk-tsk* and looked disapproving.

"*Pardonnez-moi,*" I said. Excuse me. "*Ça fait mal.*" That hurts.

The woman scowled in response. France is known for its first-rate aftercare, but she had no time for a pleasant bedside manner. She grabbed my arm and wrapped it more tightly around the baby, then pushed my back to contort it into the correct angle. I'd heard that France had lower rates of breastfeeding than other Western countries and now I had an inkling of why. She pushed and prodded and commented. Clearly, I wasn't doing a good job. My nipples weren't the kind she liked. Bigger breasts would be better. Maybe I should try sitting in a chair.

With all the instruction, I felt like a child myself, one who was failing at school. Exhausted and sore, I still jangled from the scent of death that clung to my skin. I started to weep and didn't even try to hide my tears. The nurse took my baby in her arms. As though she were doing me a favor, she let me know that I could have a moment to collect myself. She turned her back and rocked my baby, whispering in soothing tones into his small ear.

My first instinct was to jump up and snatch my baby back. Mine! Did she see what I'd done back there? I made this life and I saved it too. *Give me my goddamn baby and a cape, and I'm going to fly out of here like the hero I am.*

But I didn't say anything. Instead, I sat and wept in my blood-stained hospital gown on a mechanized bed surrounded by ugly curtains. They had given me crackers and orange juice and treated me like I was ill. I knew better than to open my mouth and tell them that I was a hero. I knew that would sound crazy.

PART IV

24.

Runt didn't come back. Girl waited patiently, without making a fuss, and still he didn't return. She pretended they were playing a game and he was hiding. Looking behind every rock and tree, she made the noise of a bison in the woods. He didn't laugh. He didn't cry out. He didn't jump out and scream *"Boh!"* at the top of his lungs. She built the fire up in case he had lost his way. She burned green branches and fanned the black smoke into the sky as a signal. If he saw it, he didn't turn and head back in her direction. She shouted and shrieked and climbed a tree to look as far as her eyes could see. It was late afternoon when she started to retrace every step he had taken that day. Runt often walked in distracted circles, and these tracks were entangled with the steps from past activity at the camp. Each found print was like another loss to Girl.

By dusk she'd reached a spot far from the slashed tree he must have set out from. He had traveled over the rock that rounded up from the land like a humped back and then hopped from stone to stone. She would find the prints of his toes and lose them again. They weren't the tracks of a child on the run, which had the looping curiosity that came with the first taste of freedom. Children who ran like that were born to the family on occasion. They were called seekers and they would run off in a new direction on a whim. More often than not, they met an early end, as one of her brothers had. The boy, the youngest next to Runt, had run into the jaws of a lion before they knew he was gone. At the meeting place, a young girl who belonged to another family had met the open mouth of the river in the same way. Sometimes, though, a seeker would find something new—a lost tool or a bowl that had been buried and forgotten—and the child would bring it back feeling proud. But Runt wasn't a seeker, not really. This was the first time he had run away. And she had thought he was old enough to know better. What surprised her about the tracks was the speed and distance that he covered. He'd traveled in a straight line and with a purpose. Unlike Girl, who had to stop often to rub her swollen feet.

The farther down the slope she went, the more her lungs puffed in the dry air. This was the opposite side of the mountain from the fish run. The family did not go on this side because it was so dry in the summer and fiercely cold in the winter. There were fewer trees to shield the body from the wind, and the snow dropped in thick slabs without anything to break its fall.

Soon it was dark and the weak moon gave her little light. She imagined there were strange, glowing eyes around each bend, and tongues licking lips at the sight of her round belly and full breasts. Despite the dark and the harder terrain, Runt hadn't stopped. In her current state, she wasn't going to catch him.

But that didn't keep Girl from tracking Runt. The urge to follow him was as strong as any she had ever had. She was the one who had to protect him. The thought of the boy out in the dark on his own brought up the same fear as when the snake slithered across his back, when the male bear raised his big head, or when she had failed to catch his fat sickness earlier. These memories clouded up in front of her eyes and made it hard to see. But when the color of the morning sun cracked into the sky, she had to stop. She looked and looked, but she had lost his tracks. Without his footprints to follow, it was impossible to keep going. For all she knew, she could be moving farther away from him. Or what if he had returned to camp and was sitting alone at the hearth, wondering where she had gone?

The walk back to camp was hard and slow, and the front edge of the storm rolled in. Snow started to fall in large flakes. Imagining Runt out in the cold made black pitch clot in Girl's chest, especially after she saw that he wasn't back at camp. Only the clouds were there to greet her, now so low they brushed against the ground. With the hut unfinished, she needed a more secure shelter. The vital part required for her to survive a storm, the large hide to cover the top, was missing. She had only the thin summer hide she had lugged from the fishing grounds. With lip curled up, she could feel the hard pressure of the air on her gums. The storm would clap down by the end of the day and it would be big. Only the first crust of snow was on the ground by then, not enough to build a snow cave. She found a tree that had grown deep in the slope. Below the root ball was the start of a burrow. It was the type of place that a bear would dig in. She found a flat rock the size of her two palms and started to scrape the dirt out.

It didn't take long to get the hole big enough for her body—even with her large belly—and Runt and Wildcat. She worked hard and fast in the hope that the boy would show up in time to take cover from the storm. Girl scooped in a side pocket for a fat lamp, then carved another as a place to store food and water. She lined the hole with fur and hide to make Runt comfortable. She lined the base of the entry with flat stones to hold the edge. She used a ripped hide from inside Big Sister's hut to cover the entrance and make a door.

All that day, as Girl worked, she would stop and scan the land for Runt, sometimes climbing a tree to look for any kind of twitch in the branches. There was a herd of beasts far out on the plains. Their vibrations came strong through the trees, but this didn't surprise her, given the time of year. The deer and caribou that roamed the plains migrated as they ate up the grasses and moved on to the protection of lower-lying forests in the winter. Without the narrows like she had on the land of the family, she had no chance of catching them by herself.

When Girl was done with the burrow, she sat in it and waited. Runt didn't come, but the storm did and it was fierce. Girl climbed outside a few times to see if there was any sign of Runt in the snow. The winds whipped and the ice lashed her face but there were no tracks coming back up the slope. The fog moved in and the snow was becoming thick on the ground when she finally went back into her shelter without him. Wildcat scampered in and she pushed two layers of hides across the small entrance.

There was enough height in the burrow to sit up and stretch, but most of the time would be spent on her side. Her hope was that the storm would break and a second thaw would come. Sometimes it happened that way, and the family would have more time to dig in for winter.

But as it was, this early cold breath blew hard and strong. Girl snuggled into Wildcat for warmth. And as she drifted off, her mind went back to the memories of wintersleep and the family. She remembered being in the pile of bodies, a leg hanging slack over her hip, an arm across the back of her thigh, the warm breath of another body on the skin of her neck. She remembered how it felt to be connected to the beating hearts, listening ears, and watching eyes. It was the thing that kept her blood warm. It was why her body had stayed alive. And it was gone. *Warm.*

25.

The winter reminded Girl of a pack of wolves howling. When she peeked outside the burrow, the land had changed into something new. It lay cloaked in white and snarling. Except for the snow and wind, nothing moved outside. During a storm as fierce as that one, all the beasts tucked themselves away. They cowered in their burrows and nests in a bid to conserve their fat. Fat was needed to keep the body warm and the heart beating. Any beast who dared to walk would find all its body fat quickly depleted. For Girl, leaving the burrow would mean she'd be up to her hips in soft powder. Trying to move around would use much more fat than could possibly be gained.

When Girl was with the family, a storm was sometimes welcome. A body could huddle down with the others and find rest. The beasts that shared the valley would all do the same. The badgers were deep in their burrows. The red squirrels had gone into their holes in the trees. The bears had found good dens that were much like the one Girl lay in. Leopards and cave lions were also hunkered down. It was a quiet time. It was a time of truce.

Every now and then, Girl peeked out to look for Runt, but she knew he wasn't there. Time passed in a blur and the storms kept coming, one after the other; they held all the beasts down. Runt wouldn't be able to move around in the deep snow. Even her hope to see him had waned, and she was alarmed to find moments where she felt nothing. Not the soft side of Wildcat's paw on her cheek, nor her weight settled on her thin hip, nor the cold on the skin of her hand when she lifted the flap to scan the land. Her body turning numb meant she was becoming indifferent to how her struggle might end.

The days and nights blurred in the dark, slow time of wintersleep, but she couldn't get into an entirely sluggish state. The baby inside kept kicking her awake. She felt more tired with each day that passed. When she got up to clear her bowels, the snow and cold air would blow into her burrow. She had to light the fat lamp to help her body dry out and to warm up the air again. She found herself continually grabbing at her stash of dried meat.

Girl had lost track of time, but it felt as though she had already waited forever when the initial crack of pain ripped along her side. At first, she thought the pain was a tremor from the mountain, perhaps waking up after so many years of deep sleep. She opened her eyes and waited to feel the rumbling from deep underneath and smell the smoke that plumed up from the earth. Long before Girl was born, the sun had buried its strength deep in the mountain. When the mountain woke up, it shook to get moving again. This was an eruption, something Girl had encountered only in Big Mother's shadow stories. The shadows made by her fingers licked up the rock walls of the cave to show fire and the burning flesh of a writhing, tortured body.

But the shaking didn't come from the mountain. It came from Girl's belly, which she clutched. After one jolt, it stopped. She patted her belly and the baby seemed to turn over and go back to sleep. She felt relief, though she knew what would soon come.

Outside, a storm raged anew and howled. The snow was continuing to build up around the door flap as the deepest part of winter arrived. At least that would help to hold in her heat. She rolled over and pulled Wildcat closer. They slowly ate what food they had stored.

He was already small and too thin, and she had him wrapped in the hides to keep out the cold, which wasn't right for a cat. During the winters before, he had been like a bear and kept himself warm. He felt her stir and moved to tuck his nose in tight. He was soft and she hummed with her cheek on his belly.

They were settled and slow. Girl lit the fat flame and watched their movements on the side of the burrow. The smoky light flickered, and she pretended Runt was there. She told him stories with her fingers casting shadows. He would grow to be the strongest on the land, even with those knobby knees. His roar would be so loud that it would scare all the big cats. His spear would drive through the chests of beasts. He would never feel fear, and all the Big Mothers would beg for him to come to their hearths. He would be more beautiful than even Him, with bigger muscles, shinier hair, and wise eyes that were hidden under his brow.

She pushed up on an elbow and looked for her shell but then remembered that it was still on a lash around Runt's neck. Since she had no shell, she put her hand over her ear instead. The effect wasn't as good, but she could pretend. Inside the cupped hand, she could hear something like the Sea. There was sand in her hair, and her skin was itching with salt. The rumble of a wave crashed on the shore. In the distance, the big fish of the ocean jumped and dived. Their tails were as broad as trees and their backs rolled like mountain ridges along the surface of the water. There was a new land inside the shell of her hand.

Time bled away and Girl looked out and saw fangs of ice pushing the door flap. Apart from her baby bulge, she was too thin. Her arms and hands looked like those of an old man—they had lost any sign of muscle. Her knuckles buckled and the skin puckered. She could feel that her cheeks had sunken in, and the bones of her face jutted out. Her hip dug painfully into the hard ground. Her knees stuck out like bulbs. Her body was eating her own meat as fuel. It was a sign that she was failing.

Girl reached over for the last piece of meat. It was a thin strip of squirrel, not enough to keep them fed for more than a day. She felt a kick inside her belly. It was hard and strong enough to hurt. She put her hand on the spot and felt the small foot. Again, it kicked, as though demanding that the meat she had just picked up go only to one place.

She broke off a length of the squirrel and put it in her mouth. She sucked at it until it was soft. Any salty juices that were left in the meat slipped down her throat. For a moment, she was surrounded by warmth. It was almost as though the sun had broken through the clouds and shone down on her. *More of that, more of that,* her body begged and pressed.

Girl took another bite and the warmth climbed up her back and helped her sit up. She did it with a strength that she hadn't had for days. She chewed and chewed, and the baby inside her settled down. The kicking stopped and the baby was quiet. The warmth bathed her skin and she knew that with a few more bites, the baby would sleep. She would sleep too, a deep sleep that would restore her blood. The sleep would keep her alive, hopefully long enough to see the long season of storms end.

She felt a nudge at her arm. Wildcat had smelled the meat and lowered his head. She kept chewing. The cat looked up with slanted eyes. It wasn't hard to know his mind. He would take the meat by force if it were possible. He might feel sad for the lack of a warm human body, but his desire for food was more important. He would eat her if he could, she knew, and she didn't blame him for it. That was just how a cat saw the world.

But Wildcat didn't try to take the squirrel from her or make a move for her throat. He knew he wasn't a match for her, especially not when he was so weak and hungry too. And maybe he had grown to like her body beside his. There was a comfort in their companionship. She lowered her head to Wildcat to show him the same respect. She broke off the tiniest corner of the squirrel to let the cat have the small pleasure of the food. She watched him chew.

She took the last bit of squirrel from her belt and reached forward to stroke Wildcat. They looked each other in the eyes and she leaned in until they touched noses. She placed the squirrel close to the cat's mouth, and he took a bite and purred.

As Wildcat chewed, she got her arms around the furry body. She could feel his contentment, and her own saliva ran as she imagined the joy of the juice running down her own throat. She pressed her cheek to the purring cat and felt his warmth. Then she moved both hands to clamp around Wildcat's jaws. She put her knee in close and pressed. In a swift move, she snapped his neck.

26.

The cat meat was gone all too quickly. The storms sank farther in and Girl realized that when the melt came, she would probably greet it from the other side of the dirt. In some ways, she had prepared for this. She had already dug herself down at the base of a tree and maybe this was why the bears burrowed the same way. If a body died during the winter storms, it was already buried come spring. But that was before she felt the first pain of labor. It ripped across her body and woke her into a state in which she was more alive than she had ever been and more alive than she might want to be. Every nerve stood on end. The baby was coming.

What happened next was nothing like what she had seen Big Mother endure. The stoic woman had made it look like a far-off rumble in her body. With closed eyes, she had moaned through labor. But Girl felt her baby come with an unexpected strength.

The baby inside her was part of the land and had the kind of force that blew the top off a mountain. Another flash, and the mountain stretched its lava fingers through her muscles from the inside. A thin line of fire surged out and cut down between her hips, then stopped. She waited and understood. The mountain connected to her through the fire, but the quake was coming from inside. It would loosen the baby and push it out. The lava flowed out from her center with the same power and force. The mountain took over the body of the mother.

There was a slick of sweat on her skin. She groaned. Her body shook. She was so far away. And the lava cut and tore and pulled. She had a hazy hope that it would not damage her body beyond what could heal, but she also knew that it wasn't concerned with her. At any other time, she might be scared to die. But in the face of the mountain's fire, bathed in its heat, she offered herself up. Her only reason for being was to birth a baby. She had to keep a family on the land. She squatted on the floor covered with hides and felt the burning rock. She let out a roar that echoed through the burrow and shook the walls so hard that there was a rumble across the land. Every part of her body pressed and pushed down. She might split in two. A shift and the pressure built. The lava flowed and the heat burned and she fell to her side. A deep breath and she opened her eyes and there was a baby. Wet. Curled. Blue. It didn't move.

Another shot of pain roused her, a last flare from the fire in her belly. The placenta slipped out from between her legs and with it went the power. She chewed through the umbilical cord, as there was no Big Mother to take that important first bite in the baby's life. She felt the hard floor of the burrow dig into her hip. The cold air clawed at her spine. Her own lips turned blue and she started to shake. She pushed up and saw the baby. With one arm, she grabbed it and pulled it against her chest. She heard a mewling and looked down to see a mouth wide open. Small fists raised into the air and a bald head like the fullest of the moon's many faces. She put her nipple into the wide mouth and the baby rooted, then latched onto her nipple. A pain traveled down a line through her body to her toes, which clenched at the feeling. This wasn't the power of the burning mountain. This pain was cold and dry.

When she next woke, the baby was quiet. He wasn't hungry or angry. She put his mouth on her breast and he rooted, but he didn't have much will. Or he wasn't strong enough to pull out the milk. She tried to coax him. She pinched her nipple between her finger and thumb and pressed it to the back of his mouth as she had seen Big Mother do many times before. He didn't latch on. His lips fell slack. After trying and trying, she could barely look at the small body. She didn't want to know it. She didn't feel anything for it. She was dying too.

The blood kept flowing out from between her legs and there was little water to drink. She placed a chunk of snow on her lips to soothe her thirst, something only the dying did. She put a stiffened water sack near their nest of hides in hopes that the edges would melt. She took sips, while the baby was too quiet. She lay a wet finger on his lips and urged him to lick. She thought of their two bodies as one. The pain of her baby's hunger was the same as hers. Her cache of food was gone. The snow outside was a trap that would hold her tight. The sun had left the sky for good.

The next morning she woke to find that the temperature had dropped further. The snow that she had left to melt had not turned into water. She licked the ice, and the tip of her tongue stuck to it, as though the moon were making a grab for her body. She ripped her tongue away and tasted blood, the warmth of her own blood down her throat. All it meant was that she was still alive.

Girl didn't feel anything except that her body was ice and a barren land. There was no meadow or sweet stink. There was no hand left to stoke the fire, no fuel to burn, no food to eat, no milk in her breasts for her baby. Her family would not be of the land. She would freeze in the well of this tree. She would never feel *warm*.

She pulled the baby close against her chest. With the back of his head in the crook of her arm, she pinched his nose and pressed her palm over his mouth. She watched the tiny arms flail and felt nothing other than the ice in her chest. The moon showed its cold face. She felt his small body struggle and then let go.

Survival

The next night came as a cluttered mix of memories, scents, and fleeting moments, each one detached from the next. I'd thought that carrying a baby through pregnancy took a toll, but nothing prepared me for what was to follow. All I wanted to do was get back to the flat and sleep. I was in a hospital room with three other mothers and their newborns. We were all in a state of disbelief. It seemed that every few minutes, there was a baby stirring, a mother struggling, or a nurse coming in to save the day. It was never quiet and I dozed only briefly, a few minutes at a time.

At some point when it was still dark, another woman was wheeled into our room. She was in the beginning stages of labor. Every ten minutes, she would writhe in pain and let out the loneliest moan I'd ever heard. My uterus would contract painfully in response, like a wolf answering the howl. But her progress was slow. I started to brace myself between her contractions, dreading the next one. By the time she was finally wheeled out of the room, I could see the first crack of light in the sky outside the window. Beside me, Jacob, a name arrived at after a phone conversation with Simon, started to mewl. I picked him up; he had such small knees and the tiniest earlobes I'd ever seen. I tried to feed him, but he wouldn't latch onto my nipple. He gummed the tip; pain shot through my network of nerves, and now I was the one to cry out. The woman beside me turned in her bed so that her back was to us and pulled the pillow over her head in dismay.

As quietly as I could, I got up to change Jacob. I was expecting a little baby poo as cute as those earlobes; I got a thick, greenish, tar-like sludge. I knew it was meconium, the substance that had stuffed his digestive pipes while he was in the womb, but it is one thing to identify and quite another to clean. Using wipe after wipe, I started to wonder if I had the wrong tools for the job. A nurse finally came over with a thick washcloth to help. She solved the problem with a few swipes and then promptly scolded me for exposing Jacob to the cold air for so long. She was right. He was shivering. The woman beside us let out a loud sigh. The nurse swaddled Jacob and put him in the crib beside my bed. His small lips shook and I knew that body heat would warm him quickly, so I picked him up and brought him under the blanket. A swift hand came in and the nurse plucked him away.

"Ne dormez pas avec le bébé dans le lit," she scolded. Don't sleep with the baby.

She put him back in the crib. There was a way of doing things in the hospital, and it wasn't mine.

I checked myself out of the hospital as soon as I could put pen to paper. The doctor expressed concern at the color of Jacob's skin. As the doctor hadn't met Simon—his early-morning flight had only just touched down on the tarmac—I explained that Jacob's father had a slightly olive complexion. I was pleased to have birthed a baby with what I saw as built-in skin protection.

"Non." The doctor shook his head. *"C'est la jaunisse."*

"Jaundice?"

"A little bit." He used his forefinger and thumb to show an inch.

He agreed to let us check out provided Jacob took lots of liquid. A midwife would be scheduled to visit in a few days. I waved my hand saying that I didn't need her, shuddering at the thought of one of those disapproving nurses coming through my door. I was too exhausted for such intrusion. We would visit the clinic. I carried my new little baby out the door.

When Simon arrived at the flat, he was ecstatic. I watched with a detached sense of confusion as his face stretched into a wide smile when he looked at Jacob sleeping. Simon's eyes were bright; his skin took on a glow, and he was full of an energy that didn't seem appropriate to the situation. I begged Simon not to pick Jacob up. I wanted a few precious minutes of sleep, but Simon couldn't help himself. He undid the little sleeper suit and looked at each part of the baby. He kissed the little tummy, counted each finger, and tried to guess the origin of the nose.

"To be honest, it looks like my uncle Alec's," he said.

"The uncle in Yorkshire?"

"Uncle Alec never grew into it." Simon laughed.

"Because he had a heart attack," I said flatly.

This stopped Simon and it was the first time he saw it on my face: my experience of birth had been more like a brush with death.

"I should have been there," he said quietly.

"There was nothing you could have done." My tears were close to the surface.

"I could have held your hand."

"It was up to me."

"I would have rubbed your back."

"Only me."

Silence. Simon looked at Jacob once more and then back at me. I watched his lips move, stop, and curl around another set of words that seemed to clog before they came from his throat. Simon, who always said the right thing, had nothing to say that could bring a measure of comfort. Maybe he finally understood that his baby had nearly died. Even if he was there, he couldn't have done anything.

"You sleep," Simon said, brushing the deep circles under my eyes with his thumb. He took Jacob out of the room, but suddenly I couldn't sleep. A kind of weight came down on me. If I was responsible for stopping Jacob's death, I was also the only one who could ensure his life continued.

"Could you bring him here, Simon? Just so I can see him."

"He's fine."

"He'll need to eat again in a minute."

And I was right. Simon didn't have the fine-tuning to Jacob's needs that I seemed to instantly acquire. Jacob wanted to eat, but he barely took my nipple. It wasn't the strong suck that I'd read about in books. Simon moved pillows in an attempt to help. I propped myself up. We moved Jacob from the left to the right. Finally, I was exhausted and starting to feel sick.

"When did you last eat?" Simon asked.

I couldn't remember.

Jacob fell asleep and Simon cooked. The smell of the frying onions made me queasy, so he put the pan outside. I realized how sore my stitches were. I kept shifting, as I couldn't find a good way to sit. It was Simon who figured out an arrangement of pillows that worked. He put two under my left knee and one under my right, which kept my weight off my stitches while also allowing me to rest. I thanked him over and over. I managed to eat an egg and I chugged back a glass of water. I slept for the first time.

When I got up, Jacob was still napping and we sat together on the daybed.

"I've got good news," Simon said.

"What's that?"

"I've got a full course load this coming semester."

My worry slipped to the side for a moment. Simon must have seen that on my face, as he made a show of beating his chest with his fists. "Your partner is a provider!"

"Thank you . . . I mean, I'm so relieved. Or glad. I mean, happy."

"You can let your worries go."

"For now."

"I'll take care of the money, Rose. And you will have to take care of Jacob for a while."

There was a hesitation in his voice. "But what?" I asked.

"I tried to register you and Jacob at the clinic down the road from our flat. I thought I'd drive you back on Sunday."

"That sounds perfect."

"It might have been."

"It will be."

"But neither of you are covered by the National Health Service."

"Sorry?"

"You don't meet the residency requirements for this year. We can't prove that you've been in London for long enough since last April. The bills, the mortgage, the council tax, they are all in my name."

I knew this had broad implications, but I was too tired to think what they could be.

"So we'll just go anyway?" I tried.

"It's risky. If something went wrong, we could end up with a huge medical bill."

I lay back and hazily tried to focus on the management problem. Every detail of the dig was accounted for and handled. But because I thought that I was engaged in a natural process, my own project had lacked supervision.

I fell in and out of sleep, but I couldn't sink down. I kept dreaming that Jacob was gone, then startling awake to check if he was still breathing. I went on for a few days like this, drifting in and out. I'd see Simon's beaming face. Jacob's bottom waving in the air. A tube of nipple cream. An impossibly small sock. The ache of stitches. It all slipped by like it wasn't happening to me. I understood the myth of the stork and assumed that Jacob had been dropped down by a bird with a large beak. A story that was clearly made up held more sense than the reality around me.

Unannounced, the midwife came on Saturday. I heard her voice and registered it only as something foreign. The midwife was talking to me. I watched her lips move but was too exhausted to speak in a language that was not my first. I smiled and did my best to look nice and kind, like a mother should. And soon Simon was tugging my arm. We were going back to the hospital.

I was conscious, but every time I blinked, the world looked like a different place. I saw a doctor with thick glasses and a concerned expression. A nurse with a long, thick braid pricked Jacob's foot to take blood for a test. Simon talked in slow English and asked me for the occasional French word. We were sent to a special ward, each set of curtains worse than the one before. Fluorescent lights buzzed above my head. The bed slid back. Simon held Jacob in his arms and tried to smile.

I dozed, and when I woke, I saw Jacob in a tanklike crib with clear plastic curving up on all sides. Bright lights shone on his skin. It was a treatment for jaundice, to help him excrete the bilirubin molecules that were building up in his blood. Jacob had little opaque goggles over his eyes, but they kept slipping. I felt the sting of the impossibly bright light as if his eyes were mine. When it got dark, the nurses sent Simon away, saying that fathers couldn't stay overnight. I sat up all night with my arm in the tank, holding the goggles in place to shield our eyes and wondering where our bilirubin would go.

Jacob got a little better but had to stay in the hospital another day. He had a bottle given to him by the nurse after every time I tried to breastfeed him. Between feedings, I worried about the next one. He had to eat every hour, as he needed sustenance to fight the jaundice. We were sent home from the hospital the next morning but told to report to the outpatient clinic the following day for a checkup. Simon started talking about missing the first week of his courses. I worried about money, but I also felt a deep fear about being alone to care for Jacob. Birth was supposed to be natural, yet I was clearly injured and needing help myself. I'm not sure if I said this aloud or if Simon sensed it but he picked up his phone to make a call.

"What are you doing?" I asked.

"You need help, Rose."

Simon hired a girl named Marie who lived two doors away. She would cook and clean and make sure I got to the clinic. She was young. I watched Simon size her up with a worried look. We had talked at length about relocating to London despite the medical coverage, but Jacob's health concerns made it seem too risky. In the end Simon decided that since Marie had opposable thumbs and could dial a phone, she would do. He gave her strict instructions on taking care of us and made sure she had the number of the midwife, the hospital, Anais, and Caitlin.

"Ugh, don't let Caitlin darken my door," I growled to him.

"She already called twice. She just wants to make sure you are okay."

"She wants to witness my ruin."

Simon reluctantly left. He must have called my mother too, as she phoned and offered to come right away. I convinced her to wait a month. I thought she could take care of Jacob when I returned to the dig, but as I limped to the bed, I doubted I'd ever be able to go back to work. My hips felt loose, as though the middle of my body might slip out from under me. I couldn't imagine ever being strong or able to walk in a straight line again. I couldn't crouch down to dig, lift heavy sample crates, or even make the hike into the camp. A new fear set in: I had lost my physical strength. I was vulnerable in a way I had never been before. And there was Jacob, solely dependent on me. When would the sweet maternal instinct kick in? The one that would help me keep my baby alive? My body shook with a deep terror that he would die because of something I did, or didn't, do. I was filled with a black dread so strong that I found myself searching for ways to stop it.

Marie made me an omelet. I somehow got Jacob and myself to the appointment at the clinic. A nurse sniffed around me in a way that made me feel like a dog, but in doing so she discovered the extent of my infection. It wasn't that I hadn't noticed it; it was more like my own body seemed like a secondary thing that I didn't have the energy to address. I was put on antibiotics for my wound, which wasn't healing properly. I worried about the effect the medication would have on my breast milk and Jacob and I tried to explain my concerns to the doctor. He suggested that I should bottle-feed but everything I'd read declared that bottle-feeding didn't give a baby the best start to life. I couldn't just stop nursing.

And the days went by this way, a blur of feedings, diaper changes, brief snatches of sleep, phone calls, checkups. Marie took a photo of me holding Jacob and sent it to Simon. I looked at her phone and it was odd to see the photo. A moment ago I had inhabited my own skin, but now I was outside of it. The woman on the phone looked tired and wan, like a giant leech had latched onto her skin and was slowly sucking her vitality away. All that remained was a bloodless face. I couldn't eat any more eggs, and Marie didn't have any other dishes in her repertoire.

Andy called one day. He was installed in the other apartment.

"Can I come visit?"

"Soon," I said.

"Later today? Caitlin offered to drive me over."

"Is she using you to get to me?"

"Sorry, what?"

"No, I just meant it's not a good time for a visit. I need to rest."

"Is everything okay?" he said, taking a slurp of something.

"Fine."

"You sure?"

"Sleep is the most important thing. I hope you aren't drinking too much soda?"

"Nice deflection, Rose."

I didn't want visitors. I didn't need misplaced concern taking up more of my energy. Marie was there a couple of hours a day to give me a chance to sleep. Whenever I lay down and drifted off, she went about keeping herself busy and I'd wake to the sound of the water tap, a chair scraping on tile, or the mop swishing in a bucket.

Finally, Marie left for the day. The stink of lavender hung in the air and coated my clothes. I fed Jacob as best I could and put him in the bassinet beside my bed. It was warm outside, but I pulled the double doors tight to fend off the lavender. All I could think about was squeezing my eyes tight to sleep because at any moment Jacob might cry.

I fell into a sort of half sleep, as if I were hovering somewhere over the bed, but the moment I started to sink down, I jumped up again. I leaned over to look at the baby. Was he alive? Still breathing? I wondered at his perfect lips, the curl of his ears, the rise and fall of his chest, and the small fingers wrapped into tiny fists. I had thought that after delivering a baby, I would feel invincible, but instead fear had filled me for days. The pull of him was so strong that it felt like falling. I had to keep him alive. I was so tired. I started to wonder how much more I could take.

I needed to sleep. I checked once more that Jacob was breathing and lay down stiff as a board on my bed. If I slept, then my muscles would relax and I wouldn't feel this urge to run. From what? I couldn't quite say. That great fear had taken up my center and blotted out anything I had been or felt before. My body ached and bled just as the day bled into my dreams, and it was hard to tell what was real.

The air in the room turned earthy, as though things could grow there. Thick vines sprouted around the edges of the old garage downstairs. They grew up through the old Peugeot and climbed out the windows. The shoots bit into a crack in the wall and burst through the windows of the flat. They grew up into tall trees and soon there were thick trunks that shot up through the ceiling. Branches ripped at the roof. They grew too tall and soon started to fall around us. The land lost its trees and opened into grassy plains. Jacob and I lay in our beds and were exposed to the sun. Our skin, too thin and white, began to blister. The light shone red through my eyelids.

I heard something stir, but my body refused to respond. The sound pushed me deeper into the pillow. A tattered blanket of leaves and dirt covered my body. I sank farther and farther down. I was being buried and didn't mind. With each clump of dirt that covered me, I felt a cool relief. Soon my head was dug in deep and the darkness soothed my burning eyes. At last I was underground. It was quiet. The dirt was thick over my body. Roots grew up through me and held me in place. And somewhere in the distance I heard a baby crying.

The tiny cries seemed to come from far away. Now I was dreaming about a cat outside the window. It was meowing, going on and on, and I tried to shoo it away. I turned on my side and woke slightly and realized that the sound wasn't coming from a cat. It was a baby in a bassinet beside my bed. It was a small baby. It was my baby. It was crying and no one was helping it. There was no one else home. Suddenly, the problem and the source settled in my mind. The baby was hungry. The baby was mine.

The dream snapped into a crisp reality, the edges sharp. A baby, my baby, was screeching for milk and I had only just gotten to sleep, a heavenly sleep that could have continued for days. I felt dry. My nipples were bullets on my chest, sore from Jacob's gnawing at me with tiny gums that should have been harmless. My body was weak. My mind was dulled to the point of uselessness. My hair was dirty. I smelled. The flap of belly lay empty and loose.

I opened my eyes and waited. I hoped he would settle, but his cries only got louder. My nerves still felt tied to his and it was as though he were shouting into the end of my spine. My heart thumped and my blood raced and suddenly I stood up, quick and furious, as though someone had stabbed me with a needle and I had leaped to my feet. My lips pulled back and my hands were in fists. From way up high, I looked down at the small body in the bassinet and willed it to stop crying.

"Shut up!" I growled.

He didn't. Jacob didn't even open his eyes, but his crying felt purposeful, driven by instinct. His body was doing things that were directly at odds with mine. My heart raced. The hair on the back of my neck stood up. My shoulders rounded and my muscles tensed. There was only so much strength to go around and it wasn't enough. I snatched him up. Only one of us could live.

27.

Winter continued to roar outside the burrow. Girl's heart slowed. Her blood moved around in her veins like a thick sludge. She had eaten every last bit of food. With nothing to consume, her body continued to feed on itself. It was not love that drove a body to live, but hunger.

When the meat on her body was close to gone, the once-thick trunks of her thighs were thin twigs. No leaves could grow. The roots couldn't reach soil. Outside the cave, the sun was weak and far away. The meadows would stay sleeping under the thick blanket of snow. There would be no bison, no hooves, and no sweet stink. The fish would live under the ice with no bears to catch them. A barren, empty land lay all around with no family. She imagined that she was on the moon.

Girl knew she was close to death and it tempted her. As Big Mother had, she felt that there would be great relief in the long dirt nap. She would finally rest. But she knew something else. There was no one else to benefit from her body in the dirt. She was the only one who could live to breed again. She was the family.

While Girl appeared to the naked eye to be dead, her thin body—like a pile of twigs under the tree where only the dead go—was still making heat. The careful observer, one who could notice very small things, one who would bother to lower a cheek to her lips, would be able to feel the faintest breath, which still held a slight trace of heat. A sharp eye might catch the twitch of her nose, just a wiggle of the fine hairs that stood up to feel the air.

A shaft of light hit her skin. She cracked one eye open and thought that she was looking up from under the earth. Maybe a badger had dug up her body, or the hyenas had come to pick at her carcass. For a moment, the light flickered. Her vision was blurry, but she realized that she was looking at the flap of the door. The sky had been the color of the snow for so long. Clouds had kept the sun away. Now the light came from the sun. And the sky outside was blue.

Girl pushed herself up to sit. Her body, now freed from the demands of the baby, could supply itself more efficiently than it had before. She didn't grow strong exactly, but something returned—a small spark, a will, like the light from a torch in the distance. And she felt a heat. It was a turn in the weather, and it provided a final chance.

Quietly and with careful movements, she reached for the horns her mother had worn. She tied them on her head. Girl became the Big Mother.

Instinct

"Rose?"

I was standing at the bassinet in a rage when I heard a sound. A voice I couldn't place. It came from behind me, somewhere in the flat. I was holding Jacob out in front of me and he was wailing. His small shoulders were bunched up. A slick of sweat came to my skin; my teeth were clenched tight. I thought only about making the sound stop.

"I'll take him." A voice sliced through my anger. I felt a cool hand on my shoulder. It seemed dark in the apartment. Was it night or day? I turned around. It was Caitlin. She was gentle but firm.

"You rest."

I let the baby go, allowing her to take him from me. All I felt was relief. I thumped down on the bed. As my breath started to even out, somewhere in the depths of my mind I realized that my baby had stopped crying. I was so grateful that he was out of my care, away from me, and away from what I had wanted to do. What I might have done. My body felt heavy. I slipped into a deep sleep.

What seemed like much later, I sat up with a start and looked around. As my eyes adjusted to the dark, I saw her again, Caitlin. A moment before, I had been sure that I had only dreamed her. She sat in the rocking chair in the corner of the room where I slept. Her T-shirt had a streak of dirt across the front, like she had been at the dig site. Her gray hair was pulled back. She looked at me but didn't smile. She held the baby softly in her arms and was giving him one of the bottles of pumped breast milk that I kept in the fridge. I guessed that she'd warmed it just right, as Jacob's eyes were rolled back and he looked drunk as he gratefully chugged it.

Caitlin nodded. She meant that it was fine to go back to sleep. Jacob drank the whole bottle and I watched. Caitlin held him close and burped him with the confident movements of an expert. I watched her gray ponytail sway. She put him on the desk I was using as a changing table and cleaned him up, then settled him into his bassinet.

I sat at the edge of the bed. My legs were shaking and I had tears in my eyes. I felt loss in the air, maybe the one that had so nearly been mine. The ceiling in the bedroom seemed lower, as if it would soon press on my head. The walls lurched and blurred around me. The floor heaved. I put my hand out to catch the bed frame and struggled to stand. Caitlin stayed by the door. She watched me carefully, as though looking for signs.

"Why did you come?" I asked her.

"I wanted to tell you," Caitlin said in a quiet voice, "about the site. That things are fine."

I stared directly at her. "That's not true, is it?"

The kitchen light shone behind her, and I could see her outline, both of the older woman she was and something else: the younger woman she had once been. For a moment, the younger body stepped forward, slightly taller, a robust frame and skin taut over sharp cheekbones. A shock of red hair and pale skin. She looked so strong and broad, as if she could do anything. Then the vision faded away and it was just Caitlin again, standing by the door and looking at me.

"No, it's not," she said.

"Why did you come?" I asked her again. I moved toward her. There were so many things that felt impossible to put into words. We were close enough that I could see the shine of tears in her eyes. I heard a breath come out from her lungs, rough and unsteady.

"I saw signs in you—"

"I'm going crazy."

"—that I'd felt in myself. I'm sorry I didn't do more to help you, Rose."

"I'm so tired."

She cupped a hand over her mouth. A tear leaked from the crease of her eye.

"I nearly . . ."

"I know. It's okay now."

"How did you know?"

"I lost my baby."

I let myself cry then, flooded with both sadness and relief that she'd stepped in when she did. I put my arms around her and held her close. The warmth from my body melted into hers. I let myself go. I cried and when I managed to calm down enough to notice, I realized she was crying too. Her shoulders shook and I held her tight. Even through my exhaustion, I knew that her grief was greater than mine.

"What happened, Caitlin?"

She answered in the softest whisper, "I was alone."

28.

Girl unfolded her body in the sunlight. Out of the burrow she came and stood to her full height, the last of the family. She was tall with a shock of red hair and muscles that, once fed again, would regain their strength. Her skin would once more gleam in the sun. She stood and tilted her face up. It was not the *warm* of a family, but it was something.

It was the sound of water that got her moving. While a body needs food, water is more immediately essential, and her body needed much more than she had been able to melt. Girl didn't know the movement of the season yet, but she did hear a small trickle of water running down the side of the tree. Any farther away and it might have been too far. She dropped to her knees and drank, and this cleared the clouds from her eyes.

The red squirrels chattered among themselves. They had been the first to notice her stirring. Perhaps she had a secret cache of food, and now that she was awake, she would reveal its location. They were excited about something else too, but she couldn't quite understand what. The chatter of the squirrels alerted the sparrows, who responded by calling to one another from the trees. That spread the news of her movement to all the other beasts.

Girl listened to the sounds of life around her. She dozed and drank and dozed and drank, and the sun warmed her skin and soon she could stand again. She walked slowly toward the hearth at the center of the camp. It took her a moment to focus, but there was something odd in the middle of it. She blinked and looked. A structure had been put there.

Three tall sticks were stuck solidly into the packed snow and tied together by a dried vine at the top. One red squirrel darted excitedly around the edge of the hearth. Its urging prompted Girl to look more closely. She soon understood what the squirrel chirps meant. The sticks had been stripped of their bark and smoothed so that squirrels couldn't get a good grip. In the middle of the sticks, hanging down, was a pouch that the squirrels hadn't been able to reach.

Inside the pouch were strips of meat, some hazelnuts, and something else. A shell. Around the area, she could see footprints in the snow, like someone had been searching. But because of her lack of movement, she hadn't left any marks in the land for them to find.

Girl ate the meat. It wasn't bison. It was another herd animal of a kind that the family didn't really have a taste for. Not even caribou, but the meat of a lean deer that ran too far and too often to keep good fat on its back. Maybe it wouldn't have been her first choice, but it was meat. She sat and ate. Then, digesting, she placed the shell to her ear. It was the Sea.

And not just any sea; it was the faint sound of the Sea. This was the shell that she had given Runt. Where was he? She looked around and sniffed. A scent came from the shell. Runt's hand had left a smell on the pouch, and there was the scent of another body on it too. She stuck her finger in the old coals of the hearth and felt the warmth of past fires. The family was alive.

She stayed and ate the food that was left in the pouch and rested. Her body had been refilled with water. She had enough strength to gather roots from the softening earth that was warmed by the trees.

She killed a few spring squirrels and roasted them. She rested more and felt some life come to her muscles.

Knowing that Runt was alive was like a pull on her skin. Soon she felt strong enough to try to find him again. The snow was melting in places during the day and froze hard at night. If she woke early in the morning, she could walk across the surface of the spring crust.

But she couldn't leave without taking something with her. She went back beside the burrow and chipped the small frozen body out of the snow. She lit a fire, melted water, and boiled the bones to clean them. After a long while, she let the bones cool and ran her fingers over the small parts of the skeleton, their smooth surfaces and delicate dips. One bone she spent more time with than the others. It was from the forearm of her baby. It was curved in a way that made the thumb jut out the wrong way, like Bent's arm. She slid her finger along this curve.

Girl buried the bones near a tree so that the baby would grow into the trunk, but she kept the small arm bone. She tied it into the softest hide, then looped the pouch to her belt. Until the day she died, she would wear that bone to remember.

She found Runt's tracks quickly after that.

29.

Runt's footprints were strong in the softer snow lower down the mountain. Girl knew them as if they were her own. She could picture every move that he'd made exactly. He stayed atop the hard crust. He wore an odd, thinned hide to protect his feet, but the print and the way his weight shifted were still familiar and clear. He, or someone he was with, had hung the meat for her. He had looked around and checked in the hut. He had been searching for something at the camp. As he was one who looked with his eyes, she wasn't surprised that her burrow had gone undetected. But when the snow was hard enough to walk along the top in the morning, he had tried to find her.

And there were other footprints. They were narrow, not large. They were slightly bigger than Runt's, but very similar to his. They were the prints she had followed from the perch by the meeting place.

Girl followed both sets of prints down the slope. It looked like the two had been walking in a relaxed manner. There were no drag marks to show that the larger body was forcing Runt. They walked close at times and in step, as if the larger body might be holding Runt's hand. If he hadn't detected danger, she felt more at ease. She had started this way when tracking him before winter sank in but had stopped and turned back before getting this far. She followed them from the river and down to the drier parts of the mountain, where the snow had nearly melted except for spots where a large boulder gave shade. She kept going downhill toward the plains. After a long stretch of walking and a rest for the night, she began again. Now the grasses bristled under her feet and the trees became more spread out. She lingered under the cover of one of them and then moved to the trunk of the next. When she was between them, her head felt bare in the glare of the sun.

Soon Girl caught the smell of a distant fire. She would have sniffed it much earlier if it weren't for the direction of the wind, which was at her back. She climbed one of those trees, its branches so broad and wide from all the sun it had to itself and still devoid of leaves from the winter, and looked out. She melted into the branches, making her body into the same shape so that she couldn't be seen. In the distance, she saw a herd. Or that's what she thought it was at first—a herd of bison, their rounded backs catching the sun. But after staring for a while, she became convinced that they weren't moving. And the fur was wrong to her eye—oddly shaped, pointed at the tip, and light in color.

Red deer? She didn't know. She gave them a good squint and tried to think. It was only later that she would learn they were a new kind of hut because just then something distracted her. She saw a body moving.

It was far in the distance, a long way away, but it was heading in her direction. It was an upright body with tight hides over its skin. Behind it was another body dressed much the same way, but smaller. It had a round head and dark hair. And she couldn't be certain, but it walked with a skipping gait that looked just like Runt's.

Girl watched the bodies approach. As they came closer, she climbed down from the tree and waited beside it. She was well aware of the risk. Anytime one kind of beast met another kind, there was danger. But she also wanted to see Runt and knew that he would signal if he approached with a hostile beast.

She walked a few steps forward and said a quiet *"Aroo"* to alert the bodies that she was aware of them. The larger body startled, as though it hadn't been sure of Girl's position. At that moment, Girl dropped her spear, to show that she didn't mean harm. She stood her ground, feet planted firmly. She lifted her hand and spread the fingers, turned her palm.

She looked at an upright body that stood on two feet in front of her. It looked like Runt in some ways, the same patch of hair like moss, the same charcoal skin, the same shine to the eyes. It had his elegance to its walking gait, a slow arch to each step, and the foot touched the ground in silence. However, it was taller than Runt, with rounded muscles and with breasts. It wore the Sea around its neck, but there were many seas all lined up in a row like a second set of teeth. It was like the family, but not of the family.

Still, the body was the closest thing to family that she had seen in months. The differences dropped back and she saw all that was the same. Her breath caught, tears came to her eyes, and the inside of her chest swelled with a sense of wonder.

The woman didn't feel like she was in mortal danger. As the girl in front of her approached, she spoke in a sharp tone to the boy she was with. Despite his protests, she instructed him to hide in a tree. He scampered up the thin trunk as told but lingered at the bottom branch so that he had a clear view. With the boy in the tree, the woman hesitated. Her weapon was still in hand, a thin spear. She shifted nervous fingers on the shaft. She didn't want to appear to be a threat, nor did she want to be without a way to defend herself. She took a last few steps and stood still.

The woman stared at the magnificent beast that was Girl. Nothing had prepared her for what she saw. She had heard stories of this kind of creature but had never seen one herself. Though the boy had described, in his halting way, the body in detail, it was a stunning sight. If Girl had been at her full size, in her hunting gear with muscles gleaming, the woman would have been terrified.

As it was, the woman still knew in one glance that she was the weaker one. Her knees started to shake. Though Girl must have been close to dead over the winter, her body was thick and looked full of power. This was a body with denser muscle mass, with great speed and strength, powerful senses, and a sharp intelligence. Her eyes were tucked in deep beneath her brow and were hard to read. She had a shock of red hair, and horns grew out from her sloping forehead.

The woman could have let her senses become swamped by the strange sight and lunged with her spear, as others of her kind in this position might have. But this woman was different. She couldn't stop staring. And she had taken care to listen to the boy. He had told her stories about the kindness, food, and safety this creature had provided for more than a year. The proof lay in the young boy's life. And he had told the woman how to greet this girl.

The woman let her weapon drop to the ground. Her curiosity won out over her fear. She decided to trust the boy's word about this creature. She walked toward Girl in slow steps, taking deep breaths to hold her fear tight to her chest. She raised her right hand and turned her palm out. As the boy had advised, she spread her fingers.

Slowly, she walked closer until she was standing directly in front of Girl. She could smell the sour odor of a starving belly and the oily residue from eating a strange kind of meat on her skin. The woman looked into Girl's eyes. As she did, tears welled up in her own. She pressed the skin of her hand against Girl's larger hand. The same blood flowed under their skin. Their hearts beat at the same time. They shared a single thought: *We are not alone.*

Human

I strap Jacob into a carrier on my chest. He's only six weeks old and I'm surprised to feel his weight; it's as if he gained a pound overnight. It's a warm autumn day and the sun is high in the sky, but I bring an extra jacket that fits over us both just in case. As I hike out from the parking lot, every step is familiar. I go up past the canvas tents and wind around to the site. When we arrive, I stand by the picnic table as I do each day and greet everyone. Jacob is the center of attention. Before long, Caitlin comes over to say hello and nods in a way that I know means she has a few things to go over. Anais, having perfected her bouncy walk the week before, takes Jacob so that Caitlin and I can talk.

Caitlin hands me a glossy photo. It is the draft layout for a museum brochure. My breath catches in my throat when I see a close-up of the skeletons, the modern human looking into my Neanderthal's eyes. Across the top, THE LOVERS is written in large letters. I've always thought of their moment as private, something I shouldn't intrude on. This shows them up close and in such intimate detail that I find I can barely look. I'm about to open my mouth, unsure what I'm going to say, but Caitlin cuts me off.

"Guy wants you to write an introduction," she tells me.

"Me?"

"Yes, you."

"The Lovers?"

"He wants to use that title to refer to them."

"We don't know that they are."

"Depends on what kind of love, I suppose," she says. "But he wants you to write the first précis. It will become the basis for how we communicate to the media and the public. Your interpretation will be the one we lead with." She lowers the brochure and looks at me. "He intends it as a great honor."

Caitlin leaves me with a wry smile, one I might have taken as pursed lips before. She walks back to the table where she was cataloging artifacts. I feel her awkward kindness lingering in me. We are so different, but I have grown fond of her. And I owe her almost too much. What will I write? It feels impossible to introduce my Neanderthal to the world. How can a few sentences correct the misinterpretation of an entire species for more than a century? I am slightly weak-kneed about it. My mind is blank. Feeding Jacob is taking a toll on my physical energy, and maybe on my cognitive ability too.

I hear the crack of a can opening.

"Andy?"

"Rose?"

I walk to the picnic table and give him a hug.

"Where's my partner in crime?"

Anais brings Jacob over and we settle into the next part of our daily routine. I care for Jacob in the morning. After lunch, I bring him to the site and talk to everyone until he is ready for his nap with Andy. We came to this arrangement after Andy pointed out that he and Jacob are on similar schedules.

"Simon back yet?" Andy asks while lowering himself carefully down into the hammock that Simon strung for him in the tent. It is specially positioned to stretch out the muscles in Andy's back.

"No, but he comes for a long weekend tomorrow."

Andy gets comfortable and I carefully lay Jacob on his belly. I arrange a blanket over the top of them both to fend off the cooler October air.

"Not too heavy?"

"He's, what, eight pounds now?"

"Nine."

"It's all that muscle. Gets that from me." Andy winks. "Hold my can?"

He wiggles into the hammock and they both settle down. I put another blanket over them and hand Andy the can, which he manages to sip from a horizontal position. Jacob coos against the warm belly. He puts a fist into his mouth. I watch as both their eyes quickly close and feel a rush of affection. My baby has a modern adaptation: the hiss of carbonation sends him to sleep.

I have only an hour or so to focus before they wake up. Simon will be back, but Jacob's afternoon feedings are frequent and I struggle to get anything done. I cinch the bungee cord on my trousers a notch tighter and push through the plastic tarp to the excavation site. In the warm glow of the lamp, I feel like I'm in a second home. Kneepads on, I pull the brush out of its case.

The day before, I found a protrusion at the same depth and in the same quadrant as my Neanderthal's pelvis, as though it had been dropped, placed, or attached to her in some way before decay. All night I thought about it, wondering what it could be. Now I start to brush. Soon I can see the outline and I adjust my headlamp. It is only about eighty millimeters in length and gently curved. I can't think what it is: An ornament? A piece of horn? If it is a tool, it is unlike any that I've seen.

I blow at the dust as I quietly get to work. Any dirt I lift out goes into a tray for sifting. What will I write? I glance up at the two skeletons. I let my mind go as I brush.

My scientific training won't let me make the leap to think of them as the Lovers, but something about the name sticks with me. We can imagine ourselves as superior to Neanderthals and envision killing them off, but how did we come to have sex with them? That's the more interesting question. I understand that it's one that Guy is trying to provoke. The proof that it happened is in our DNA. And because all this is running through my mind, it takes me a moment longer than usual to understand what I've found.

It's a piece of bone. I lean over and blow gently at the dust. I grab my magnifying glass for a closer look. It has a crook along its length, like a deformity. Soon I realize from the distinct shape that it is a small radius bone, the forearm of a baby who was probably around the same age as Jacob is now. The ends are well preserved. From the width and the squat shape, I think it might be Neanderthal, though I can't tell for sure.

I look up at the Neanderthal skull from where I'm sitting by her pelvis. She is my constant companion, but she looks to someone else. She lies in the dirt, gazing into the eyes of . . . who? A son, a partner, or maybe even a foe—a modern human is all I can say for sure— who once lay down or was laid down beside her. Her arm bones are stretched out as though she is reaching toward him, wanting to hold or be held. His arms are extended in the same way. The position makes me certain that they knew each other. That they, or the people who buried them, didn't feel they were different from each other.

What have we lost? I glance toward the plastic door to make sure that no one is coming. All I hear from the tents outside is the soft saw of Andy's snore. I lean in to put my hands on the pads that I set down to protect the earth around her. I get close to her skull, tilting my head to look into her eye sockets.

For a moment, I feel nothing. I wait, and slowly, I start to warm. These rock walls are what kept her safe. The heat of the day radiates up from them; it might have been the warmth of her body. She had the same skin as mine. The same blood ran through her veins. Our hearts both beat. All our differences drop away. I know that if I had ever been fortunate enough to meet her, I would look into her eyes and know her. And maybe she could know me. We are so much the same.

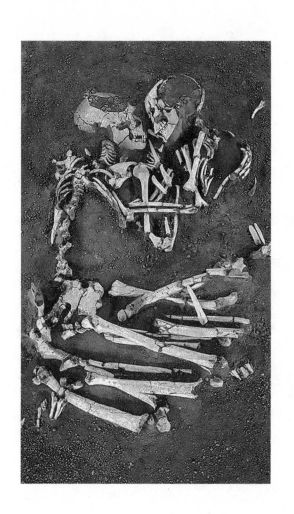

Acknowledgments

A heartfelt thank you to Asya Muchnick, Reagan Arthur, Zea Moscone, Ashley Marudas, and Karen Landry at Little, Brown; to Kristin Cochrane, Kiara Kent, Amy Black, and Sharon Klein at Penguin Random House Canada; and to my literary agent, Denise Bukowski.

Thank you to John Shea, professor of anthropology at Stony Brook University in New York, and to Hilary Duke of Stony Brook University, both of whom provided invaluable guidance on the science that underpins much of this novel. Thank you also to Adrian Haimovich of Yale University, who tackled my many questions about DNA. This novel benefited greatly from Yuval Noah Harari's thoughtful feedback. Ian Tattersall's books gave me a line through the science, and I appreciate his willingness to answer my questions.

Barbara Gowdy's novel *The White Bone* gave me the courage to write this book.

Last but not least, thank you to my early readers and true believers: Elizabeth Boyden, Michael Bourne, Jim Bull, Dave, Ben, and Max Cameron, Ian Cameron, Susannah Cameron, Wendy Cameron, Seanna Doherty, Laurie Grassi, Danielle Gideon, Leigh Anne Graham, Amy Fisher, Keith Lawton, Sarah Murphy, Lindsay Oughtred, Angelique Palozzi, Emily Sewell, Laura Tisdel, Melissa van der Wagt, and Sarah Wright.

About the Author

Claire Cameron's novel *The Bear* became a number one bestseller in Canada and was long-listed for the 2014 Baileys Women's Prize for Fiction. Cameron's writing has appeared in the *New York Times*, the *Globe and Mail*, the *Los Angeles Review of Books*, and *Salon*. She is a staff writer at *The Millions*. She lives in Toronto with her husband and two sons.